THE TREMBLING OF A LEAF

Little Stories of the South Sea Islands

W. SOMERSET MAUGHAM

SANAGE
PUBLISHING HOUSE

Paperback: 978-936205726-6
Hardback: 978-936205463-0
eBook: 978-936205065-6

Printed by: Manipal Technologies Limited, Manipal

Sanage Publishing House LLP
Mumbai, India

sanagepublishing@gmail.com

William Somerset Maugham was an English writer, known for his plays, novels and short stories. His first novel, Liza of Lambeth (1897), a study of life in the slums, attracted attention, but it was as a playwright that he first achieved national celebrity.

Maugham's novels after Liza of Lambeth include Of Human Bondage (1915), The Moon and Sixpence (1919), The Painted Veil (1925), Cakes and Ale (1930) and The Razor's Edge (1944). His short stories were published in collections such as The Casuarina Tree (1926) and The Mixture as Before (1940).

TO
BERTRAM ALANSON

L'extrême félicité à peine séparée par une feuille tremblante de l'extrême désespoir, n'est-ce pas la vie?

Sainte-Beuve.

CONTENTS

I

THE PACIFIC

The Pacific is inconstant and uncertain like the soul of man. Sometimes it is grey like the English Channel off Beachy Head, with a heavy swell, and sometimes it is rough, capped with white crests, and boisterous. It is not so often that it is calm and blue. Then, indeed, the blue is arrogant. The sun shines fiercely from an unclouded sky. The trade wind gets into your blood, and you are filled with an impatience for the unknown. The billows, magnificently rolling, stretch widely on all sides of you, and you forget your vanished youth, with its memories, cruel and sweet, in a restless, intolerable desire for life. On such a sea as this Ulysses sailed when he sought the Happy Isles. But there are days also when the Pacific is like a lake. The sea is flat and shining. The flying fish, a gleam of shadow on the brightness of a mirror, make little fountains of sparkling drops when they dip. There are fleecy clouds on the horizon, and at sunset they take strange shapes so that it is impossible not to believe that you see a range of lofty mountains. They are the mountains of the country of your dreams. You sail through an unimaginable silence upon a magic sea. Now and then a few gulls suggest that land is not far off, a forgotten island hidden in a wilderness of waters; but the gulls, the melancholy gulls, are the only sign you have of it. You see never a tramp, with its friendly smoke, no stately bark or trim schooner, not a fishing boat even: it is an empty desert; and presently the emptiness fills you with a vague foreboding.

II

MACKINTOSH

He splashed about for a few minutes in the sea; it was too shallow to swim in and for fear of sharks he could not go out of his depth; then he got out and went into the bath-house for a shower. The coldness of the fresh water was grateful after the heavy stickiness of the salt Pacific, so warm, though it was only just after seven, that to bathe in it did not brace you but rather increased your languor; and when he had dried himself, slipping into a bath-gown, he called out to the Chinese cook that he would be ready for breakfast in five minutes. He walked barefoot across the patch of coarse grass which Walker, the administrator, proudly thought was a lawn, to his own quarters and dressed. This did not take long, for he put on nothing but a shirt and a pair of duck trousers and then went over to his chief's house on the other side of the compound. The two men had their meals together, but the Chinese cook told him that Walker had set out on horseback at five and would not be back for another hour.

Mackintosh had slept badly, and he looked with distaste at the paw-paw and the eggs and bacon which were set before him. The mosquitoes had been maddening that night; they flew about the net under which he slept in such numbers that their humming, pitiless and menacing, had the effect of a note, infinitely drawn out, played on a distant organ, and whenever he dozed off he awoke with a start in the belief that one had found its way inside his curtains. It was so hot that he lay naked. He turned from side to side. And gradually the dull roar of the breakers on the reef, so unceasing and so regular that generally you did not hear it, grew distinct on his consciousness, its rhythm hammered on his tired nerves, and he held himself with clenched hands in the effort to bear it. The thought that nothing could stop that sound, for it would continue to all eternity, was almost impossible to bear, and, as though his strength were a match for the ruthless forces of nature, he had an insane impulse to do some violent thing. He felt he must cling to his self-control, or he would go mad. And now, looking out of the window at the lagoon and the strip of foam which marked the reef, he shuddered with hatred of the brilliant scene. The cloudless sky was like an inverted bowl that hemmed it in. He lit his pipe and turned over the pile of Auckland papers that had come over from Apia a few days before. The newest of them was three weeks old. They gave an impression of incredible dullness.

Then he went into the office. It was a large, bare room with two desks in it and a bench along one side. A number of natives were seated on this, and a couple of women. They gossiped while they waited for the administrator, and when Mackintosh came in they greeted him.

"Talofa li."

He returned their greeting and sat down at his desk. He began to write, working on a report which the governor of Samoa had been clamouring for and which Walker, with his usual dilatoriness, had neglected to prepare. Mackintosh as he made his notes reflected vindictively that Walker was late with his report because he was so illiterate that he had an invincible distaste for anything to do with pens and paper; and now when it was at last ready, concise and neatly official, he would accept his subordinate's work without a word of appreciation, with a sneer rather or a gibe, and send it on to his own superior as though it were his own composition. He could not have written a word of it. Mackintosh thought with rage that if his chief pencilled in some insertion it would be childish in expression and faulty in language. If he remonstrated or sought to put his meaning into an intelligible phrase, Walker would fly into a passion and cry:

"What the hell do I care about grammar? That's what I want to say and that's how I want to say it."

At last Walker came in. The natives surrounded him as he entered, trying to get his immediate attention, but he turned on them roughly and told them to sit down and hold their tongues. He threatened that if they were not quiet he would have them all turned out and see none of them that day. He nodded to Mackintosh.

"Hulloa, Mac; up at last? I don't know how you can waste the best part of the day in bed. You ought to have been up before dawn like me. Lazy beggar."

He threw himself heavily into his chair and wiped his face with a large bandana.

"By heaven, I've got a thirst."

He turned to the policeman who stood at the door, a picturesque figure in his white jacket and *lava-lava*, the loin cloth of the Samoan, and told him to bring *kava*. The *kava* bowl stood on the floor in the corner of the room, and the policeman filled a half coconut shell and brought it to Walker. He poured a few drops on the ground, murmured the customary words to the company, and drank with relish. Then he told the policeman to serve the waiting natives, and the shell was handed to each one in order of birth or importance and emptied with the same ceremonies.

Then he set about the day's work. He was a little man, considerably less than of middle height, and enormously stout; he had a large, fleshy face, clean-shaven, with the cheeks hanging on each side in great dew-laps, and three vast chins; his small features were all dissolved in fat; and, but for a crescent of white hair at the back of his head, he was completely bald. He reminded you of Mr. Pickwick. He was grotesque, a figure of fun, and yet, strangely enough, not without dignity. His blue eyes, behind large gold-rimmed spectacles, were shrewd and vivacious, and there was a great deal of determination in his face. He was sixty, but his native vitality triumphed over advancing years. Notwithstanding his corpulence his movements were quick, and he walked with a heavy, resolute tread as though he sought to impress his weight upon the earth. He spoke in a loud, gruff voice.

It was two years now since Mackintosh had been appointed Walker's assistant. Walker, who had been for a quarter of a century administrator of Talua, one of the larger islands in the Samoan group, was a man known in person or by report through the length and breadth of the South Seas; and it was with lively curiosity that Mackintosh looked forward to his first meeting with him. For one reason or another he stayed a couple of weeks at Apia before he took up his post and both at Chaplin's hotel and at the English club he heard innumerable stories about the administrator. He thought now with irony of his interest in them. Since then, he had heard them a hundred times from Walker himself. Walker knew that he was a character, and, proud of his reputation, deliberately acted up to it. He was jealous of his "legend" and anxious that you should know the exact details of any of the celebrated stories that were told of him. He was ludicrously angry with anyone who had told them to the stranger incorrectly.

There was a rough cordiality about Walker which Mackintosh at first found not unattractive, and Walker, glad to have a listener to whom all he said was fresh, gave of his best. He was good-humoured, hearty, and considerate. To Mackintosh, who had lived the sheltered life of a government official in London till at the age of thirty-four an attack of pneumonia, leaving him with the threat of tuberculosis, had forced him to seek a post in the Pacific, Walker's existence seemed extraordinarily romantic. The adventure with which he started on his conquest of circumstance was typical of the man. He ran away to sea when he was fifteen and for over a year was employed in shovelling coal on a collier. He was an undersized boy and both men and mates were kind to him, but the captain for some reason conceived a savage dislike of him. He used the lad cruelly so that, beaten and kicked, he often could not sleep for the pain that racked his limbs. He loathed the captain with all his soul. Then he was given a tip for some race and managed to borrow twenty-five pounds from a friend he had picked up in Belfast. He put it on the horse, an outsider, at long odds. He had no means of repaying the money if he lost, but it never occurred to him that he could lose. He felt himself in luck. The horse won and he found himself with something over a thousand pounds in hard cash. Now his chance had come. He found out who was the best solicitor in the town—the collier lay then somewhere on the Irish coast—went to him, and, telling him that he heard the ship was for sale, asked him to arrange the purchase for him. The solicitor was amused at his small client, he was only sixteen and did not look so old, and moved perhaps by sympathy, promised not only to arrange the matter for him but to see that he made a good bargain. After a little while Walker found himself the owner of the ship. He went back to her and had what he described as the most glorious moment of his life when he gave the skipper notice and told him that he must get off his ship in half an hour. He made the mate captain and sailed on the collier for another nine months, at the end of which he sold her at a profit.

He came out to the islands at the age of twenty-six as a planter. He was one of the few white men settled in Talua at the time of the German occupation and had then already some influence with the natives. The Germans made him administrator, a position which he occupied for twenty years, and when the island was seized by the British he was confirmed in his post. He ruled the island despotically, but with complete success. The prestige of this success was another reason for the interest that Mackintosh took in him.

But the two men were not made to get on. Mackintosh was an ugly man, with ungainly gestures, a tall thin fellow, with a narrow chest and bowed shoulders. He had sallow, sunken cheeks, and his eyes were large and sombre. He was a great reader, and when his books arrived and were unpacked Walker came over to his quarters and looked at them. Then he turned to Mackintosh with a coarse laugh.

"What in Hell have you brought all this muck for?" he asked.

Mackintosh flushed darkly.

"I'm sorry you think it muck. I brought my books because I want to read them."

"When you said you'd got a lot of books coming I thought there'd be something for me to read. Haven't you got any detective stories?"

"Detective stories don't interest me."

"You're a damned fool then."

"I'm content that you should think so."

Every mail brought Walker a mass of periodical literature, papers from New Zealand and magazines from America, and it exasperated him that Mackintosh showed his contempt for these ephemeral publications. He had no patience with the books that absorbed Mackintosh's leisure and thought it only a pose that he read Gibbon's *Decline and Fall* or Burton's *Anatomy of Melancholy*. And since he had never learned to put any restraint on his tongue, he expressed his opinion of his assistant freely. Mackintosh began to see the real man, and under the boisterous good-humour he discerned a vulgar cunning which was hateful; he was vain and domineering, and it was strange that he had notwithstanding a shyness which made him dislike people who were not quite of his kidney. He judged others, naïvely, by their language, and if it was free from the oaths and the obscenity which made up the greater part of his own conversation, he looked upon them with suspicion. In the evening the two men played piquet. He played badly but vaingloriously, crowing over his opponent when he won and losing his temper when he lost. On rare occasions a couple of planters or traders would drive over to play bridge, and then Walker showed himself in what Mackintosh considered a characteristic light. He played regardless of his partner, calling up in his desire to play the hand, and argued interminably, beating down opposition by the loudness of his voice. He constantly revoked, and when he did so said with an ingratiating whine: "Oh, you wouldn't count it against an old man who can hardly see." Did he know that his opponents thought it as well to keep on the right side of him and hesitated to insist on the rigour of the game? Mackintosh watched him with an icy contempt. When the game was over, while they smoked their pipes and drank whisky, they would begin telling stories. Walker told with gusto the story of his marriage. He had got so drunk at the wedding feast that the bride had fled, and he had never seen her since. He had had numberless adventures, commonplace and sordid, with the women of the island and he described them with a pride in his own prowess which was an offence to Mackintosh's fastidious ears. He was a gross, sensual old man. He thought Mackintosh a poor fellow because he would not share his promiscuous amours and remained sober when the company was drunk.

He despised him also for the orderliness with which he did his official work. Mackintosh liked to do everything just so. His desk was always tidy, his papers were always neatly docketed, he could put his hand on any document that was needed, and he had at his fingers' ends all the regulations that were required for the business of their administration.

"Fudge, fudge," said Walker. "I've run this island for twenty years without red tape, and I don't want it now."

"Does it make it any easier for you that when you want a letter you have to hunt half an hour for it?" answered Mackintosh.

"You're nothing but a damned official. But you're not a bad fellow, when you've been out here a year or two you'll be all right. What's wrong about you is that you won't drink. You wouldn't be a bad sort if you got soused once a week."

The curious thing was that Walker remained perfectly unconscious of the dislike for him which every month increased in the breast of his subordinate. Although he laughed at him, as he grew accustomed to him, he began almost to like him. He had a certain tolerance for the peculiarities of others, and he accepted Mackintosh as a queer fish. Perhaps he liked him, unconsciously, because he could chaff him. His humour consisted of coarse banter, and he wanted a butt. Mackintosh's exactness, his morality, his sobriety, were all fruitful subjects; his Scot's name gave an opportunity for the usual jokes about

Scotland; he enjoyed himself thoroughly when two or three men were there, and he could make them all laugh at the expense of Mackintosh. He would say ridiculous things about him to the natives, and Mackintosh, his knowledge of Samoan still imperfect, would see their unrestrained mirth when Walker had made an obscene reference to him. He smiled good-humouredly.

"I'll say this for you, Mac," Walker would say in his gruff loud voice, "you can take a joke."

"Was it a joke?" smiled Mackintosh. "I didn't know."

"Scots wha hae!" shouted Walker, with a bellow of laughter. "There's only one way to make a Scotchman see a joke and that's by a surgical operation."

Walker little knew that there was nothing Mackintosh could stand less than chaff. He would wake in the night, the breathless night of the rainy season, and brood sullenly over the gibe that Walker had uttered carelessly days before. It rankled. His heart swelled with rage, and he pictured to himself ways in which he might get even with the bully. He had tried answering him, but Walker had a gift of repartee, coarse and obvious, which gave him an advantage. The dullness of his intellect made him impervious to a delicate shaft. His self-satisfaction made it impossible to wound him. His loud voice, his bellow of laughter, were weapons against which Mackintosh had nothing to counter, and he learned that the wisest thing was never to betray his irritation. He learned to control himself. But his hatred grew till it was a monomania. He watched Walker with an insane vigilance. He fed his own self-esteem by every instance of meanness on Walker's part, by every exhibition of childish vanity, of cunning and of vulgarity. Walker ate greedily, noisily, filthily, and Mackintosh watched him with satisfaction. He took note of the foolish things he said and of his mistakes in grammar.

He knew that Walker held him in small esteem, and he found a bitter satisfaction in his chief's opinion of him; it increased his own contempt for the narrow, complacent old man. And it gave him a singular pleasure to know that Walker was entirely unconscious of the hatred he felt for him. He was a fool who liked popularity, and he blandly fancied that everyone admired him. Once Mackintosh had overheard Walker speaking of him.

"He'll be all right when I've licked him into shape," he said. "He's a good dog and he loves his master."

Mackintosh silently, without a movement of his long, sallow face, laughed long and heartily.

But his hatred was not blind; on the contrary, it was peculiarly clear-sighted, and he judged Walker's capabilities with precision. He ruled his small kingdom with efficiency. He was just and honest. With opportunities to make money he was a poorer man than when he was first appointed to his post, and his only support for his old age was the pension which he expected when at last he retired from official life. His pride was that with an assistant and a half-caste clerk he was able to administer the island more competently than Upolu, the island of which Apia is the chief town, was administered with its army of functionaries. He had a few native policemen to sustain his authority, but he made no use of them. He governed by bluff and his Irish humour.

"They insisted on building a jail for me," he said. "What the devil do I want a jail for? I'm not going to put the natives in prison. If they do wrong I know how to deal with them."

One of his quarrels with the higher authorities at Apia was that he claimed entire jurisdiction over the natives of his island. Whatever their crimes he would not give them up to courts competent to deal with them, and several times an angry correspondence had passed between him and the

Governor at Upolu. For he looked upon the natives as his children. And that was the amazing thing about this coarse, vulgar, selfish man; he loved the island on which he had lived so long with passion, and he had for the natives a strange rough tenderness which was quite wonderful.

He loved to ride about the island on his old grey mare and he was never tired of its beauty. Sauntering along the grassy roads among the coconut trees he would stop every now and then to admire the loveliness of the scene. Now and then he would come upon a native village and stop while the head man brought him a bowl of *kava*. He would look at the little group of bell-shaped huts with their high thatched roofs, like beehives, and a smile would spread over his fat face. His eyes rested happily on the spreading green of the bread-fruit trees.

"By George, it's like the garden of Eden."

Sometimes his rides took him along the coast and through the trees he had a glimpse of the wide sea, empty, with never a sail to disturb the loneliness; sometimes he climbed a hill so that a great stretch of country, with little villages nestling among the tall trees, was spread out before him like the kingdom of the world, and he would sit there for an hour in an ecstasy of delight. But he had no words to express his feelings and to relieve them would utter an obscene jest; it was as though his emotion was so violent that he needed vulgarity to break the tension.

Mackintosh observed this sentiment with an icy disdain. Walker had always been a heavy drinker, he was proud of his capacity to see men half his age under the table when he spent a night in Apia, and he had the sentimentality of the toper. He could cry over the stories he read in his magazines and yet would refuse a loan to some trader in difficulties whom he had known for twenty years. He was close with his money. Once Mackintosh said to him:

"No one could accuse you of giving money away."

He took it as a compliment. His enthusiasm for nature was but the drivelling sensibility of the drunkard. Nor had Mackintosh any sympathy for his chief's feelings towards the natives. He loved them because they were in his power, as a selfish man loves his dog, and his mentality was on a level with theirs. Their humour was obscene, and he was never at a loss for the lewd remark. He understood them and they understood him. He was proud of his influence over them. He looked upon them as his children and he mixed himself in all their affairs. But he was very jealous of his authority; if he ruled them with a rod of iron, brooking no contradiction, he would not suffer any of the white men on the island to take advantage of them. He watched the missionaries suspiciously and, if they did anything of which he disapproved, was able to make life so unendurable to them that if he could not get them removed they were glad to go of their own accord. His power over the natives was so great that on his word they would refuse labour and food to their pastor. On the other hand, he showed the traders no favour. He took care that they should not cheat the natives; he saw that they got a fair reward for their work and their copra and that the traders made no extravagant profit on the wares they sold them. He was merciless to a bargain that he thought unfair. Sometimes the traders would complain at Apia that they did not get fair opportunities. They suffered for it. Walker then hesitated at no calumny, at no outrageous lie, to get even with them, and they found that if they wanted not only to live at peace, but to exist at all, they had to accept the situation on his own terms. More than once the store of a trader obnoxious to him had been burned down, and there was only the appositeness of the event to show that the administrator had instigated it. Once a Swedish half-caste, ruined by the burning, had gone to him and roundly accused him of arson. Walker laughed in his face.

"You dirty dog. Your mother was a native and you try to cheat the natives. If your rotten old store is burned down it's a judgment of Providence; that's what it is, a judgment of Providence. Get out."

And as the man was hustled out by two native policemen the administrator laughed fatly.

"A judgment of Providence."

And now Mackintosh watched him enter upon the day's work. He began with the sick, for Walker added doctoring to his other activities, and he had a small room behind the office full of drugs. An elderly man came forward, a man with a crop of curly grey hair, in a blue *lava-lava*, elaborately tatooed, with the skin of his body wrinkled like a wine-skin.

"What have you come for?" Walker asked him abruptly.

In a whining voice the man said that he could not eat without vomiting and that he had pains here and pains there.

"Go to the missionaries," said Walker. "You know that I only cure children."

"I have been to the missionaries, and they do me no good."

"Then go home and prepare yourself to die. Have you lived so long and still want to go on living? You're a fool."

The man broke into querulous expostulation, but Walker, pointing to a woman with a sick child in her arms, told her to bring it to his desk. He asked her questions and looked at the child.

"I will give you medicine," he said. He turned to the half-caste clerk. "Go into the dispensary and bring me some calomel pills."

He made the child swallow one there and then and gave another to the mother.

"Take the child away and keep it warm. To-morrow it will be dead or better."

He leaned back in his chair and lit his pipe.

"Wonderful stuff, calomel. I've saved more lives with it than all the hospital doctors at Apia put together."

Walker was very proud of his skill, and with the dogmatism of ignorance had no patience with the members of the medical profession.

"The sort of case I like," he said, "is the one that all the doctors have given up as hopeless. When the doctors have said they can't cure you, I say to them, 'come to me.' Did I ever tell you about the fellow who had a cancer?"

"Frequently," said Mackintosh.

"I got him right in three months."

"You've never told me about the people you haven't cured."

He finished this part of the work and went on to the rest. It was a queer medley. There was a woman who could not get on with her husband and a man who complained that his wife had run away from him.

"Lucky dog," said Walker. "Most men wish their wives would too."

There was a long-complicated quarrel about the ownership of a few yards of land. There was a dispute about the sharing out of a catch of fish. There was a complaint against a white trader because he had given short measure. Walker listened attentively to every case, made up his mind quickly, and gave his decision. Then he would listen to nothing more; if the complainant went on he was hustled out of the office by a policeman. Mackintosh listened to it all with sullen irritation. On the whole, perhaps, it might be admitted that rough justice was done, but it exasperated the assistant that his chief trusted his instinct rather than the evidence. He would not listen to reason. He browbeat the witnesses and when they did not see what he wished them to have called them thieves and liars.

He left to the last a group of men who were sitting in the corner of the room. He had deliberately ignored them. The party consisted of an old chief, a tall, dignified man with short, white hair, in a new *lava-lava*, bearing a huge fly wisp as a badge of office, his son, and half a dozen of the important men of the village. Walker had had a feud with them and had beaten them. As was characteristic of him he meant now to rub in his victory, and because he had them down to profit by their helplessness. The facts were peculiar. Walker had a passion for building roads. When he had come to Talua there were but a few tracks here and there, but in course of time he had cut roads through the country, joining the villages together, and it was to this that a great part of the island's prosperity was due. Whereas in the old days it had been impossible to get the produce of the land, copra chiefly, down to the coast where it could be put on schooners or motor launches and so taken to Apia, now transport was easy and simple. His ambition was to make a road right round the island and a great part of it was already built.

"In two years, I shall have done it, and then I can die, or they can fire me, I don't care."

His roads were the joy of his heart, and he made excursions constantly to see that they were kept in order. They were simple enough, wide tracks, grass covered, cut through the scrub or through the plantations; but trees had to be rooted out, rocks dug up or blasted, and here and there levelling had been necessary. He was proud that he had surmounted by his own skill such difficulties as they presented. He rejoiced in his disposition of them so that they were not only convenient but showed off the beauties of the island which his soul loved. When he spoke of his roads he was almost a poet. They meandered through those lovely scenes, and Walker had taken care that here and there they should run in a straight line, giving you a green vista through the tall trees, and here and there should turn and curve so that the heart was rested by the diversity. It was amazing that this coarse and sensual man should exercise so subtle an ingenuity to get the effects which his fancy suggested to him. He had used in making his roads all the fantastic skill of a Japanese gardener. He received a grant from headquarters for the work but took a curious pride in using but a small part of it, and the year before had spent only a hundred pounds of the thousand assigned to him.

"What do they want money for?" he boomed. "They'll only spend it on all kinds of muck they don't want; what the missionaries leave them, that is to say."

For no particular reason, except perhaps pride in the economy of his administration and the desire to contrast his efficiency with the wasteful methods of the authorities at Apia, he got the natives to do the work he wanted for wages that were almost nominal. It was owing to this that he had lately had difficulty with the village whose chief men now were come to see him. The chief's son had been in Upolu for a year and on coming back had told his people of the large sums that were paid at Apia for the public works. In long, idle talks he had inflamed their hearts with the desire for gain. He held out to them visions of vast wealth and they thought of the whisky they could buy—it was dear, since there was a law that it must not be sold to natives, and so it cost them double what the white man had to pay for it—they thought of the great sandal-wood boxes in which they kept their treasures, and the scented soap and potted salmon, the luxuries for which the Kanaka will sell his soul; so that when the administrator sent for them and told them he wanted a road made from their village to a certain point along the coast and offered them twenty pounds, they asked him a hundred. The chief's son was called Manuma. He was a tall, handsome fellow, copper-coloured, with his fuzzy hair dyed red with lime, a wreath of red berries round his neck, and behind his ear a flower like a scarlet flame against his brown face. The upper part of his body was naked, but to show that he was no longer a savage, since he had lived in Apia, he wore a pair of dungarees instead of a *lava-lava*. He told them that if they held together the administrator would be obliged to accept their terms. His heart was set on building the road and when he found they would not work for less he would give them what they asked. But they must not move; whatever he said they must not abate their claim; they had asked a hundred and that they must keep to. When they mentioned the figure, Walker burst into a shout of his long, deep-voiced laughter. He told them not to make fools of themselves, but to set about the work at once. Because he was in a good humour that day he promised to give them a feast when the road was finished. But when he found that no attempt was made to start work, he went to the village and asked the men what silly game they were playing. Manuma had coached them well. They were quite calm, they did not attempt to argue—and argument is a passion with the Kanaka—they merely shrugged their shoulders: they would do it for a hundred pounds, and if he would not give them that they would do no work. He could please himself. They did not care. Then Walker flew into a passion. He was ugly then. His short fat neck swelled ominously, his red face grew purple, he foamed at the mouth. He set upon the natives with invective. He knew well how to wound and how to humiliate. He was terrifying. The older men grew pale and uneasy. They hesitated. If it had not been for Manuma, with his knowledge of the great world, and their dread of his ridicule, they would have yielded. It was Manuma who answered Walker.

"Pay us a hundred pounds and we will work."

Walker, shaking his fist at him, called him every name he could think of. He riddled him with scorn. Manuma sat still and smiled. There may have been more bravado than confidence in his smile, but he had to make a good show before the others. He repeated his words.

"Pay us a hundred pounds and we will work."

They thought that Walker would spring on him. It would not have been the first time that he had thrashed a native with his own hands; they knew his strength, and though Walker was three times the age of the young man and six inches shorter they did not doubt that he was more than a match for Manuma. No one had ever thought of resisting the savage onslaught of the administrator. But Walker said nothing. He chuckled.

"I am not going to waste my time with a pack of fools," he said. "Talk it over again. You know what I have offered. If you do not start in a week, take care."

He turned round and walked out of the chief's hut. He untied his old mare, and it was typical of the relations between him and the natives that one of the elder men hung on to the off stirrup while Walker from a convenient boulder hoisted himself heavily into the saddle.

That same night when Walker according to his habit was strolling along the road that ran past his house, he heard something whizz past him and with a thud strike a tree.

Something had been thrown at him. He ducked instinctively. With a shout, "Who's that"? he ran towards the place from which the missile had come, and he heard the sound of a man escaping through the bush. He knew it was hopeless to pursue in the darkness, and besides he was soon out of breath, so he stopped and made his way back to the road. He looked about for what had been thrown but could find nothing. It was quite dark. He went quickly back to the house and called Mackintosh and the Chinese boy.

"One of those devils has thrown something at me. Come along and let's find out what it was."

He told the boy to bring a lantern and the three of them made their way back to the place. They hunted about the ground but could not find what they sought. Suddenly the boy gave a guttural cry. They turned to look. He held up the lantern, and there, sinister in the light that cut the surrounding darkness, was a long knife sticking into the trunk of a coconut tree. It had been thrown with such force that it required quite an effort to pull it out.

"By George, if he hadn't missed me I'd have been in a nice state."

Walker handled the knife. It was one of those knives, made in imitation of the sailor knives brought to the islands a hundred years before by the first white men, used to divide the coconuts in two so that the copra might be dried. It was a murderous weapon, and the blade, twelve inches long, was very sharp. Walker chuckled softly.

"The devil, the impudent devil."

He had no doubt it was Manuma who had flung the knife. He had escaped death by three inches. He was not angry. On the contrary, he was in high spirits; the adventure exhilarated him, and when they got back to the house, calling for drinks, he rubbed his hands gleefully.

"I'll make them pay for this!"

His little eyes twinkled. He blew himself out like a turkey-cock, and for the second time within half an hour insisted on telling Mackintosh every detail of the affair. Then he asked him to play piquet, and while they played he boasted of his intentions. Mackintosh listened with tightened lips.

"But why should you grind them down like this?" he asked. "Twenty pounds is precious little for the work you want them to do."

"They ought to be precious thankful I give them anything."

"Hang it all, it's not your own money. The government allots you a reasonable sum. They won't complain if you spend it."

"They're a bunch of fools at Apia."

Mackintosh saw that Walker's motive was merely vanity. He shrugged his shoulders.

"It won't do you much good to score off the fellows at Apia at the cost of your life."

"Bless you, they wouldn't hurt me, these people. They couldn't do without me. They worship me. Manuma is a fool. He only threw that knife to frighten me."

The next day Walker rode over again to the village. It was called Matautu. He did not get off his horse. When he reached the chief's house he saw that the men were sitting round the floor in a circle, talking, and he guessed they were discussing again the question of the road. The Samoan huts are formed in this way: Trunks of slender trees are placed in a circle at intervals of perhaps five or six feet; a tall tree is set in the middle and from this downwards slopes the thatched roof.

Venetian blinds of coconut leaves can be pulled down at night or when it is raining. Ordinarily the hut is open all round so that the breeze can blow through freely. Walker rode to the edge of the hut and called out to the chief.

"Oh, there, Tangatu, your son left his knife in a tree last night. I have brought it back to you."

He flung it down on the ground in the midst of the circle, and with a low burst of laughter ambled off.

On Monday he went out to see if they had started work. There was no sign of it. He rode through the village. The inhabitants were about their ordinary avocations. Some were weaving mats of the pandanus leaf, one old man was busy with a *kava* bowl, the children were playing, the women went about their household chores. Walker, a smile on his lips, came to the chief's house.

"*Talofa-li*," said the chief.

"*Talofa*," answered Walker.

Manuma was making a net. He sat with a cigarette between his lips and looked up at Walker with a smile of triumph.

"You have decided that you will not make the road?"

The chief answered.

"Not unless you pay us one hundred pounds."

"You will regret it." He turned to Manuma. "And you, my lad, I shouldn't wonder if your back was very sore before you're much older."

He rode away chuckling. He left the natives vaguely uneasy. They feared the fat sinful old man, and neither the missionaries' abuse of him nor the scorn which Manuma had learnt in Apia made them forget that he had a devilish cunning and that no man had ever braved him without in the long run suffering for it. They found out within twenty-four hours what scheme he had devised. It was characteristic. For next morning a great band of men, women, and children came into the village and the chief men said that they had made a bargain with Walker to build the road. He had offered them twenty pounds and they had accepted. Now the cunning lay in this, that the Polynesians have rules of hospitality which have all the force of laws; an etiquette of absolute rigidity made it necessary for the people of the village not only to give lodging to the strangers, but to provide them with food and drink as long as they wished to stay. The inhabitants of Matautu were outwitted. Every morning the workers went out in a joyous band, cut down trees, blasted rocks, levelled here and there and then in the evening tramped back again, and ate and drank, ate heartily, danced, sang hymns, and enjoyed life. For them it was a picnic. But soon their hosts began to wear long faces; the strangers had enormous appetites, and the plantains and the bread-fruit vanished before their rapacity; the alligator-pear trees, whose fruit sent to Apia might sell for good money, were stripped bare. Ruin stared them in the face. And then they found that the strangers were working very slowly. Had they received a hint from Walker that they might take their time? At this rate by the time the road was finished there would not be a scrap of food in the village. And worse than this, they were a laughing-stock; when one or other of them went to some distant hamlet on an errand he found that the story had got there before him, and he was met with derisive laughter. There is nothing the Kanaka can endure less than ridicule. It was not long before much angry talk passed among the sufferers. Manuma was no longer a hero; he had to put up with a good deal of plain speaking, and one day what Walker had suggested came to pass: a heated argument turned into a quarrel and half a dozen of the young men set upon the chief's son and gave him such a beating that for a week he lay bruised and sore on the pandanus mats. He turned from side to side and could find no ease. Every day or two the administrator rode over on his old mare and watched the progress of the road. He was not a man to resist the temptation of taunting the fallen foe, and he missed no opportunity to rub into the shamed inhabitants of Matautu the bitterness of their humiliation. He broke their spirit. And one morning, putting their pride in their pockets, a figure of speech, since pockets they had not, they all set out with the strangers and started working on the road. It was urgent to get it done quickly if they wanted to save any food at all, and the whole village joined in. But they worked silently, with rage and mortification in their hearts, and even the children toiled in silence. The women wept as they carried away bundles of brushwood. When Walker saw them he laughed so much that he almost rolled out of his saddle. The news spread quickly and tickled the people of the island to death. This was the greatest joke of all, the crowning triumph of that cunning old white man whom no Kanaka had ever been able to circumvent; and they came from distant villages, with their wives and children, to look at the foolish folk who had refused twenty pounds to make the road and now were forced to work for nothing. But the harder they worked the more easily went the guests. Why should they hurry, when they were getting good food for nothing and the longer they took about the job the better the joke became? At last, the wretched villagers could stand it no longer, and they had come this morning to beg the administrator to send the strangers back to their own homes. If he would do this they promised to finish the road themselves for nothing. For him it was a victory complete and unqualified. They were humbled. A look of arrogant complacence spread over his large, naked face, and he seemed to swell in his chair like a great bullfrog. There was something sinister in his appearance, so that Mackintosh shivered with disgust. Then in his booming tones he began to speak.

"Is it for my good that I make the road? What benefit do you think I get out of it? It is for you, so that you can walk in comfort and carry your copra in comfort. I offered to pay you for your work, though it was for your own sake the work was done. I offered to pay you generously. Now *you* must pay. I will send the people of Manua back to their homes if you will finish the road and pay the twenty pounds that I have to pay them."

There was an outcry. They sought to reason with him. They told him they had not the money. But to everything they said he replied with brutal gibes. Then the clock struck.

"Dinner time," he said. "Turn them all out."

He raised himself heavily from his chair and walked out of the room. When Mackintosh followed him he found him already seated at table, a napkin tied round his neck, holding his knife and fork in readiness for the meal the Chinese cook was about to bring. He was in high spirits.

"I did 'em down fine," he said, as Mackintosh sat down. "I shan't have much trouble with the roads after this."

"I suppose you were joking," said Mackintosh icily.

"What do you mean by that?"

"You're not really going to make them pay twenty pounds?"

"You bet your life I am."

"I'm not sure you've got any right to."

"Ain't you? I guess I've got the right to do any damned thing I like on this island."

"I think you've bullied them quite enough."

Walker laughed fatly. He did not care what Mackintosh thought.

"When I want your opinion I'll ask for it." Mackintosh grew very white. He knew by bitter experience that he could do nothing but keep silence, and the violent effort at self-control made him sick and faint. He could not eat the food that was before him and with disgust he watched Walker shovel meat into his vast mouth. He was a dirty feeder, and to sit at table with him needed a strong stomach. Mackintosh shuddered. A tremendous desire seized him to humiliate that gross and cruel man; he would give anything in the world to see him in the dust, suffering as much as he had made others suffer. He had never loathed the bully with such loathing as now.

The day wore on. Mackintosh tried to sleep after dinner, but the passion in his heart prevented him; he tried to read, but the letters swam before his eyes. The sun beat down pitilessly, and he longed for rain; but he knew that rain would bring no coolness; it would only make it hotter and steamier. He was a native of Aberdeen and his heart yearned suddenly for the icy winds that whistled through the granite streets of that city. Here he was a prisoner, imprisoned not only by that placid sea, but by his hatred for that horrible old man. He pressed his hands to his aching head. He would like to kill him. But he pulled himself together. He must do something to distract his mind, and since he could not read he thought he would set his private papers in order. It was a job which he had long meant to do and which he had constantly put off. He unlocked the drawer of his desk and took out a handful of letters. He caught sight of his revolver. An impulse no sooner realised than set aside, to put a bullet through his head and so escape from the intolerable bondage of life flashed through his mind. He noticed that in the damp air the revolver was slightly rusted, and he got an oil rag and began to clean it. It was while he was thus occupied that he grew aware of someone slinking round the door. He looked up and called:

"Who is there?"

There was a moment's pause, then Manuma showed himself.

"What do you want?"

The chief's son stood for a moment, sullen and silent, and when he spoke it was with a strangled voice.

"We can't pay twenty pounds. We haven't the money."

"What am I to do?" said Mackintosh. "You heard what Mr. Walker said."

Manuma began to plead, half in Samoan and half in English. It was a sing-song whine, with the quavering intonations of a beggar, and it filled Mackintosh with disgust. It outraged him that the man should let himself be so crushed. He was a pitiful object.

"I can do nothing," said Mackintosh irritably. "You know that Mr. Walker is master here."

Manuma was silent again. He still stood in the doorway.

"I am sick," he said at last. "Give me some medicine."

"What is the matter with you?"

"I do not know. I am sick. I have pains in my body."

"Don't stand there," said Mackintosh sharply. "Come in and let me look at you."

Manuma entered the little room and stood before the desk.

"I have pains here and here."

He put his hands to his loins and his face assumed an expression of pain. Suddenly Mackintosh grew conscious that the boy's eyes were resting on the revolver which he had laid on the desk when Manuma appeared in the doorway. There was a silence between the two which to Mackintosh was endless. He seemed to read the thoughts which were in the Kanaka's mind. His heartbeat violently. And then he felt as though something possessed him so that he acted under the compulsion of a foreign will. Himself did not make the movements of his body, but a power that was strange to him. His throat was suddenly dry, and he put his hand to it mechanically in order to help his speech. He was impelled to avoid Manuma's eyes.

"Just wait here," he said, his voice sounded as though someone had seized him by the windpipe, "and I'll fetch you something from the dispensary."

He got up. Was it his fancy that he staggered a little? Manuma stood silently, and though he kept his eyes averted, Mackintosh knew that he was looking dully out of the door. It was this other person that possessed him that drove him out of the room, but it was himself that took a handful of muddled papers and threw them on the revolver in order to hide it from view. He went to the dispensary. He got a pill and poured out some blue draught into a small bottle, and then came out into the compound. He did not want to go back into his own bungalow, so he called to Manuma.

"Come here."

He gave him the drugs and instructions how to take them. He did not know what it was that made it impossible for him to look at the Kanaka. While he was speaking to him he kept his eyes on his shoulder. Manuma took the medicine and slunk out of the gate.

Mackintosh went into the dining-room and turned over once more the old newspapers. But he could not read them. The house was very still. Walker was upstairs in his room asleep, the Chinese cook was busy in the kitchen, the two policemen were out fishing. The silence that seemed to brood over the house was unearthly, and there hammered in Mackintosh's head the question whether the revolver still lay where he had placed it. He could not bring himself to look. The uncertainty was horrible, but the certainty would be more horrible still. He sweated. At last, he could stand the silence no longer, and he made up his mind to go down the road to the trader's, a man named Jervis, who had a store about a mile away. He was a half-caste, but even that amount of white blood made him possible to talk to. He wanted to get away from his bungalow, with the desk littered with untidy papers, and underneath them something, or nothing. He walked along the road. As he passed the fine hut of a chief a greeting was called out to him. Then he came to the store. Behind the counter sat the trader's daughter, a swarthy broad-featured girl in a pink blouse and a white drill skirt. Jervis hoped he would marry her. He had money, and he had told Mackintosh that his daughter's husband would be well-to-do. She flushed a little when she saw Mackintosh.

"Father's just unpacking some cases that have come in this morning. I'll tell him you're here."

He sat down and the girl went out behind the shop. In a moment her mother waddled in, a huge old woman, a chiefess, who owned much land in her own right; and gave him her hand. Her monstrous obesity was an offence, but she managed to convey an impression of dignity. She was cordial without obsequiousness; affable, but conscious of her station.

"You're quite a stranger, Mr. Mackintosh. Teresa was saying only this morning: 'Why, we never see Mr. Mackintosh now.'"

He shuddered a little as he thought of himself as that old native's son-in-law. It was notorious that she ruled her husband, notwithstanding his white blood, with a firm hand. Hers was the authority and hers the business head. She might be no more than Mrs. Jervis to the white people, but her father had been a chief of the blood royal, and his father and his father's father had ruled as kings. The trader came in, small beside his imposing wife, a dark man with a black beard going grey, in ducks, with handsome eyes and flashing teeth. He was very British, and his conversation was slangy, but you felt he spoke English as a foreign tongue; with his family he used the language of his native mother. He was a servile man, cringing and obsequious.

"Ah, Mr. Mackintosh, this is a joyful surprise. Get the whisky, Teresa; Mr. Mackintosh will have a gargle with us."

He gave all the latest news of Apia, watching his guest's eyes the while, so that he might know the welcome thing to say.

"And how is Walker? We've not seen him just lately. Mrs. Jervis is going to send him a sucking-pig one day this week."

"I saw him riding home this morning," said Teresa.

"Here's how," said Jervis, holding up his whisky.

Mackintosh drank. The two women sat and looked at him, Mrs. Jervis in her black Mother Hubbard, placid and haughty, and Teresa, anxious to smile whenever she caught his eye, while the trader gossiped insufferably.

"They were saying in Apia it was about time Walker retired. He ain't so young as he was. Things have changed since he first come to the islands and he ain't changed with them."

"He'll go too far," said the old chiefess. "The natives aren't satisfied."

"That was a good joke about the road," laughed the trader. "When I told them about it in Apia they fair split their sides with laughing. Good old Walker."

Mackintosh looked at him savagely. What did he mean by talking of him in that fashion? To a half-caste trader he was Mr. Walker. It was on his tongue to utter a harsh rebuke for the impertinence. He did not know what held him back.

"When he goes I hope you'll take his place, Mr. Mackintosh," said Jervis. "We all like you on the island. You understand the natives. They're educated now, they must be treated differently to the old days. It wants an educated man to be administrator now. Walker was only a trader same as I am."

Teresa's eyes glistened.

"When the time comes if there's anything anyone can do here, you bet your bottom dollar we'll do it. I'd get all the chiefs to go over to Apia and make a petition."

Mackintosh felt horribly sick. It had not struck him that if anything happened to Walker it might be he who would succeed him. It was true that no one in his official position knew the island so well. He got up suddenly and scarcely taking his leave walked back to the compound. And now he went straight to his room. He took a quick look at his desk. He rummaged among the papers.

The revolver was not there.

His heart thumped violently against his ribs. He looked for the revolver everywhere. He hunted in the chairs and in the drawers. He looked desperately, and all the time he knew he would not find it. Suddenly he heard Walker's gruff, hearty voice.

"What the devil are you up to, Mac?"

He started. Walker was standing in the doorway and instinctively he turned round to hide what lay upon his desk.

"Tidying up?" quizzed Walker. "I've told 'em to put the grey in the trap. I'm going down to Tafoni to bathe. You'd better come along."

"All right," said Mackintosh.

So long as he was with Walker nothing could happen. The place they were bound for was about three miles away, and there was a fresh-water pool, separated by a thin barrier of rock from the sea, which the administrator had blasted out for the natives to bathe in. He had done this at spots round the island, wherever there was a spring; and the fresh water, compared with the sticky warmth of the sea, was cool and invigorating. They drove along the silent grassy road, splashing now and then through fords, where the sea had forced its way in, past a couple of native villages, the bell-shaped huts spaced out roomily and the white chapel in the middle, and at the third village they got out of the trap, tied up the horse, and walked down to the pool. They were accompanied by four or five girls and a dozen children. Soon they were all splashing about, shouting and laughing, while Walker, in a *lava-lava*, swam to and fro like an unwieldy porpoise. He made lewd jokes with the girls, and they amused themselves by diving under him and wriggling away when he tried to catch them. When he was tired he lay down on a rock, while the girls and children surrounded him; it was a happy family; and the old man, huge, with his crescent of white hair and his shining bald crown, looked like some old sea god. Once Mackintosh caught a queer soft look in his eyes.

"They're dear children," he said. "They look upon me as their father."

And then without a pause he turned to one of the girls and made an obscene remark which sent them all into fits of laughter. Mackintosh started to dress. With his thin legs and thin arms, he made a grotesque figure, a sinister Don Quixote, and Walker began to make coarse jokes about him. They were acknowledged with little smothered laughs. Mackintosh struggled with his shirt. He knew he looked absurd, but he hated being laughed at. He stood silent and glowering.

"If you want to get back in time for dinner you ought to come soon."

"You're not a bad fellow, Mac. Only you're a fool. When you're doing one thing you always want to do another. That's not the way to live."

But all the same he raised himself slowly to his feet and began to put on his clothes. They sauntered back to the village, drank a bowl of *kava* with the chief, and then, after a joyful farewell from all the lazy villagers, drove home.

After dinner, according to his habit, Walker, lighting his cigar, prepared to go for a stroll. Mackintosh was suddenly seized with fear.

"Don't you think it's rather unwise to go out at night by yourself just now?"

Walker stared at him with his round blue eyes.

"What the devil do you mean?"

"Remember the knife the other night. You've got those fellows' backs up."

"Pooh! They wouldn't dare."

"Someone dared before."

"That was only a bluff. They wouldn't hurt me. They look upon me as a father. They know that whatever I do is for their own good."

Mackintosh watched him with contempt in his heart. The man's self-complacency outraged him, and yet something, he knew not what, made him insist.

"Remember what happened this morning. It wouldn't hurt you to stay at home just tonight. I'll play piquet with you."

"I'll play piquet with you when I come back. The Kanaka isn't born yet who can make me alter my plans."

"You'd better let me come with you."

"You stay where you are."

Mackintosh shrugged his shoulders. He had given the man full warning. If he did not heed it that was his own lookout. Walker put on his hat and went out. Mackintosh began to read; but then he thought of something; perhaps it would be as well to have his own whereabouts quite clear. He crossed over to the kitchen and, inventing some pretext, talked for a few minutes with the cook. Then he got out the gramophone and put a record on it, but while it ground out its melancholy tune, some comic song of a London music-hall, his ear was strained for a sound away there in the night. At his elbow the record reeled out its loudness, the words were raucous, but notwithstanding he seemed to be surrounded by an unearthly silence. He heard the dull roar of the breakers against the reef. He heard the breeze sigh, far up, in the leaves of the coconut trees. How long would it be? It was awful.

He heard a hoarse laugh.

"Wonders will never cease. It's not often you play yourself a tune, Mac."

Walker stood at the window, red-faced, bluff and jovial.

"Well, you see I'm alive and kicking. What were you playing for?"

Walker came in.

"Nerves a bit dicky, eh? Playing a tune to keep your pecker up?"

"I was playing your requiem."

"What the devil's that?"

"'Alf o' bitter an' a pint of stout."

"A rattling good song too. I don't mind how often I hear it. Now I'm ready to take your money off you at piquet."

They played and Walker bullied his way to victory, bluffing his opponent, chaffing him, jeering at his mistakes, up to every dodge, browbeating him, exulting. Presently Mackintosh recovered his coolness, and standing outside himself, as it were, he was able to take a detached pleasure in watching the overbearing old man and in his own cold reserve. Somewhere Manuma sat quietly and awaited his opportunity.

Walker won game after game and pocketed his winnings at the end of the evening in high good humour.

"You'll have to grow a little bit older before you stand much chance against me, Mac. The fact is I have a natural gift for cards."

"I don't know that there's much gift about it when I happen to deal you fourteen aces."

"Good cards come to good players," retorted Walker. "I'd have won if I'd had your hands."

He went on to tell long stories of the various occasions on which he had played cards with notorious sharpers and to their consternation had taken all their money from them. He boasted. He praised himself. And Mackintosh listened with absorption. He wanted now to feed his hatred; and everything Walker said, every gesture, made him more detestable. At last Walker got up.

"Well, I'm going to turn in," he said with a loud yawn. "I've got a long day to-morrow."

"What are you going to do?"

"I'm driving over to the other side of the island. I'll start at five, but I don't expect I shall get back to dinner till late."

They generally dined at seven.

"We'd better make it half past seven then."

"I guess it would be as well."

Mackintosh watched him knock the ashes out of his pipe. His vitality was rude and exuberant. It was strange to think that death hung over him. A faint smile flickered in Mackintosh's cold, gloomy eyes.

"Would you like me to come with you?"

"What in God's name should I want that for? I'm using the mare, and she'll have enough to do to carry me; she don't want to drag you over thirty miles of road."

"Perhaps you don't quite realise what the feeling is at Matautu. I think it would be safer if I came with you."

Walker burst into contemptuous laughter.

"You'd be a fine lot of use in a scrap. I'm not a great hand at getting the wind up."

Now the smile passed from Mackintosh's eyes to his lips. It distorted them painfully.

"Quem deus vult perdere prius dementat."

"What the hell is that?" said Walker.

"Latin," answered Mackintosh as he went out.

And now he chuckled. His mood had changed. He had done all he could, and the matter was in the hands of fate. He slept more soundly than he had done for weeks. When he awoke next morning he went out. After a good night he found a pleasant exhilaration in the freshness of the early air. The sea was a more vivid blue, the sky more brilliant, than on most days, the trade wind was fresh, and there was a ripple on the lagoon as the breeze brushed over it like velvet brushed the wrong way. He felt himself stronger and younger. He entered upon the day's work with zest. After luncheon he slept again, and as evening drew on he had the bay saddled and sauntered through the bush. He seemed to see it all with new eyes. He felt more normal. The extraordinary thing was that he was able to put Walker out of his mind altogether. So far as he was concerned he might never have existed.

He returned late, hot after his ride, and bathed again. Then he sat on the verandah, smoking his pipe, and looked at the day declining over the lagoon. In the sunset the lagoon, rosy and purple and green, was very beautiful. He felt at peace with the world and with himself. When the cook came out to say that dinner was ready and to ask whether he should wait, Mackintosh smiled at him with friendly eyes. He looked at his watch.

"It's half-past seven. Better not wait. One can't tell when the boss'll be back."

The boy nodded, and in a moment Mackintosh saw him carry across the yard a bowl of steaming soup. He got up lazily, went into the dining-room, and ate his dinner. Had it happened? The uncertainty was amusing, and Mackintosh chuckled in the silence. The food did not seem so monotonous as usual, and even though there was Hamburger steak, the cook's invariable dish when his poor invention failed him, it tasted by some miracle succulent and spiced. After dinner he strolled over lazily to his bungalow to get a book. He liked the intense stillness, and now that the night had fallen the stars were blazing in the sky. He shouted for a lamp and in a moment the Chink pattered over on his bare feet, piercing the darkness with a ray of light. He put the lamp on the desk and noiselessly slipped out of the room. Mackintosh stood rooted to the floor, for there, half hidden by untidy papers, was his revolver. His heart throbbed painfully, and he broke into a sweat. It was done then.

He took up the revolver with a shaking hand. Four of the chambers were empty. He paused a moment and looked suspiciously out into the night, but there was no one there. He quickly slipped four cartridges into the empty chambers and locked the revolver in his drawer.

He sat down to wait.

An hour passed; a second hour passed. There was nothing. He sat at his desk as though he were writing, but he neither wrote nor read. He merely listened. He strained his ears for a sound travelling from a far distance. At last, he heard hesitating footsteps and knew it was the Chinese cook.

"Ah-Sung," he called.

The boy came to the door.

"Boss velly late," he said. "Dinner no good."

Mackintosh stared at him, wondering whether he knew what had happened, and whether, when he knew, he would realise on what terms he and Walker had been. He went about his work, sleek, silent, and smiling, and who could tell his thoughts?

"I expect he's had dinner on the way, but you must keep the soup hot at all events."

The words were hardly out of his mouth when the silence was suddenly broken into by a confusion, cries, and a rapid patter of naked feet. A number of natives ran into the compound, men and women and children; they crowded round Mackintosh, and they all talked at once. They were unintelligible. They were excited and frightened and some of them were crying. Mackintosh pushed his way through them and went to the gateway. Though he had scarcely understood what they said he knew quite well what had happened. And as he reached the gate the dog-cart arrived. The old mare was being led by a tall Kanaka, and in the dog-cart crouched two men, trying to hold Walker up. A little crowd of natives surrounded it.

The mare was led into the yard and the natives surged in after it. Mackintosh shouted to them to stand back and the two policemen, sprang suddenly from God knows where, pushed them violently aside. By now he had managed to understand that some lads who had been fishing, on their way back to their village had come across the cart on the home side of the ford. The mare was nuzzling about the herbage and in the darkness they could just see the great white bulk of the old man sunk between the seat and the dashboard. At first they thought he was drunk, and they peered in, grinning, but then they heard him groan, and guessed that something was amiss. They ran to the village and called for help. It was when they returned, accompanied by half a hundred people, that they discovered Walker had been shot.

With a sudden thrill of horror Mackintosh asked himself whether he was already dead. The first thing at all events was to get him out of the cart, and that, owing to Walker's corpulence, was a difficult job. It took four strong men to lift him. They jolted him and he uttered a dull groan. He was still alive. At last, they carried him into the house, up the stairs, and placed him on his bed. Then Mackintosh was able to see him, for in the yard, lit only by half a dozen hurricane lamps, everything had been obscured. Walker's white ducks were stained with blood, and the men who had carried him wiped their hands, red and sticky, on their *lava-lavas*. Mackintosh held up the lamp. He had not expected the old man to be so pale. His eyes were closed. He was breathing still, his pulse could be just felt, but it was obvious that he was dying. Mackintosh had not bargained for the shock of horror that convulsed him. He saw that the native clerk was there, and in a voice hoarse with fear told him to go into the dispensary and get what was necessary for a hypodermic injection. One of the policemen had brought up the whisky, and Mackintosh forced a little into the old man's mouth. The room was crowded with natives. They sat about the floor, speechless now and terrified, and every now and then one wailed aloud. It was very hot, but Mackintosh felt cold, his hands and his feet were like ice, and he had to make a violent effort not to tremble in all his limbs. He did not know what to do. He did not know if Walker was bleeding still, and if he was, how he could stop the bleeding.

The clerk brought the hypodermic needle.

"You give it to him," said Mackintosh. "You're more used to that sort of thing than I am."

His head ached horribly. It felt as though all sorts of little savage things were beating inside it, trying to get out. They watched for the effect of the injection. Presently Walker opened his eyes slowly. He did not seem to know where he was.

"Keep quiet," said Mackintosh. "You're at home. You're quite safe."

Walker's lips outlined a shadowy smile.

"They've got me," he whispered.

"I'll get Jervis to send his motor-boat to Apia at once. We'll get a doctor out by to-morrow afternoon."

There was a long pause before the old man answered,

"I shall be dead by then."

A ghastly expression passed over Mackintosh's pale face. He forced himself to laugh.

"What rot! You keep quiet and you'll be as right as rain."

"Give me a drink," said Walker. "A stiff one."

With shaking hand Mackintosh poured out whisky and water, half and half, and held the glass while Walker drank greedily. It seemed to restore him. He gave a long sigh and a little colour came into his great fleshy face. Mackintosh felt extraordinarily helpless. He stood and stared at the old man.

"If you'll tell me what to do I'll do it," he said.

"There's nothing to do. Just leave me alone. I'm done for."

He looked dreadfully pitiful as he lay on the great bed, a huge, bloated, old man; but so wan, so weak, it was heart-rending. As he rested, his mind seemed to grow clearer.

"You were right, Mac," he said presently. "You warned me."

"I wish to God I'd come with you."

"You're a good chap, Mac, only you don't drink."

There was another long silence, and it was clear that Walker was sinking. There was an internal hæmorrhage and even Mackintosh in his ignorance could not fail to see that his chief had but an hour or two to live. He stood by the side of the bed stock still. For half an hour perhaps, Walker lay with his eyes closed, then he opened them.

"They'll give you my job," he said, slowly. "Last time I was in Apia I told them you were all right. Finish my road. I want to think that'll be done. All round the island."

"I don't want your job. You'll get all right."

Walker shook his head wearily.

"I've had my day. Treat them fairly, that's the great thing. They're children. You must always remember that. You must be firm with them, but you must be kind. And you must be just. I've never made a bob out of them. I haven't saved a hundred pounds in twenty years. The road's the great thing. Get the road finished."

Something very like a sob was wrung from Mackintosh.

"You're a good fellow, Mac. I always liked you."

He closed his eyes, and Mackintosh thought that he would never open them again. His mouth was so dry that he had to get himself something to drink. The Chinese cook silently put a chair for him. He sat down by the side of the bed and waited. He did not know how long a time passed. The night was endless. Suddenly one of the men sitting there broke into uncontrollable sobbing, loudly, like a child, and Mackintosh grew aware that the room was crowded by this time with natives. They sat all over the floor on their haunches, men and women, staring at the bed.

"What are all these people doing here?" said Mackintosh. "They've got no right. Turn them out, turn them out, all of them."

His words seemed to rouse Walker, for he opened his eyes once more, and now they were all misty. He wanted to speak, but he was so weak that Mackintosh had to strain his ears to catch what he said.

"Let them stay. They're my children. They ought to be here."

Mackintosh turned to the natives.

"Stay where you are. He wants you. But be silent."

A faint smile came over the old man's white face.

"Come nearer," he said.

Mackintosh bent over him. His eyes were closed and the words he said were like a wind sighing through the fronds of the coconut trees.

"Give me another drink. I've got something to say."

This time Mackintosh gave him his whisky neat. Walker collected his strength in a final effort of will.

"Don't make a fuss about this. In 'ninety-five when there were troubles white men were killed, and the fleet came and shelled the villages. A lot of people were killed who'd had nothing to do with it. They're damned fools at Apia. If they make a fuss they'll only punish the wrong people. I don't want anyone punished."

He paused for a while to rest.

"You must say it was an accident. No one's to blame. Promise me that."

"I'll do anything you like," whispered Mackintosh.

"Good chap. One of the best. They're children. I'm their father. A father don't let his children get into trouble if he can help it."

A ghost of a chuckle came out of his throat. It was astonishingly weird and ghastly.

"You're a religious chap, Mac. What's that about forgiving them?You know."

For a while Mackintosh did not answer. His lips trembled.

"Forgive them, for they know not what they do?"

"That's right. Forgive them. I've loved them, you know, always loved them."

He sighed. His lips faintly moved, and now Mackintosh had to put his ears quite close to them in order to hear.

"Hold my hand," he said.

Mackintosh gave a gasp. His heart seemed wrenched. He took the old man's hand, so cold and weak, a coarse, rough hand, and held it in his own. And thus, he sat until he nearly started out of his seat, for the silence was suddenly broken by a long rattle. It was terrible and unearthly. Walker was dead. Then the natives broke out with loud cries. The tears ran down their faces, and they beat their breasts.

Mackintosh disengaged his hand from the dead man's and staggering like one drunk with sleep he went out of the room. He went to the locked drawer in his writing-desk and took out the revolver. He walked down to the sea and walked into the lagoon; he waded out cautiously, so that he should not trip against a coral rock, till the water came to his arm-pits. Then he put a bullet through his head.

An hour later half a dozen slim brown sharks were splashing and struggling at the spot where he fell.

III

THE FALL OF EDWARD BARNARD

Bateman Hunter slept badly. For a fortnight on the boat that brought him from Tahiti to San Francisco he had been thinking of the story he had to tell, and for three days on the train he had repeated to himself the words in which he meant to tell it. But in a few hours now he would be in Chicago, and doubts assailed him. His conscience, always very sensitive, was not at ease. He was uncertain that he had done all that was possible, it was on his honour to do much more than the possible, and the thought was disturbing that, in a matter which so nearly touched his own interest, he had allowed his interest to prevail over his quixotry. Self-sacrifice appealed so keenly to his imagination that the inability to exercise it gave him a sense of disillusion. He was like the philanthropist who with altruistic motives builds model dwellings for the poor and finds that he has made a lucrative investment. He cannot prevent the satisfaction he feels in the ten per cent which rewards the bread he had cast upon the waters, but he has an awkward feeling that it detracts somewhat from the savour of his virtue. Bateman Hunter knew that his heart was pure, but he was not quite sure how steadfastly, when he told her his story, he would endure the scrutiny of Isabel Longstaffe's cool grey eyes. They were far-seeing and wise. She measured the standards of others by her own meticulous uprightness and there could be no greater censure than the cold silence with which she expressed her disapproval of a conduct that did not satisfy her exacting code. There was no appeal from her judgment, for, having made up her mind, she never changed it. But Bateman would not have had her different. He loved not only the beauty of her person, slim and straight, with the proud carriage of her head, but still more the beauty of her soul. With her truthfulness, her rigid sense of honour, her fearless outlook, she seemed to him to collect in herself all that was most admirable in his countrywomen. But he saw in her something more than the perfect type of the American girl, he felt that her exquisiteness was peculiar in a way to her environment, and he was assured that no city in the world could have produced her but Chicago. A pang seized him when he remembered that he must deal so bitter a blow to her pride, and anger flamed up in his heart when he thought of Edward Barnard.

But at last, the train steamed into Chicago, and he exulted when he saw the long streets of grey houses. He could hardly bear his impatience at the thought of State and Wabash with their crowded pavements, their hustling traffic, and their noise. He was at home. And he was glad that he had been born in the most important city in the United States. San Francisco was provincial, New York was effete; the future of America lay in the development of its economic possibilities, and Chicago, by its position and by the energy of its citizens, was destined to become the real capital of the country.

"I guess I shall live long enough to see it the biggest city in the world," Bateman said to himself as he stepped down to the platform.

His father had come to meet him, and after a hearty handshake, the pair of them, tall, slender, and well-made, with the same fine, ascetic features and thin lips, walked out of the station. Mr Hunter's automobile was waiting for them, and they got in. Mr. Hunter caught his son's proud and happy glance as he looked at the street.

"Glad to be back, son?" he asked.

"I should just think I was," said Bateman.

His eyes devoured the restless scene.

"I guess there's a bit more traffic here than in your South Sea island," laughed Mr Hunter. "Did you like it there?"

"Give me Chicago, dad," answered Bateman.

"You haven't brought Edward Barnard back with you."

"No."

"How was he?"

Bateman was silent for a moment, and his handsome, sensitive face darkened.

"I'd sooner not speak about him, dad," he said at last.

"That's all right, my son. I guess your mother will be a happy woman today."

They passed out of the crowded streets in the Loop and drove along the lake till they came to the imposing house, an exact copy of a château on the Loire, which Mr Hunter had built himself some years before. As soon as Bateman was alone in his room he asked for a number on the telephone. His heart leaped when he heard the voice that answered him.

"Good-morning, Isabel," he said gaily.

"Good-morning, Bateman."

"How did you recognise my voice?"

"It is not so long since I heard it last. Besides, I was expecting you."

"When may I see you?"

"Unless you have anything better to do perhaps you'll dine with us tonight."

"You know very well that I couldn't possibly have anything better to do."

"I suppose that you're full of news?"

He thought he detected in her voice a note of apprehension.

"Yes," he answered.

"Well, you must tell me tonight. Good-bye."

She rang off. It was characteristic of her that she should be able to wait so many unnecessary hours to know what so immensely concerned her. To Bateman there was an admirable fortitude in her restraint.

At dinner, at which beside himself and Isabel no one was present but her father and mother, he watched her guide the conversation into the channels of an urbane small-talk, and it occurred to him that in just such a manner would a marquise under the shadow of the guillotine toy with the affairs of a day that would know no morrow. Her delicate features, the aristocratic shortness of her upper lip, and her wealth of fair hair suggested the marquise again, and it must have been obvious, even if it were not notorious, that in her veins flowed the best blood in Chicago. The dining-room was a fitting frame to her fragile beauty, for Isabel had caused the house, a replica of a palace on the Grand Canal at Venice, to be furnished by an English expert in the style of Louis XV; and the graceful decoration linked with the name of that amorous monarch enhanced her loveliness and at the same time acquired from it a more profound significance. For Isabel's mind was richly stored, and her conversation, however light, was never flippant. She spoke now of the *Musicale* to which she and her mother had been in the afternoon, of the lectures which an English poet was giving at the Auditorium, of the political situation, and of the Old Master which her father had recently bought for fifty thousand dollars in New York. It comforted Bateman to hear her. He felt that he was once more in the civilised world, at the Centre of culture and distinction; and certain voices, troubling and yet against his will refusing to still their clamour, were at last silent in his heart.

"Gee, but it's good to be back in Chicago," he said.

At last dinner was over, and when they went out of the dining-room Isabel said to her mother:

"I'm going to take Bateman along to my den. We have various things to talk about."

"Very well, my dear," said Mrs. Longstaffe. "You'll find your father and me in the Madame du Barry room when you're through."

Isabel led the young man upstairs and showed him into the room of which he had so many charming memories. Though he knew it so well he could not repress the exclamation of delight which it always wrung from him. She looked round with a smile.

"I think it's a success," she said. "The main thing is that it's right. There's not even an ashtray that isn't of the period."

"I suppose that's what makes it so wonderful. Like all you do it's so superlatively right."

They sat down in front of a log fire and Isabel looked at him with calm grave eyes.

"Now what have you to say to me?" she asked.

"I hardly know how to begin."

"Is Edward Barnard coming back?"

"No."

There was a long silence before Bateman spoke again, and with each of them it was filled with many thoughts. It was a difficult story he had to tell, for there were things in it which were so offensive to her sensitive ears that he could not bear to tell them, and yet in justice to her, no less than in justice to himself, he must tell her the whole truth.

It had all begun long ago when he and Edward Barnard, still at college, had met Isabel Longstaffe at the tea-party given to introduce her to society. They had both known her when she was a child and they long-legged boys, but for two years she had been in Europe to finish her education, and it was with a surprised delight that they renewed acquaintance with the lovely girl who returned. Both of them fell desperately in love with her, but Bateman saw quickly that she had eyes only for Edward, and, devoted to his friend, he resigned himself to the role of confidant. He passed bitter moments, but he could not deny that Edward was worthy of his good fortune, and, anxious that nothing should impair the friendship he so greatly valued, he took care never by a hint to disclose his own feelings. In six months, the young couple were engaged. But they were very young, and Isabel's father decided that they should not marry at least till Edward graduated. They had to wait a year. Bateman remembered the winter at the end of which Isabel and Edward were to be married, a winter of dances and theatre-parties and of informal gaieties at which he, the constant third, was always present. He loved her no less because she would shortly be his friend's wife; her smile, a gay word she flung him, the confidence of her affection, never ceased to delight him; and he congratulated himself, somewhat complacently, because he did not envy them their happiness. Then an accident happened. A great bank failed, there was a panic on the exchange, and Edward Barnard's father found himself a ruined man. He came home one night, told his wife that he was penniless, and after dinner, going into his study, shot himself.

A week later, Edward Barnard, with a tired, white face, went to Isabel and asked her to release him. Her only answer was to throw her arms round his neck and burst into tears.

"Don't make it harder for me, sweet," he said.

"Do you think I can let you go now? I love you."

"How can I ask you to marry me? The whole thing's hopeless. Your father would never let you. I haven't a cent."

"What do I care? I love you."

He told her his plans. He had to earn money at once, and George Braunschmidt, an old friend of his family, had offered to take him into his own business. He was a South Sea merchant, and he had agencies in many of the islands of the Pacific. He had suggested that Edward should go to Tahiti for a year or two, where under the best of his managers he could learn the details of that varied trade, and at the end of that time he promised the young man a position in Chicago. It was a wonderful opportunity, and when he had finished his explanations Isabel was once more all smiles.

"You foolish boy, why have you been trying to make me miserable?"

His face lit up at her words and his eyes flashed.

"Isabel, you don't mean to say you'll wait for me?"

"Don't you think you're worth it?" she smiled.

"Ah, don't laugh at me now. I beseech you to be serious. It may be for two years."

"Have no fear. I love you, Edward. When you come back I will marry you."

Edward's employer was a man who did not like delay, and he had told him that if he took the post he offered he must sail that day week from San Francisco. Edward spent his last evening with Isabel. It was after dinner that Mr. Longstaffe, saying he wanted a word with Edward, took him into the smoking-room. Mr. Longstaffe had accepted good-naturedly the arrangement which his daughter had told him of, and Edward could not imagine what mysterious communication he had now to make. He was not a little perplexed to see that his host was embarrassed. He faltered. He talked of trivial things. At last, he blurted it out.

"I guess you've heard of Arnold Jackson," he said, looking at Edward with a frown.

Edward hesitated. His natural truthfulness obliged him to admit some knowledge he would gladly have been able to deny.

"Yes, I have. But it's a long time ago. I guess I didn't pay very much attention."

"There are not many people in Chicago who haven't heard of Arnold Jackson," said Mr. Longstaffe bitterly, "and if there are they'll have no difficulty in finding someone who'll be glad to tell them. Did you know he was Mrs. Longstaffe's brother?"

"Yes, I knew that."

"Of course we've had no communication with him for many years. He left the country as soon as he was able to, and I guess the country wasn't sorry to see the last of him. We understand he lives in Tahiti. My advice to you is to give him a wide berth, but if you do hear anything about him Mrs. Longstaffe and I would be very glad if you'd let us know."

"Sure."

"That was all I wanted to say to you. Now I daresay you'd like to join the ladies."

There are few families that have not among their members one whom, if their neighbours permitted, they would willingly forget, and they are fortunate when the lapse of a generation or two has invested his vagaries with a romantic glamour. But when he is actually alive, if his peculiarities are not of the kind that can be condoned by the phrase, "he is nobody's enemy but his own," a safe one when the culprit has no worse to answer for than alcoholism or wandering affections, the only possible course is silence. And it was this which the Longstaffes had adopted towards Arnold Jackson. They never talked of him. They would not even pass through the street in which he had lived. Too kind to make his wife and children suffer for his misdeeds, they had supported them for years, but on the understanding that they should live in Europe. They did everything they could to blot out all recollection of Arnold Jackson and yet were conscious that the story was as fresh in the public mind as when first the scandal burst upon a gaping world. Arnold Jackson was as black a sheep as any family could suffer from. A wealthy banker, prominent in his church, a philanthropist, a man respected by all, not only for his connections (in his veins ran the blue blood of Chicago), but also for his upright character, he was arrested one day on a charge of fraud; and the dishonesty which the trial brought to light was not of the sort which could be explained by a sudden temptation; it was deliberate and systematic. Arnold Jackson was a rogue. When he was sent to the penitentiary for seven years there were few who did not think he had escaped lightly.

When at the end of this last evening the lovers separated it was with many protestations of devotion. Isabel, all tears, was consoled a little by her certainty of Edward's passionate love. It was a strange feeling that she had. It made her wretched to part from him and yet she was happy because he adored her.

This was more than two years ago.

He had written to her by every mail since then, twenty-four letters in all, for the mail went but once a month, and his letters had been all that a lover's letters should be. They were intimate and charming, humorous sometimes, especially of late, and tender. At first they suggested that he was homesick, they were full of his desire to get back to Chicago and Isabel; and a little anxiously, she wrote begging him to persevere. She was afraid that he might throw up his opportunity and come racing back. She did not want her lover to lack endurance, and she quoted to him the lines:

"I could not love thee, dear, so much,
Loved I not honour more."

But presently he seemed to settle down and it made Isabel very happy to observe his growing enthusiasm to introduce American methods into that forgotten corner of the world. But she knew him, and at the end of the year, which was the shortest time he could possibly stay in Tahiti, she expected to have to use all her influence to dissuade him from coming home. It was much better that he should learn the business thoroughly, and if they had been able to wait a year there seemed no reason why they should not wait another. She talked it over with Bateman Hunter, always the most generous of friends (during those first few days after Edward went she did not know what she would have done without him), and they decided that Edward's future must stand before everything. It was with relief that she found as the time passed that he made no suggestion of returning.

"He's splendid, isn't he?" she exclaimed to Bateman.

"He's white, through and through."

"Reading between the lines of his letter I know he hates it over there, but he's sticking it out because...."

She blushed a little and Bateman, with the grave smile, which was so attractive in him, finished the sentence for her.

"Because he loves you."

"It makes me feel so humble," she said.

"You're wonderful, Isabel, you're perfectly wonderful."

But the second year passed, and every month Isabel continued to receive a letter from Edward, and presently it began to seem a little strange that he did not speak of coming back. He wrote as though he were settled definitely in Tahiti, and what was more, comfortably settled. She was surprised. Then she read his letters again, all of them, several times; and now, reading between the lines indeed, she was puzzled to notice a change which had escaped her. The later letters were as tender and as delightful as the first, but the tone was different. She was vaguely suspicious of their humour, she had the instinctive mistrust of her sex for that unaccountable quality, and she discerned in them now a flippancy which perplexed her. She was not quite certain that the Edward who wrote to her now was the same Edward that she had known. One afternoon, the day after a mail had arrived from Tahiti, when she was driving with Bateman he said to her:

"Did Edward tell you when he was sailing?"

"No, he didn't mention it. I thought he might have said something to you about it."

"Not a word."

"You know what Edward is," she laughed in reply, "he has no sense of time. If it occurs to you next time you write you might ask him when he's thinking of coming."

Her manner was so unconcerned that only Bateman's acute sensitiveness could have discerned in her request a very urgent desire. He laughed lightly.

"Yes. I'll ask him. I can't imagine what he's thinking about."

A few days later, meeting him again, she noticed that something troubled him. They had been much together since Edward left Chicago; they were both devoted to him and each in his desire to talk of the absent one found a willing listener; the consequence was that Isabel knew every expression of Bateman's face, and his denials now were useless against her keen instinct. Something told her that his harassed look had to do with Edward, and she did not rest till she had made him confess.

"The fact is," he said at last, "I heard in a round-about way that Edward was no longer working for Braunschmidt and Co., and yesterday I took the opportunity to ask Mr. Braunschmidt himself."

"Well?"

"Edward left his employment with them nearly a year ago."

"How strange he should have said nothing about it!"

Bateman hesitated, but he had gone so far now that he was obliged to tell the rest. It made him feel dreadfully embarrassed.

"He was fired."

"In heaven's name what for?"

"It appears they warned him once or twice, and at last they told him to get out. They say he was lazy and incompetent."

"Edward?"

They were silent for a while, and then he saw that Isabel was crying. Instinctively he seized her hand.

"Oh, my dear, don't, don't," he said. "I can't bear to see it."

She was so unstrung that she let her hand rest in his. He tried to console her.

"It's incomprehensible, isn't it? It's so unlike Edward. I can't help feeling there must be some mistake."

She did not say anything for a while, and when she spoke it was hesitatingly.

"Has it struck you that there was anything queer in his letters lately?" she asked, looking away, her eyes all bright with tears.

He did not quite know how to answer.

"I have noticed a change in them," he admitted. "He seems to have lost that high seriousness which I admired so much in him. One would almost think that the things that matter—well, don't matter."

Isabel did not reply. She was vaguely uneasy.

"Perhaps in his answer to your letter he'll say when he's coming home. All we can do is to wait for that."

Another letter came from Edward for each of them, and still he made no mention of his return; but when he wrote he could not have received Bateman's enquiry. The next mail would bring them an answer to that. The next mail came, and Bateman brought Isabel the letter he had just received; but the first glance of his face was enough to tell her that he was disconcerted. She read it through carefully and then, with slightly tightened lips, read it again.

"It's a very strange letter," she said. "I don't quite understand it."

"One might almost think that he was joshing me," said Bateman, flushing.

"It reads like that, but it must be unintentional. That's so unlike Edward."

"He says nothing about coming back."

"If I weren't so confident of his love I should think.... I hardly know what I should think."

It was then that Bateman had broached the scheme which during the afternoon had formed itself in his brain. The firm, founded by his father, in which he was now a partner, a firm which manufactured all manner of motor vehicles, was about to establish agencies in Honolulu, Sidney, and Wellington; and Bateman proposed that himself should go instead of the manager who had been suggested. He could return by Tahiti; in fact, travelling from Wellington, it was inevitable to do so; and he could see Edward.

"There's some mystery and I'm going to clear it up. That's the only way to do it."

"Oh, Bateman, how can you be so good and kind?" she exclaimed.

"You know there's nothing in the world I want more than your happiness, Isabel."

She looked at him and she gave him her hands.

"You're wonderful, Bateman. I didn't know there was anyone in the world like you. How can I ever thank you?"

"I don't want your thanks. I only want to be allowed to help you."

She dropped her eyes and flushed a little. She was so used to him that she had forgotten how handsome he was. He was as tall as Edward and as well made, but he was dark and pale of face, while Edward was ruddy. Of course, she knew he loved her. It touched her. She felt very tenderly towards him.

It was from this journey that Bateman Hunter was now returned.

The business part of it took him somewhat longer than he expected, and he had much time to think of his two friends. He had come to the conclusion that it could be nothing serious that prevented Edward from coming home, a pride, perhaps, which made him determined to make good before he claimed the bride he adored; but it was a pride that must be reasoned with. Isabel was unhappy. Edward must come back to Chicago with him and marry her at once. A position could be found for him in the works of the Hunter Motor Traction and Automobile Company. Bateman, with a bleeding heart, exulted at the prospect of giving happiness to the two persons he loved best in the world at the cost of his own. He would never marry. He would be godfather to the children of Edward and Isabel, and many years later when they were both dead he would tell Isabel's daughter how long, long ago he had loved her mother. Bateman's eyes were veiled with tears when he pictured this scene to himself.

Meaning to take Edward by surprise he had not cabled to announce his arrival, and when at last he landed at Tahiti he allowed a youth, who said he was the son of the house, to lead him to the Hotel de la Fleur. He chuckled when he thought of his friend's amazement on seeing him, the most unexpected of visitors, walk into his office.

"By the way," he asked, as they went along, "can you tell me where I shall find Mr. Edward Barnard?"

"Barnard?" said the youth. "I seem to know the name."

"He's an American. A tall fellow with light brown hair and blue eyes. He's been here over two years."

"Of course. Now I know who you mean. You mean Mr. Jackson's nephew."

"Whose nephew?"

"Mr. Arnold Jackson."

"I don't think we're speaking of the same person," answered Bateman, frigidly.

He was startled. It was queer that Arnold Jackson, known apparently to all and sundry, should live here under the disgraceful name in which he had been convicted. But Bateman could not imagine whom it was that he passed off as his nephew. Mrs. Longstaffe was his only sister, and he had never had a brother. The young man by his side talked volubly in an English that had something in it of the intonation of a foreign tongue, and Bateman, with a sidelong glance, saw, what he had not noticed before, that there was in him a good deal of native blood. A touch of hauteur involuntarily entered into his manner. They reached the hotel. When he had arranged about his room Bateman asked to be directed to the premises of Braunschmidt & Co. They were on the front, facing the lagoon, and, glad to feel the solid earth under his feet after eight days at sea, he sauntered down the sunny road to the water's edge. Having found the place he sought, Bateman sent in his card to the manager and was led through a lofty barn-like room, half store and half warehouse, to an office in which sat a stout, spectacled, bald-headed man.

"Can you tell me where I shall find Mr. Edward Barnard? I understand he was in this office for some time."

"That is so. I don't know just where he is."

"But I thought he came here with a particular recommendation from Mr. Braunschmidt. I know Mr. Braunschmidt very well."

The fat man looked at Bateman with shrewd, suspicious eyes. He called to one of the boys in the warehouse.

"Say, Henry, where's Barnard now, d'you know?"

"He's working at Cameron's, I think," came the answer from someone who did not trouble to move.

The fat man nodded.

"If you turn to your left when you get out of here you'll come to Cameron's in about three minutes."

Bateman hesitated.

"I think I should tell you that Edward Barnard is my greatest friend. I was very much surprised when I heard he'd left Braunschmidt & Co."

The fat man's eyes contracted till they seemed like pin-points, and their scrutiny made Bateman so uncomfortable that he felt himself blushing.

"I guess Braunschmidt & Co. and Edward Barnard didn't see eye to eye on certain matters," he replied.

Bateman did not quite like the fellow's manner, so he got up, not without dignity, and with an apology for troubling him bade him good-day. He left the place with a singular feeling that the man he had just interviewed had much to tell him, but no intention of telling it. He walked in the direction indicated and soon found himself at Cameron's. It was a trader's store, such as he had passed half a dozen of on his way, and when he entered the first person he saw, in his shirt sleeves, measuring out a length of trade cotton, was Edward. It gave him a start to see him engaged in so humble an occupation. But he had scarcely appeared when Edward, looking up, caught sight of him, and gave a joyful cry of surprise.

"Bateman! Who ever thought of seeing you here?"

He stretched his arm across the counter and wrung Bateman's hand. There was no self-consciousness in his manner and the embarrassment was all on Bateman's side.

"Just wait till I've wrapped this package."

With perfect assurance he ran his scissors across the stuff, folded it, made it into a parcel, and handed it to the dark-skinned customer.

"Pay at the desk, please."

Then, smiling, with bright eyes, he turned to Bateman.

"How did you show up here? Gee, I am delighted to see you. Sit down, old man. Make yourself at home."

"We can't talk here. Come along to my hotel. I suppose you can get away?"

This he added with some apprehension.

"Of course I can get away. We're not so businesslike as all that in Tahiti." He called out to a Chinese who was standing behind the opposite counter. "Ah-Ling, when the boss comes tell him a friend of mine's just arrived from America and I've gone out to have a drain with him."

"All-light," said the Chinese, with a grin.

Edward slipped on a coat and, putting on his hat, accompanied Bateman out of the store. Bateman attempted to put the matter facetiously.

"I didn't expect to find you selling three and a half yards of rotten cotton to a greasy nigger," he laughed.

"Braunschmidt fired me, you know, and I thought that would do as well as anything else."

Edward's candour seemed to Bateman very surprising, but he thought it indiscreet to pursue the subject.

"I guess you won't make a fortune where you are," he answered, somewhat dryly.

"I guess not. But I earn enough to keep body and soul together, and I'm quite satisfied with that."

"You wouldn't have been two years ago."

"We grow wiser as we grow older," retorted Edward, gaily.

Bateman took a glance at him. Edward was dressed in a suit of shabby white ducks, none too clean, and a large straw hat of native make. He was thinner than he had been, deeply burned by the sun, and he was certainly better looking than ever. But there was something in his appearance that disconcerted Bateman. He walked with a new jauntiness; there was a carelessness in his demeanour, a gaiety about nothing in particular, which Bateman could not precisely blame, but which exceedingly puzzled him.

"I'm blest if I can see what he's got to be so darned cheerful about," he said to himself.

They arrived at the hotel and sat on the terrace. A Chinese boy brought them cocktails. Edward was most anxious to hear all the news of Chicago and bombarded his friend with eager questions. His interest was natural and sincere. But the odd thing was that it seemed equally divided among a multitude of subjects. He was as eager to know how Bateman's father was as what Isabel was doing. He talked of her without a shade of embarrassment, but she might just as well have been his sister as his promised wife; and before Bateman had done analysing the exact meaning of Edward's remarks he found that the conversation had drifted to his own work and the buildings his father had lately erected. He was determined to bring the conversation back to Isabel and was looking for the occasion when he saw Edward wave his hand cordially. A man was advancing towards them on the terrace, but Bateman's back was turned to him, and he could not see him.

"Come and sit down," said Edward gaily.

The new-comer approached. He was a very tall, thin man, in white ducks, with a fine head of curly white hair. His face was thin too, long, with a large, hooked nose and a beautiful, expressive mouth.

"This is my old friend Bateman Hunter. I've told you about him," said Edward, his constant smile breaking on his lips.

"I'm pleased to meet you, Mr. Hunter. I used to know your father."

The stranger held out his hand and took the young men in a strong, friendly grasp. It was not till then that Edward mentioned the other's name.

"Mr. Arnold Jackson."

Bateman turned white and he felt his hands grow cold. This was the forger, the convict, this was Isabel's uncle. He did not know what to say. He tried to conceal his confusion. Arnold Jackson looked at him with twinkling eyes.

"I daresay my name is familiar to you."

Bateman did not know whether to say yes or no, and what made it more awkward was that both Jackson and Edward seemed to be amused. It was bad enough to have forced on him the acquaintance of the one man on the island he would rather have avoided, but worse to discern that he was being made a fool of. Perhaps, however, he had reached this conclusion too quickly, for Jackson, without a pause, added:

"I understand you're very friendly with the Longstaffes. Mary Longstaffe is my sister."

Now Bateman asked himself if Arnold Jackson could think him ignorant of the most terrible scandal that Chicago had ever known. But Jackson put his hand on Edward's shoulder.

"I can't sit down, Teddie," he said. "I'm busy. But you two boys had better come up and dine tonight."

"That'll be fine," said Edward.

"It's very kind of you, Mr. Jackson," said Bateman, frigidly, "but I'm here for so short a time; my boat sails to-morrow, you know; I think if you'll forgive me, I won't come."

"Oh, nonsense. I'll give you a native dinner. My wife's a wonderful cook. Teddie will show you the way. Come early so as to see the sunset. I can give you both a shake-down if you like."

"Of course we'll come," said Edward. "There's always the devil of a row in the hotel on the night a boat arrives, and we can have a good yarn up at the bungalow."

"I can't let you off, Mr. Hunter," Jackson continued with the utmost cordiality. "I want to hear all about Chicago and Mary."

He nodded and walked away before Bateman could say another word.

"We don't take refusals in Tahiti," laughed Edward. "Besides, you'll get the best dinner on the island."

"What did he mean by saying his wife was a good cook? I happen to know his wife's in Geneva."

"That's a long way off for a wife, isn't it?" said Edward. "And it's a long time since he saw her. I guess it's another wife he's talking about."

For some time, Bateman was silent. His face was set in grave lines. But looking up he caught the amused look in Edward's eyes, and he flushed darkly.

"Arnold Jackson is a despicable rogue," he said.

"I greatly fear he is," answered Edward, smiling.

"I don't see how any decent man can have anything to do with him."

"Perhaps I'm not a decent man."

"Do you see much of him, Edward?"

"Yes, quite a lot. He's adopted me as his nephew."

Bateman leaned forward and fixed Edward with his searching eyes.

"Do you like him?"

"Very much."

"But don't you know, doesn't everyone here know, that he's a forger and that he's been a convict? He ought to be hounded out of civilised society."

Edward watched a ring of smoke that floated from his cigar into the still, scented air.

"I suppose he is a pretty unmitigated rascal," he said at last. "And I can't flatter myself that any repentance for his misdeeds offers one an excuse for condoning them. He was a swindler and a hypocrite. You can't get away from it. I never met a more agreeable companion. He's taught me everything I know."

"What has he taught you?" cried Bateman in amazement.

"How to live."

Bateman broke into ironical laughter.

"A fine master. Is it owing to his lessons that you lost the chance of making a fortune and earn your living now by serving behind a counter in a ten-cent store?"

"He has a wonderful personality," said Edward, smiling good-naturedly. "Perhaps you'll see what I mean tonight."

"I'm not going to dine with him if that's what you mean. Nothing would induce me to set foot within that man's house."

"Come to oblige me, Bateman. We've been friends for so many years, you won't refuse me a favour when I ask it."

Edward's tone had in it a quality new to Bateman. Its gentleness was singularly persuasive.

"If you put it like that, Edward, I'm bound to come," he smiled.

Bateman reflected, moreover, that it would be as well to learn what he could about Arnold Jackson. It was plain that he had a great ascendency over Edward, and if it was to be combated it was necessary to discover in what exactly it consisted of. The more he talked with Edward the more conscious he became that a change had taken place in him. He had an instinct that it behooved him to walk warily, and he made up his mind not to broach the real purport of his visit till he saw his way more clearly. He began to talk of one thing and another, of his journey and what he had achieved by it, of politics in Chicago, of this common friend and that, of their days together at college.

At last Edward said he must get back to his work and proposed that he should fetch Bateman at five so that they could drive out together to Arnold Jackson's house.

"By the way, I rather thought you'd be living at this hotel," said Bateman, as he strolled out of the garden with Edward. "I understand it's the only decent one here."

"Not I," laughed Edward. "It's a deal too grand for me. I rent a room just outside the town. It's cheap and clean."

"If I remember right those weren't the points that seemed most important to you when you lived in Chicago."

"Chicago!"

"I don't know what you mean by that, Edward. It's the greatest city in the world."

"I know," said Edward.

Bateman glanced at him quickly, but his face was inscrutable.

"When are you coming back to it?"

"I often wonder," smiled Edward.

This answer, and the manner of it, staggered Bateman, but before he could ask for an explanation Edward waved to a half-caste who was driving a passing motor.

"Give us a ride down, Charlie," he said.

He nodded to Bateman and ran after the machine that had pulled up a few yards in front. Bateman was left to piece together a mass of perplexing impressions.

Edward called for him in a rickety trap drawn by an old mare, and they drove along a road that ran by the sea. On each side of it were plantations, coconut and vanilla; and now and then they saw a great mango, its fruit yellow and red and purple among the massy green of the leaves; now and then they had a glimpse of the lagoon, smooth and blue, with here and there a tiny islet graceful with tall palms. Arnold Jackson's house stood on a little hill and only a path led to it, so they unharnessed the mare and tied her to a tree, leaving the trap by the side of the road. To Bateman it seemed a happy-go-lucky way of doing things. But when they went up to the house they were met by a tall, handsome native woman, no longer young, with whom Edward cordially shook hands. He introduced Bateman to her.

"This is my friend Mr. Hunter. We're going to dine with you, Lavina."

"All right," she said, with a quick smile. "Arnold ain't back yet."

"We'll go down and bathe. Let us have a couple of *pareos*."

The woman nodded and went into the house.

"Who is that?" asked Bateman.

"Oh, that's Lavina. She's Arnold's wife."

Bateman tightened his lips but said nothing. In a moment the woman returned with a bundle, which she gave to Edward; and the two men, scrambling down a steep path, made their way to a grove of coconut trees on the beach. They undressed and Edward showed his friend how to make the strip of red trade cotton which is called a *pareo* into a very neat pair of bathing-drawers. Soon they were splashing in the warm, shallow water. Edward was in great spirits. He laughed and shouted and sang. He might have been fifteen. Bateman had never seen him so gay, and afterwards when they lay on the beach, smoking cigarettes, in the limpid air, there was such an irresistible light-heartedness in him that Bateman was taken aback.

"You seem to find life mighty pleasant," said he.

"I do."

They heard a soft movement and looking round saw that Arnold Jackson was coming towards them.

"I thought I'd come down and fetch you two boys back," he said. "Did you enjoy your bath, Mr. Hunter?"

"Very much," said Bateman.

Arnold Jackson, no longer in spruce ducks, wore nothing but a *pareo* round his loins and walked barefoot. His body was deeply browned by the sun. With his long, curling white hair and his ascetic face he made a fantastic figure in the native dress, but he bore himself without a trace of self-consciousness.

"If you're ready we'll go right up," said Jackson.

"I'll just put on my clothes," said Bateman.

"Why, Teddie, didn't you bring a *pareo* for your friend?"

"I guess he'd rather wear clothes," smiled Edward.

"I certainly would," answered Bateman, grimly, as he saw Edward gird himself in the loincloth and stand ready to start before he himself had got his shirt on.

"Won't you find it rough walking without your shoes?" he asked Edward. "It struck me the path was a trifle rocky."

"Oh, I'm used to it."

"It's a comfort to get into a *pareo* when one gets back from town," said Jackson. "If you were going to stay here I would strongly recommend you adopt it. It's one of the most sensible costumes I have ever come across. It's cool, convenient, and inexpensive."

They walked up to the house, and Jackson took them into a large room with white-washed walls and an open ceiling in which a table was laid for dinner. Bateman noticed that it was set for five.

"Eva, come and show yourself to Teddie's friend, and then shake us a cocktail," called Jackson.

Then he led Bateman to a long low window.

"Look at that," he said, with a dramatic gesture. "Look well."

Below them coconut trees tumbled down steeply to the lagoon, and the lagoon in the evening light had the colour, tender and varied, of a dove's breast. On a creek, at a little distance, were the clustered huts of a native village, and towards the reef was a canoe, sharply silhouetted, in which were a couple of natives fishing. Then, beyond, you saw the vast calmness of the Pacific and twenty miles away, airy and unsubstantial like the fabric of a poet's fancy, the unimaginable beauty of the island which is called Murea. It was all so lovely that Bateman stood abashed.

"I've never seen anything like it," he said at last.

Arnold Jackson stood staring in front of him, and in his eyes was a dreamy softness. His thin, thoughtful face was very grave. Bateman, glancing at it, was once more conscious of its intense spirituality.

"Beauty," murmured Arnold Jackson. "You seldom see beauty face to face. Look at it well, Mr. Hunter, for what you see now you will never see again, since the moment is transitory, but it will be an imperishable memory in your heart. You touch eternity."

His voice was deep and resonant. He seemed to breathe forth the purest idealism, and Bateman had to urge himself to remember that the man who spoke was a criminal and a cruel cheat. But Edward, as though he heard a sound, turned round quickly.

"Here is my daughter, Mr. Hunter."

Bateman shook hands with her. She had dark, splendid eyes and a red mouth tremulous with laughter; but her skin was brown, and her curling hair, rippling down her-shoulders, was coal black. She wore but one garment, a Mother Hubbard of pink cotton, her feet were bare, and she was crowned with a wreath of white scented flowers. She was a lovely creature. She was like a goddess of the Polynesian spring.

She was a little shy, but not more shy than Bateman, to whom the whole situation was highly embarrassing, and it did not put him at his ease to see this sylph-like thing take a shaker and with a practised hand mix three cocktails.

"Let us have a kick in them, child," said Jackson.

She poured them out and smiling delightfully handed one to each of the men. Bateman flattered himself on his skill in the subtle art of shaking cocktails and he was not a little astonished, on tasting this one, to find that it was excellent. Jackson laughed proudly when he saw his guest's involuntary look of appreciation.

"Not bad, is it? I taught the child myself, and in the old days in Chicago I considered that there wasn't a bar-tender in the city that could hold a candle to me. When I had nothing better to do in the penitentiary I used to amuse myself by thinking out new cocktails, but when you come down to brass-tacks there's nothing to beat a dry Martini."

Bateman felt as though someone had given him a violent blow on the funny-bone and he was conscious that he turned red and then white. But before he could think of anything to say a native boy brought in a great bowl of soup and the whole party sat down to dinner. Arnold Jackson's remark seemed to have aroused in him a train of recollections, for he began to talk of his prison days. He talked quite naturally, without malice, as though he were relating his experiences at a foreign university. He addressed himself to Bateman and Bateman was confused and then confounded. He saw Edward's eyes fixed on him and there was in them a flicker of amusement. He blushed scarlet, for it struck him that Jackson was making a fool of him, and then because he felt absurd—and knew there was no reason why he should—he grew angry. Arnold Jackson was impudent—there was no other word for it—and his callousness, whether assumed or not, was outrageous. The dinner proceeded. Bateman was asked to eat sundry messes, raw fish and he knew not what, which only his civility induced him to swallow, but which he was amazed to find very good eating. Then an incident happened which to Bateman was the most mortifying experience of the evening. There was a little circlet of flowers in front of him, and for the sake of conversation he hazarded a remark about it.

"It's a wreath that Eva made for you," said Jackson, "but I guess she was too shy to give it you."

Bateman took it up in his hand and made a polite little speech of thanks to the girl.

"You must put it on," she said, with a smile and a blush.

"I? I don't think I'll do that."

"It's the charming custom of the country," said Arnold Jackson.

There was one in front of him, and he placed it on his hair. Edward did the same.

"I guess I'm not dressed for the part," said Bateman, uneasily.

"Would you like a *pareo*?" said Eva quickly. "I'll get you one in a minute."

"No, thank you. I'm quite comfortable as I am."

"Show him how to put it on, Eva," said Edward.

At that moment Bateman hated his greatest friend. Eva got up from the table and with much laughter placed the wreath on his black hair.

"It suits you very well," said Mrs Jackson. "Don't it suit him, Arnold?"

"Of course it does."

Bateman sweated at every pore.

"Isn't it a pity it's dark?" said Eva. "We could photograph you all three together."

Bateman thanked his stars it was. He felt that he must look prodigiously foolish in his blue serge suit and high collar—very neat and gentlemanly—with that ridiculous wreath of flowers on his head. He was seething with indignation, and he had never in his life exercised more self-control than now when he presented an affable exterior. He was furious with that old man, sitting at the head of the table, half-naked, with his saintly face and the flowers on his handsome white locks. The whole position was monstrous.

Then dinner came to an end, and Eva and her mother remained to clear away while the three men sat on the verandah. It was very warm, and the air was scented with the white flowers of the night. The full moon, sailing across an unclouded sky, made a pathway on the broad sea that led to the boundless realms of Forever. Arnold Jackson began to talk. His voice was rich and musical. He talked now of the natives and of the old legends of the country. He told strange stories of the past, stories of hazardous expeditions into the unknown, of love and death, of hatred and revenge. He told of the adventurers who had discovered those distant islands, of the sailors who, settling in them, had married the daughters of great chieftains, and of the beach-combers who had led their varied lives on those silvery shores. Bateman mortified and exasperated at first listened sullenly, but presently some magic in the words possessed him and he sat entranced. The mirage of romance obscured the light of common day. Had he forgotten that Arnold Jackson had a tongue of silver, a tongue by which he had charmed vast sums out of the credulous public, a tongue which very nearly enabled him to escape the penalty of his crimes? No one had a sweeter eloquence, and no one had a more acute sense of climax. Suddenly he rose.

"Well, you two boys haven't seen one another for a long time. I shall leave you to have a yarn. Teddie will show you your quarters when you want to go to bed."

"Oh, but I wasn't thinking of spending the night, Mr. Jackson," said Bateman.

"You'll find it more comfortable. We'll see that you're called in good time."

Then with a courteous shake of the hand, stately as though he were a bishop in canonicals, Arnold Jackson took leave of his guest.

"Of course, I'll drive you back to Papeete if you like," said Edward, "but I advise you to stay. It's bully driving in the early morning."

For a few minutes neither of them spoke. Bateman wondered how he should begin on the conversation which all the events of the day made him think more urgent.

"When are you coming back to Chicago?" he asked, suddenly.

For a moment Edward did not answer. Then he turned rather lazily to look at his friend and smiled.

"I don't know. Perhaps never."

"What in heaven's name do you mean?" cried Bateman.

"I'm very happy here. Wouldn't it be folly to make a change?"

"Man alive, you can't live here all your life. This is no life for a man. It's a living death. Oh, Edward, come away at once, before it's too late. I've felt that something was wrong. You're infatuated with the place, you've succumbed to evil influences, but it only requires a wrench, and when you're free from these surroundings you'll thank all the gods there be. You'll be like a dope-fiend when he's broken from his drug. You'll see then that for two years you've been breathing poisoned air. You can't imagine what a relief it will be when you fill your lungs once more with the fresh, pure air of your native country."

He spoke quickly, the words tumbling over one another in his excitement, and there was in his voice sincere and affectionate emotion. Edward was touched.

"It is good of you to care so much, old friend."

"Come with me to-morrow, Edward. It was a mistake that you ever came to this place. This is no life for you."

"You talk of this sort of life and that. How do you think a man gets the best out of life?"

"Why, I should have thought there could be no two answers to that. By doing his duty, by hard work, by meeting all the obligations of his state and station."

"And what is his reward?"

"His reward is the consciousness of having achieved what he set out to do."

"It all sounds a little portentous to me," said Edward, and in the lightness of the night Bateman could see that he was smiling. "I'm afraid you'll think I've degenerated sadly. There are several things I think now which I daresay would have seemed outrageous to me three years ago."

"Have you learnt them from Arnold Jackson?" asked Bateman, scornfully.

"You don't like him? Perhaps you couldn't be expected to. I didn't when I first came. I had just the same prejudice as you. He's a very extraordinary man. You saw for yourself that he makes no secret of the fact that he was in a penitentiary. I do not know that he regrets it or the crimes that led him there. The only complaint he ever made in my hearing was that when he came out his health was impaired. I think he does not know what remorse is. He is completely unmoral. He accepts everything and he accepts himself as well. He's generous and kind."

"He always was," interrupted Bateman, "on other people's money."

"I've found him a very good friend. Is it unnatural that I should take a man as I find him?"

"The result is that you lose the distinction between right and wrong."

"No, they remain just as clearly divided in my mind as before, but what has become a little confused in me is the distinction between the bad man and the good one. Is Arnold Jackson a bad man who does good things or a good man who does bad things? It's a difficult question to answer. Perhaps we make too much of the difference between one man and another. Perhaps even the best of us are sinners and the worst of us are saints. Who knows?"

"You will never persuade me that white is black, and that black is white," said Bateman.

"I'm sure I shan't, Bateman."

Bateman could not understand why the flicker of a smile crossed Edward's lips when he thus agreed with him. Edward was silent for a minute.

"When I saw you this morning, Bateman," he said then, "I seemed to see myself as I was two years ago. The same collar, and the same shoes, the same blue suit, the same energy. The same determination. By God, I was energetic. The sleepy methods of this place made my blood tingle. I went about and everywhere I saw possibilities for development and enterprise. There were fortunes to be made here. It seemed to me absurd that the copra should be taken away from here in sacks and the oil extracted in America. It would be far more economical to do all that on the spot, with cheap labour, and save freight, and I saw already the vast factories springing up on the island. Then the way they extracted it from the coconut seemed to me hopelessly inadequate, and I invented a machine which divided the nut and scooped out the meat at the rate of two hundred and forty an hour. The harbour was not large enough. I made plans to enlarge it, then to form a syndicate to buy land, put up two or three large hotels, and bungalows for occasional residents; I had a scheme for improving the steamer service in order to attract visitors from California. In twenty years, instead of this half French, lazy little town of Papeete I saw a great American city with ten-story buildings and street-cars, a theatre and an opera house, a stock exchange and a mayor."

"But go ahead, Edward," cried Bateman, springing up from the chair in excitement. "You've got the ideas and the capacity. Why, you'll become the richest man between Australia and the States."

Edward chuckled softly.

"But I don't want to," he said.

"Do you mean to say you don't want money, big money, money running into millions? Do you know what you can do with it? Do you know the power it brings? And if you don't care about it for yourself think what you can do, opening new channels for human enterprise, giving occupation to thousands. My brain reels at the visions your words have conjured up."

"Sit down, then, my dear Bateman," laughed Edward. "My machine for cutting the coconuts will always remain unused, and so far as I'm concerned street-cars shall never run in the idle streets of Papeete."

Bateman sank heavily into his chair.

"I don't understand you," he said.

"It came upon me little by little. I came to like the life here, with its ease and its leisure, and the people, with their good-nature and their happy smiling faces. I began to think. I'd never had time to do that before. I began to read."

"You always read."

"I read for examinations. I read in order to be able to hold my own in conversation. I read for instruction. Here I learned to read for pleasure. I learned to talk. Do you know that conversation is one of the greatest pleasures in life? But it wants leisure. I'd always been too busy before. And gradually all the life that had seemed so important to me began to seem rather trivial and vulgar. What is the use of all this hustle and this constant striving? I think of Chicago now and I see a dark, grey city, all stone—it is like a prison—and a ceaseless turmoil. And what does all that activity amount to? Does one get there the best out of life? Is that what we come into the world for, to hurry to an office, and work hour after hour till night, then hurry home and dine and go to a theatre? Is that how I must spend my youth? Youth lasts so short a time, Bateman. And when I am old, what have I to look forward to? To hurry from my home in the morning to my office and work hour after hour till night, and then hurry home again, and dine and go to a theatre? That may be worthwhile if you make a fortune; I don't know, it depends on your nature; but if you don't, is it worthwhile then? I want to make more out of my life than that, Bateman."

"What do you value in life then?"

"I'm afraid you'll laugh at me. Beauty, truth, and goodness."

"Don't you think you can have those in Chicago?"

"Some men can, perhaps, but not I." Edward sprang up now. "I tell you when I think of the life I led in the old days I am filled with horror," he cried violently. "I tremble with fear when I think of the danger I have escaped. I never knew I had a soul till I found it here. If I had remained a rich man I might have lost it for good and all."

"I don't know how you can say that" cried Bateman indignantly. "We often used to have discussions about it."

"Yes, I know. They were about as effectual as the discussions of deaf mutes about harmony. I shall never come back to Chicago, Bateman."

"And what about Isabel?"

Edward walked to the edge of the verandah and leaning overlooked intently at the blue magic of the night. There was a slight smile on his face when he turned back to Bateman.

"Isabel is infinitely too good for me. I admire her more than any woman I have ever known. She has a wonderful brain and she's as good as she's beautiful. I respect her energy and her ambition. She was born to make a success of life. I am entirely unworthy of her."

"She doesn't think so."

"But you must tell her so, Bateman."

"I?" cried Bateman. "I'm the last person who could ever do that."

Edward had his back to the vivid light of the moon and his face could not be seen. Is it possible that he smiled again?

"It's no good your trying to conceal anything from her, Bateman. With her quick intelligence she'll turn you inside out in five minutes. You'd better make a clean breast of it right away."

"I don't know what you mean. Of course I shall tell her I've seen you." Bateman spoke in some agitation. "Honestly I don't know what to say to her."

"Tell her that I haven't made good. Tell her that I'm not only poor, but that I'm content to be poor. Tell her I was fired from my job because I was idle and inattentive. Tell her all you've seen tonight and all I've told you."

The idea which on a sudden flashed through Bateman's brain brought him to his feet and in uncontrollable perturbation he faced Edward.

"Man alive, don't you want to marry her?"

Edward looked at him gravely.

"I can never ask her to release me. If she wishes to hold me to my word I will do my best to make her a good and loving husband."

"Do you wish me to give her that message, Edward? Oh, I can't. It's terrible. It's never dawned on her for a moment that you don't want to marry her. She loves you. How can I inflict such a mortification on her?"

Edward smiled again.

"Why don't you marry her yourself, Bateman? You've been in love with her for ages. You're perfectly suited to one another. You'll make her very happy."

"Don't talk to me like that. I can't bear it."

"I resign in your favour, Bateman. You are the better man."

There was something in Edward's tone that made Bateman look up quickly, but Edward's eyes were grave and unsmiling. Bateman did not know what to say. He was disconcerted. He wondered whether Edward could possibly suspect that he had come to Tahiti on a special errand. And though he knew it was horrible he could not prevent the exultation in his heart.

"What will you do if Isabel writes and puts an end to her engagement with you?" he said, slowly.

"Survive," said Edward.

Bateman was so agitated that he did not hear the answer.

"I wish you had ordinary clothes on," he said, somewhat irritably. "It's such a tremendously serious decision you're taking. That fantastic costume of yours makes it seem terribly casual."

"I assure you, I can be just as solemn in a *pareo* and a wreath of roses, as in a high hat and a cut-away coat."

Then another thought struck Bateman.

"Edward, it's not for my sake you're doing this? I don't know, but perhaps this is going to make a tremendous difference to my future. You're not sacrificing yourself for me? I couldn't stand for that, you know."

"No, Bateman, I have learnt not to be silly and sentimental here. I should like you and Isabel to be happy, but I have not the least wish to be unhappy myself."

The answer somewhat chilled Bateman. It seemed to him a little cynical. He would not have been sorry to act a noble part.

"Do you mean to say you're content to waste your life here? It's nothing less than suicide. When I think of the great hopes you had when we left college it seems terrible that you should be content to be no more than a salesman in a cheap-John store."

"Oh, I'm only doing that for the present, and I'm gaining a great deal of valuable experience. I have another plan in my head. Arnold Jackson has a small island in the Paumotas, about a thousand miles from here, a ring of land round a lagoon. He's planted coconut there. He's offered to give it me."

"Why should he do that?" asked Bateman.

"Because if Isabel releases me I shall marry his daughter."

"You?" Bateman was thunderstruck. "You can't marry a half-caste. You wouldn't be so crazy as that."

"She's a good girl, and she has a sweet and gentle nature. I think she would make me very happy."

"Are you in love with her?"

"I don't know," answered Edward reflectively. "I'm not in love with her as I was in love with Isabel. I worshipped Isabel. I thought she was the most wonderful creature I had ever seen. I was not half good enough for her. I don't feel like that with Eva. She's like a beautiful exotic flower that must be sheltered from bitter winds. I want to protect her. No one ever thought of protecting Isabel. I think she loves me for myself and not for what I may become. Whatever happens to me I shall never disappoint her. She suits me."

Bateman was silent.

"We must turn out early in the morning," said Edward at last. "It's really about time we went to bed."

Then Bateman spoke and his voice had in it a genuine distress.

"I'm so bewildered, I don't know what to say. I came here because I thought something was wrong. I thought you hadn't succeeded in what you set out to do and were ashamed to come back when you'd failed. I never guessed I should be faced with this. I'm so desperately sorry, Edward. I'm so disappointed. I hoped you would do great things. It's almost more than I can bear to think of you wasting your talents and your youth and your chance in this lamentable way."

"Don't be grieved, old friend," said Edward. "I haven't failed. I've succeeded. You can't think with what zest I look forward to life, how full it seems to me and how significant. Sometimes, when you are married to Isabel, you will think of me. I shall build myself a house on my coral island and I shall live there, looking after my trees—getting the fruit out of the nuts in the same old way that they have done for unnumbered years—I shall grow all sorts of things in my garden, and I shall fish. There will be enough work to keep me busy and not enough to make me dull. I shall have my books and Eva, children, I hope, and above all, the infinite variety of the sea and the sky, the freshness of the dawn and the beauty of the sunset, and the rich magnificence of the night. I shall make a garden out of what so short a while ago was a wilderness. I shall have created something. The years will pass insensibly, and when I am an old man I hope that I shall be able to look back on a happy, simple, peaceful life. In my small way I too shall have lived in beauty. Do you think it is so little to have enjoyed contentment? We know that it will profit a man little if he gain the whole world and lose his soul. I think I have won mine."

Edward led him to a room in which there were two beds, and he threw himself on one of them. In ten minutes, Bateman knew by his regular breathing, peaceful as a child's, that Edward was asleep. But for his part he had no rest, he was disturbed in mind, and it was not till the dawn crept into the room, ghostlike and silent, that he fell asleep.

Bateman finished telling Isabel his long story. He had hidden nothing from her except what he thought would wound her or what made himself ridiculous. He did not tell her that he had been forced to sit at dinner with a wreath of flowers round his head and he did not tell her that Edward was prepared to marry her uncle's half-caste daughter the moment she set him free. But perhaps Isabel had keener intuitions than he knew, for as he went on with his tale her eyes grew colder, and her lips closed upon one another more tightly. Now and then she looked at him closely, and if he had been less intent on his narrative he might have wondered at her expression.

"What was this girl like?" she asked when he finished. "Uncle Arnold's daughter. Would you say there was any resemblance between her and me?"

Bateman was surprised at the question.

"It never struck me. You know I've never had eyes for anyone, but you and I could never think that anyone was like you. Who could resemble you?"

"Was she pretty?" said Isabel, smiling slightly at his words.

"I suppose so. I daresay some men would say she was very beautiful."

"Well, it's of no consequence. I don't think we need give her any more of our attention."

"What are you going to do, Isabel?" he asked then.

Isabel looked down at the hand which still bore the ring Edward had given her on their betrothal.

"I wouldn't let Edward break our engagement because I thought it would be an incentive to him. I wanted to be an inspiration to him. I thought if anything could enable him to achieve success it was the thought that I loved him. I have done all I could. It's hopeless. It would only be weakness on my part not to recognise the facts. Poor Edward, he's nobody's enemy but his own. He was a dear, nice fellow, but there was something lacking in him, I suppose it was backbone. I hope he'll be happy."

She slipped the ring off her finger and placed it on the table. Bateman watched her with a heart beating so rapidly that he could hardly breathe.

"You're wonderful, Isabel, you're simply wonderful."

She smiled, and, standing up, held out her hand to him.

"How can I ever thank you for what you've done for me?" she said. "You've done me a great service. I knew I could trust you."

He took her hand and held it. She had never looked more beautiful.

"Oh, Isabel, I would do so much more for you than that. You know that I only ask to be allowed to love and serve you."

"You're so strong, Bateman," she sighed. "It gives me such a delicious feeling of confidence."

"Isabel, I adore you."

He hardly knew how the inspiration had come to him, but suddenly he clasped her in his arms, and she, all unresisting, smiled into his eyes.

"Isabel, you know I wanted to marry you the very first day I saw you," he cried passionately.

"Then why on earth didn't you ask me?" she replied.

She loved him. He could hardly believe it was true. She gave him her lovely lips to kiss. And as he held her in his arms he had a vision of the works of the Hunter Motor Traction and Automobile Company growing in size and importance till they covered a hundred acres, and of the millions of motors they would turn out, and of the great collection of pictures he would form which should beat anything they had in New York. He would wear horn spectacles. And she, with the delicious pressure of his arms about her, sighed with happiness, for she thought of the exquisite house she would have, full of antique furniture, and of the concerts she would give, and of the *thés dansants*, and the dinners to which only the most cultured people would come. Bateman should wear horn spectacles.

"Poor Edward," she sighed.

IV

RED

The skipper thrust his hand into one of his trouser pockets and with difficulty, for they were not at the sides but in front and he was a portly man, pulled out a large silver watch. He looked at it and then looked again at the declining sun. The Kanaka at the wheel gave him a glance but did not speak. The skipper's eyes rested on the island they were approaching. A white line of foam marked the reef. He knew there was an opening large enough to get his ship through, and when they came a little nearer he counted on seeing it. They had nearly an hour of daylight still before them. In the lagoon the water was deep, and they could anchor comfortably. The chief of the village which he could already see among the coconut trees was a friend of the mates and it would be pleasant to go ashore for the night. The mate came forward at that minute and the skipper turned to him.

"We'll take a bottle of booze along with us and get some girls in to dance," he said.

"I don't see the opening," said the mate.

He was a Kanaka, a handsome, swarthy fellow, with somewhat the look of a later Roman emperor, inclined to stoutness; but his face was fine and clean-cut.

"I'm dead sure there's one right here," said the captain, looking through his glasses. "I can't understand why I can't pick it up. Send one of the boys up the mast to have a look."

The mate called one of the crew and gave him the order. The captain watched the Kanaka climb and waited for him to speak. But the Kanaka shouted down that he could see nothing but the unbroken line of foam. The captain spoke Samoan like a native, and he cursed him freely.

"Shall he stay up there?" asked the mate.

"What the hell good does that do?" answered the captain. "The blame fool can't see worth a cent. You bet your sweet life I'd find the opening if I was up there."

He looked at the slender mast with anger. It was all very well for a native who had been used to climbing up coconut trees all his life. He was fat and heavy.

"Come down," he shouted. "You're no more use than a dead dog. We'll just have to go along the reef till we find the opening."

It was a seventy-ton schooner with paraffin auxiliary, and it ran, when there was no head wind, between four and five knots an hour. It was a bedraggled object; it had been painted white a very long time ago, but it was now dirty, dingy, and mottled. It smelt strongly of paraffin and of the copra which was its usual cargo. They were within a hundred feet of the reef now and the captain told the steersman to run along it till they came to the opening. But when they had gone a couple of miles he realised that they had missed it. He went about and slowly worked back again. The white foam of the reef continued without interruption and now the sun was setting. With a curse at the stupidity of the crew the skipper resigned himself to waiting till next morning.

"Put her about," he said. "I can't anchor here."

They went out to sea a little and presently it was quite dark. They anchored. When the sail was furled the ship began to roll a good deal. They said in Apia that one day she would roll right over; and the owner, a German-American who managed one of the largest stores, said that no money was big enough to induce him to go out in her. The cook, a Chinese in white trousers, very dirty and ragged, and a thin white tunic, came to say that supper was ready, and when the skipper went into the cabin he found the engineer already seated at table. The engineer was a long, lean man with a scraggy neck. He was dressed in blue overalls and a sleeveless jersey which showed his thin arms tatooed from elbow to wrist.

"Hell, having to spend the night outside," said the skipper.

The engineer did not answer, and they ate their supper in silence. The cabin was lit by a dim oil lamp. When they had eaten the canned apricots with which the meal finished the Chink brought them a cup of tea. The skipper lit a cigar and went on the upper deck. The island now was only a darker mass against the night. The stars were very bright. The only sound was the ceaseless breaking of the surf. The skipper sank into a deck-chair and smoked idly. Presently three or four members of the crew came up and sat down. One of them had a banjo and another a concertina. They began to play, and one of them sang. The native song sounded strange on these instruments. Then to the singing a couple began to dance. It was a barbaric dance, savage and primeval, rapid, with quick movements of the hands and feet and contortions of the body; it was sensual, sexual even, but sexual without passion. It was very animal, direct, weird without mystery, natural in short, and one might almost say childlike. At last, they grew tired. They stretched themselves on the deck and slept, and all was silent. The skipper lifted himself heavily out of his chair and clambered down the companion. He went into his cabin and got out of his clothes. He climbed into his bunk and lay there. He panted a little in the heat of the night.

But next morning, when the dawn crept over the tranquil sea, the opening in the reef which had eluded them the night before was seen a little to the east of where they lay. The schooner entered the lagoon. There was not a ripple on the surface of the water. Deep down among the coral rocks you saw little coloured fish swim. When he had anchored his ship the skipper ate his breakfast and went on deck. The sun shone from an unclouded sky, but in the early morning the air was grateful and cool. It was Sunday, and there was a feeling of quietness, a silence as though nature were at rest, which gave him a peculiar sense of comfort. He sat, looking at the wooded coast, and felt lazy and well at ease. Presently a slow smile moved his lips, and he threw the stump of his cigar into the water.

"I guess I'll go ashore," he said. "Get the boat out."

He climbed stiffly down the ladder and was rowed to a little cove. The coconut trees came down to the water's edge, not in rows, but spaced out with an ordered formality. They were like a ballet of spinsters, elderly but flippant, standing in affected attitudes with the simpering graces of a bygone age. He sauntered idly through them, along a path that could be just seen winding its tortuous way, and it led him presently to a broad creek. There was a bridge across it, but a bridge constructed of single trunks of coconut trees, a dozen of them, placed end to end and supported where they met by a forked branch driven into the bed of the creek. You walked on a smooth, round surface, narrow and slippery, and there was no support for the hand. To cross such a bridge required sure feet and a stout heart. The skipper hesitated. But he saw on the other side, nestling among the trees, a white man's house;

he made up his mind and, rather gingerly, began to walk. He watched his feet carefully, and where one trunk joined on to the next and there was a difference of level, he tottered a little. It was with a gasp of relief that he reached the last tree and finally set his feet on the firm ground of the other side. He had been so intent on the difficult crossing that he never noticed anyone was watching him, and it was with surprise that he heard himself spoken to.

"It takes a bit of nerve to cross these bridges when you're not used to them."

He looked up and saw a man standing in front of him. He had evidently come out of the house which he had seen.

"I saw you hesitate," the man continued, with a smile on his lips, "and I was watching to see you fall in."

"Not on your life," said the captain, who had now recovered his confidence.

"I've fallen in myself before now. I remember, one evening I came back from shooting, and I fell in, gun and all. Now I get a boy to carry my gun for me."

He was a man no longer young, with a small beard, now somewhat grey, and a thin face. He was dressed in a singlet, without arms, and a pair of duck trousers. He wore neither shoes nor socks. He spoke English with a slight accent.

"Are you Neilson?" asked the skipper.

"I am."

"I've heard about you. I thought you lived somewheres round here."

The skipper followed his host into the little bungalow and sat down heavily in the chair which the other motioned him to take. While Neilson went out to fetch whisky and glasses he took a look round the room. It filled him with amazement. He had never seen so many books. The shelves reached from floor to ceiling on all four walls, and they were closely packed. There was a grand piano littered with music, and a large table on which books and magazines lay in disorder. The room made him feel embarrassed. He remembered that Neilson was a queer fellow. No one knew very much about him, although he had been in the islands for so many years, but those who knew him agreed that he was queer. He was a Swede.

"You've got one big heap of books here," he said, when Neilson returned.

"They do no harm," answered Neilson with a smile.

"Have you read them all?" asked the skipper.

"Most of them."

"I'm a bit of a reader myself. I have the *Saturday Evening Post* sent me regular."

Neilson poured his visitor a good stiff glass of whisky and gave him a cigar. The skipper volunteered a little information.

"I got in last night, but I couldn't find the opening, so I had to anchor outside. I never been this run before, but my people had some stuff they wanted to bring over here. Gray, d'you know him?"

"Yes, he's got a store a little way along."

"Well, there was a lot of canned stuff that he wanted over, an' he's got some copra. They thought I might just as well come over as lie idle at Apia. I run between Apia and Pago-Pago mostly, but they've got smallpox there just now, and there's nothing stirring."

He took a drink of his whisky and lit a cigar. He was a taciturn man, but there was something in Neilson that made him nervous, and his nervousness made him talk. The Swede was looking at him with large dark eyes in which there was an expression of faint amusement.

"This is a tidy little place you've got here."

"I've done my best with it."

"You must do pretty well with your trees. They look fine. With copra at the price, it is now. I had a bit of a plantation myself once, in Upolu it was, but I had to sell it."

He looked round the room again, where all those books gave him a feeling of something incomprehensible and hostile.

"I guess you must find it a bit lonesome here though," he said.

"I've got used to it. I've been here for twenty-five years."

Now the captain could think of nothing more to say, and he smoked in silence. Neilson had apparently no wish to break it. He looked at his guest with a meditative eye. He was a tall man, more than six feet high, and very stout. His face was red and blotchy, with a network of little purple veins on the cheeks, and his features were sunk into its fatness. His eyes were bloodshot. His neck was buried in rolls of fat. But for a fringe of long curly hair, nearly white, at the back of his head, he was quite bald; and that immense, shiny surface of forehead, which might have given him a false look of intelligence, on the contrary gave him one of peculiar imbecility. He wore a blue flannel shirt, open at the neck and showing his fat chest covered with a mat of reddish hair, and a very old pair of blue serge trousers. He sat in his chair in a heavy ungainly attitude, his great belly thrust forward, and his fat legs uncrossed. All elasticity had gone from his limbs. Neilson wondered idly what sort of man he had been in his youth. It was almost impossible to imagine that this creature of vast bulk had ever been a boy who ran about. The skipper finished his whisky, and Neilson pushed the bottle towards him.

"Help yourself."

The skipper leaned forward and with his great hand seized it.

"And how come you in these parts anyways?" he said.

"Oh, I came out to the islands for my health. My lungs were bad, and they said I hadn't a year to live. You see they were wrong."

"I meant, how come you to settle down right here?"

"I am a sentimentalist."

"Oh!"

Neilson knew that the skipper had not an idea what he meant, and he looked at him with an ironical twinkle in his dark eyes. Perhaps just because the skipper was so gross and dull a man the whim seized him to talk further.

"You were too busy keeping your balance to notice, when you crossed the bridge, but this spot is generally considered rather pretty."

"It's a cute little house you've got here."

"Ah, that wasn't here when I first came. There was a native hut, with its beehive roof and its pillars, overshadowed by a great tree with red flowers; and the croton bushes, their leaves yellow and red and golden, made a pied fence around it. And then all about were the coconut trees, as fanciful as women, and as vain. They stood at the water's edge and spent all day looking at their reflections. I was a young man then—Good Heavens, it's a quarter of a century ago—and I wanted to enjoy all the loveliness of the world in the short time allotted to me before I passed into the darkness. I thought it was the most beautiful spot I had ever seen. The first time I saw it I had a catch at my heart, and I was afraid I was going to cry. I wasn't more than twenty-five, and though I put the best face I could on it, I didn't want to die. And somehow it seemed to me that the very beauty of this place made it easier for me to accept my fate. I felt when I came here that all my past life had fallen away, Stockholm and its University, and then Bonn: it all seemed the life of somebody else, as though now at last I had achieved the reality which our Doctor of Philosophy—I am one myself, you know—had discussed so much. 'A year,' I cried to myself. 'I have a year. I will spend it here and then I am content to die.'"

"We are foolish and sentimental and melodramatic at twenty-five, but if we weren't perhaps we should be less wise at fifty."

"Now drink, my friend. Don't let the nonsense I talk interfere with you."

He waved his thin hand towards the bottle, and the skipper finished what remained in his glass.

"You ain't drinking nothin," he said, reaching for the whisky.

"I am of a sober habit," smiled the Swede. "I intoxicate myself in ways which I fancy are more subtle. But perhaps that is only vanity. Anyhow, the effects are more lasting and the results less deleterious."

"They say there's a deal of cocaine taken in the States now," said the captain.

Neilson chuckled.

"But I do not see a white man often," he continued, "and for once I don't think a drop of whisky can do me any harm."

He poured himself out a little, added some soda, and took a sip.

"And presently I found out why the spot had such an unearthly loveliness. Here love had tarried for a moment like a migrant bird that happens on a ship in mid-ocean and for a little while folds its tired wings. The fragrance of a beautiful passion hovered over it like the fragrance of hawthorn in May in the meadows of my home. It seems to me that the places where men have loved or suffered keep about them always some faint aroma of something that has not wholly died. It is as though they had acquired a spiritual significance which mysteriously affects those who pass. I wish I could make myself clear." He smiled a little. "Though I cannot imagine that if I did you would understand."

He paused.

"I think this place was beautiful because here I had been loved beautifully." And now he shrugged his shoulders. "But perhaps it is only that my æsthetic sense is gratified by the happy conjunction of young love and a suitable setting."

Even a man less thick-witted than the skipper might have been forgiven if he were bewildered by Neilson's words. For he seemed faintly to laugh at what he said. It was as though he spoke from emotion which his intellect found ridiculous. He had said himself that he was a sentimentalist, and when sentimentality is joined with scepticism there is often the devil to pay.

He was silent for an instant and looked at the captain with eyes in which there was a sudden perplexity.

"You know, I can't help thinking that I've seen you before somewhere or other," he said.

"I couldn't say as I remember you," returned the skipper.

"I have a curious feeling as though your face were familiar to me. It's been puzzling me for some time. But I can't situate my recollection in any place or at any time."

The skipper massively shrugged his heavy shoulders.

"It's thirty years since I first come to the islands. A man can't figure on remembering all the folk he meets in a while like that."

The Swede shook his head.

"You know how one sometimes has the feeling that a place one has never been to before is strangely familiar. That's how I seem to see you." He gave a whimsical smile. "Perhaps I knew you in some past existence. Perhaps, perhaps you were the master of a galley in ancient Rome, and I was a slave at the oar. Thirty years have you been here?"

"Every bit of thirty years."

"I wonder if you knew a man called Red?"

"Red?"

"That is the only name I've ever known him by. I never knew him personally. I never even set eyes on him. And yet I seem to see him more clearly than many men, my brothers, for instance, with whom I passed my daily life for many years. He lives in my imagination with the distinctness of a Paolo Malatesta or a Romeo. But I daresay you have never read Dante or Shakespeare?"

"I can't say as I have," said the captain.

Neilson, smoking a cigar, leaned back in his chair and looked vacantly at the ring of smoke which floated in the still air. A smile played on his lips, but his eyes were grave. Then he looked at the captain. There was in his gross obesity something extraordinarily repellent. He had the plethoric self-satisfaction of the very fat. It was an outrage. It set Neilson's nerves on edge. But the contrast between the man before him and the man he had in mind was pleasant.

"It appears that Red was the comeliest thing you ever saw. I've talked to quite a number of people who knew him in those days, white men, and they all agree that the first time you saw him his beauty just took your breath away. They called him Red on account of his flaming hair. It had a natural wave, and he wore it long. It must have been of that wonderful colour that the pre-Raphaelites raved over. I don't think he was vain of it, he was much too ingenuous for that, but no one could have blamed him if he had been. He was tall, six feet and an inch or two—in the native house that used to stand here was the mark of his height cut with a knife on the central trunk that supported the roof—and he was made like a Greek god, broad in the shoulders and thin in the flanks; he was like Apollo, with just that soft roundness which Praxiteles gave him, and that suave, feminine grace which has in it something troubling and mysterious. His skin was dazzling white, milky, like satin; his skin was like a woman's."

"I had kind of a white skin myself when I was a kiddie," said the skipper, with a twinkle in his bloodshot eyes.

But Neilson paid no attention to him. He was telling his story now and interruption made him impatient.

"And his face was just as beautiful as his body. He had large blue eyes, very dark, so that some say they were black, and unlike most red-haired people he had dark eyebrows and long dark lashes. His features were perfectly regular, and his mouth was like a scarlet wound. He was twenty."

On these words the Swede stopped with a certain sense of the dramatic. He took a sip of whisky.

"He was unique. There never was anyone more beautiful. There was no more reason for him than for a wonderful blossom to flower on a wild plant. He was a happy accident of nature."

"One day he landed at that cove into which you must have put this morning. He was an American sailor, and he had deserted from a man-of-war in Apia. He had induced some good-humoured native to give him a passage on a cutter that happened to be sailing from Apia to Safoto and he had been put ashore here in a dugout. I do not know why he deserted. Perhaps life on a man-of-war with its restrictions irked him, perhaps he was in trouble, and perhaps it was the South Seas and these romantic islands that got into his bones. Every now and then they take a man strangely, and he finds himself like a fly in a spider's web. It may be that there was a softness of fibre in him and these green hills with their soft airs, this blue sea, took the northern strength from him as Delilah took the Nazarite's. Anyhow, he wanted to hide himself, and he thought he would be safe in this secluded nook till his ship had sailed from Samoa."

"There was a native hut at the cove and as he stood there, wondering where exactly he should turn his steps, a young girl came out and invited him to enter. He knew scarcely two words of the native tongue and she as little English. But he understood well enough what her smiles meant, and her pretty gestures, and he followed her. He sat down on a mat, and she gave him slices of pineapple to eat. I can speak of Red only from hearsay, but I saw the girl three years after he first met her, and she was scarcely nineteen then. You cannot imagine how exquisite she was. She had the passionate grace of the hibiscus and the rich colour. She was rather tall, slim, with the delicate features of her race, and large eyes like pools of still water under the palm trees; her hair, black and curling, fell down her back, and she wore a wreath of scented flowers. Her hands were lovely. They were so small, so exquisitely formed, they gave your heart-strings a wrench. And in those days she laughed easily. Her smile was so delightful that it made your knees shake. Her skin was like a field of ripe corn on a summer day. Good Heavens, how can I describe her? She was too beautiful to be real."

"And these two young things, she was sixteen and he was twenty, fell in love with one another at first sight. That is the real love, not the love that comes from sympathy, common interests, or intellectual community, but love pure and simple. That is the love that Adam felt for Eve when he awoke and found her in the garden gazing at him with dewy eyes. That is the love that draws the beasts to one another, and the Gods. That is the love that makes the world a miracle. That is the love which gives life its pregnant meaning. You have never heard of the wise, cynical French duke who said that with two lovers there is always one who loves and one who lets himself be loved; it is a bitter truth to which most of us have to resign ourselves; but now and then there are two who love and two who let themselves be loved. Then one might fancy that the sun stands still as it stood when Joshua prayed to the God of Israel."

"And even now after all these years, when I think of these two, so young, so fair, so simple, and of their love, I feel a pang. It tears my heart just as my heart is torn when on certain nights I watch the full moon shining on the lagoon from an unclouded sky. There is always pain in the contemplation of perfect beauty."

"They were children. She was good and sweet and kind. I know nothing of him, and I like to think that then at all events he was ingenuous and frank. I like to think that his soul was as comely as his body. But I daresay he had no more soul than the creatures of the woods and forests who made pipes from reeds and bathed in the mountain streams when the world was young, and you might catch sight of little fawns galloping through the glade on the back of a bearded centaur. A soul is a troublesome possession and when man developed it he lost the Garden of Eden."

"Well, when Red came to the island it had recently been visited by one of those epidemics which the white man has brought to the South Seas, and one third of the inhabitants had died. It seems that the girl had lost all her near kin, and she lived now in the house of distant cousins. The household consisted of two ancient crones, bowed and wrinkled, two younger women, and a man and a boy. For a few days he stayed there. But perhaps he felt himself too near the shore, with the possibility that he might fall in with white men who would reveal his hiding-place; perhaps the lovers could not bear that the company of others should rob them for an instant of the delight of being together. One morning they set out, the pair of them, with the few things that belonged to the girl, and walked along a grassy path under the coconuts, till they came to the creek you see. They had to cross the bridge you crossed, and the girl laughed gleefully because he was afraid. She held his hand till they came to the end of the first tree, and then his courage failed him, and he had to go back. He was obliged to take off all his clothes before he could risk it, and she carried them over for him on her head. They settled down in the empty hut that stood here. Whether she had any rights over it (land tenure is a complicated business in the islands), or whether the owner had died during the epidemic, I do not know, but anyhow no one questioned them, and they took possession. Their furniture consisted of a couple of grass-mats on which they slept, a fragment of looking-glass, and a bowl or two. In this pleasant land that is enough to start housekeeping on."

"They say that happy people have no history, and certainly a happy love has none. They did nothing all day long and yet the days seemed all too short. The girl had a native name, but Red called her Sally. He picked up the easy language very quickly, and he used to lie on the mat for hours while she chattered gaily to him. He was a silent fellow, and perhaps his mind was lethargic. He smoked incessantly the cigarettes which she made him out of the native tobacco and pandanus leaf, and he watched her while with deft fingers she made grass mats. Often natives would come in and tell long stories of the old days when the island was disturbed by tribal wars. Sometimes he would go fishing on the reef and bring home a basket full of coloured fish. Sometimes at night he would go out with a lantern to catch lobster. There were plantains round the hut and Sally would roast them for their frugal meal. She knew how to make delicious messes from coconuts, and the bread-fruit tree by the side of the creek gave them its fruit. On feast-days they killed a little pig and cooked it on hot stones. They bathed together in the creek; and in the evening they went down to the lagoon and paddled about in a dugout, with its great outrigger. The sea was deep blue, wine-coloured at sundown, like the sea of Homeric Greece; but in the lagoon the colour had an infinite variety, aquamarine and amethyst and emerald; and the setting sun turned it for a short moment to liquid gold. Then there was the colour of the coral, brown, white, pink, red, purple; and the shapes it took were marvellous. It was like a magic garden, and the hurrying fish were like butterflies. It strangely lacked reality. Among the coral were pools with a floor of white sand and here, where the water was dazzling clear, it was very good to bathe. Then, cool and happy, they wandered back in the gloaming over the soft grass road to the creek, walking hand in hand, and now the mynah birds filled the coconut trees with their clamour. And then the night, with that great, sky shining with gold, that seemed to stretch more widely than the skies of Europe, and the soft airs that blew gently through the open hut, the long night again was all too short. She was sixteen and he was barely twenty. The dawn crept in among the wooden pillars of the hut and looked at those lovely children sleeping in one another's arms. The sun hid behind the great tattered leaves of the plantains so that it might not disturb them, and then, with playful malice, shot a golden ray, like the outstretched paw of a Persian cat, on their faces. They opened their sleepy eyes, and they smiled to welcome another day. The weeks lengthened into months, and a year passed. They seemed to love one another as—I hesitate to say passionately, for passion has in it always a shade of sadness, a touch of bitterness or anguish, but as whole heartedly, as simply and naturally as on that first day on which, meeting, they had recognised that a god was in them."

"If you had asked them I have no doubt that they would have thought it impossible to suppose their love could ever cease. Do we not know that the essential element of love is a belief in its own eternity? And yet perhaps in Red there was already a very little seed, unknown to himself and unsuspected by the girl, which would in time have grown to weariness. For one day one of the natives from the cove told them that some way down the coast at the anchorage was a British whaling-ship."

"'Gee,' he said, 'I wonder if I could make a trade of some nuts and plantains for a pound or two of tobacco.'"

"The pandanus cigarettes that Sally made him with untiring hands were strong and pleasant enough to smoke, but they left him unsatisfied; and he yearned on a sudden for real tobacco, hard, rank, and pungent. He had not smoked a pipe for many, months. His mouth watered at the thought of it. One would have thought some premonition of harm would have made Sally seek to dissuade him, but love possessed her so completely that it never occurred to her any power on earth could take him from her. They went up into the hills together and gathered a great basket of wild oranges, green, but sweet and juicy; and they picked plantains from around the hut, and coconuts from their trees, and breadfruit and mangoes; and they carried them down to the cove. They loaded the unstable canoe with them, and Red and the native boy who had brought them the news of the ship paddled along outside the reef."

"It was the last time she ever saw him."

"Next day the boy came back alone. He was all in tears. This is the story he told. When after their long paddle they reached the ship and Red hailed it, a white man looked over the side and told them to come on board. They took the fruit they had brought with them and Red piled it up on the deck. The white man and he began to talk, and they seemed to come to some agreement. One of them went below and brought up tobacco. Red took some at once and lit a pipe. The boy imitated the zest with which he blew a great cloud of smoke from his mouth. Then they said something to him, and he went into the cabin. Through the open door the boy, watching curiously, saw a bottle brought out and glasses. Red drank and smoked. They seemed to ask him something, for he shook his head and laughed. The man, the first man who had spoken to them, laughed too, and he filled Red's glass once more. They went on talking and drinking, and presently, growing tired of watching a sight that meant nothing to him, the boy curled himself up on the deck and slept. He was awakened by a kick; and, jumping to his feet, he saw that the ship was slowly sailing out of the lagoon. He caught sight of Red seated at the table, with his head resting heavily on his arms, fast asleep. He made a movement towards him, intending to wake him, but a rough hand seized his arm, and a man, with a scowl and words which he did not understand, pointed to the side. He shouted to Red, but in a moment he was seized and flung overboard. Helpless, he swam round to his canoe which was drifting a little way off and pushed it on to the reef. He climbed in and, sobbing all the way, paddled back to shore."

"What had happened was obvious enough. The whaler, by desertion or sickness, was short of hands, and the captain when Red came aboard had asked him to sign on; on his refusal he had made him drunk and kidnapped him."

"Sally was beside herself with grief. For three days she screamed and cried. The natives did what they could to comfort her, but she would not be comforted. She would not eat. And then, exhausted, she sank into a sullen apathy. She spent long days at the cove, watching the lagoon, in the vain hope that Red somehow or other would manage to escape. She sat on the white sand, hour after hour, with the tears running down her cheeks, and at night dragged herself wearily back across the creek to the little hut where she had been happy. The people with whom she had lived before Red came to the island wished her to return to them, but she would not; she was convinced that Red would come back, and she wanted him to find her where he had left her. Four months later she was delivered of a still-born child, and the old woman who had come to help her through her confinement remained with her in the hut. All joy was taken from her life. If her anguish with time became less intolerable it was replaced by a settled melancholy. You would not have thought that among these people, whose emotions, though so violent, are very transient, a woman could be found capable of so enduring a passion. She never lost the profound conviction that sooner or later Red would come back. She watched for him, and every time someone crossed this slender little bridge of coconut trees she looked. It might at last be he."

Neilson stopped talking and gave a faint sigh.

"And what happened to her in the end?" asked the skipper.

Neilson smiled bitterly.

"Oh, three years afterwards she took up with another white man."

The skipper gave a fat, cynical chuckle.

"That's generally what happens to them," he said.

The Swede shot him a look of hatred. He did not know why that gross, obese man excited in him so violent a repulsion. But his thoughts wandered, and he found his mind filled with memories of the past. He went back five and twenty years. It was when he first came to the island, weary of Apia, with its heavy drinking, its gambling and coarse sensuality, a sick man, trying to resign himself to the loss of the career which had fired his imagination with ambitious thoughts. He set behind him resolutely all his hopes of making a great name for himself and strove to content himself with the few poor months of careful life which was all that he could count on. He was boarding with a half-caste trader who had a store a couple of miles along the coast at the edge of a native village; and one day, wandering aimlessly along the grassy paths of the coconut groves, he had come upon the hut in which Sally lived. The beauty of the spot had filled him with a rapture so great that it was almost painful, and then he had seen Sally. She was the loveliest creature he had ever seen, and the sadness in those dark, magnificent eyes of hers affected him strangely. The Kanakas were a handsome race, and beauty was not rare among them, but it was the beauty of shapely animals. It was empty. But those tragic eyes were dark with mystery, and you felt in them the bitter complexity of the groping, human soul. The trader told him the story and it moved him.

"Do you think he'll ever come back?" asked Neilson.

"No fear. Why, it'll be a couple of years before the ship is paid off, and by then he'll have forgotten all about her. I bet he was pretty mad when he woke up and found he'd been shanghaied, and I shouldn't wonder but he wanted to fight somebody. But he'd got to grin and bear it, and I guess in a month he was thinking it the best thing that had ever happened to him that he got away from the island."

But Neilson could not get the story out of his head. Perhaps because he was sick and weakly, the radiant health of Red appealed to his imagination. Himself an ugly man, insignificant of appearance, he prized very highly comeliness in others. He had never been passionately in love, and certainly he had never been passionately loved. The mutual attraction of those two young things gave him a singular delight. It had the ineffable beauty of the Absolute. He went again to the little hut by the creek. He had a gift for languages and an energetic mind, accustomed to work, and he had already given much time to the study of the local tongue. Old habit was strong in him, and he was gathering together material for a paper on the Samoan speech. The old crone who shared the hut with Sally invited him to come in and sit down. She gave him *kava* to drink and cigarettes to smoke. She was glad to have someone to chat with and while she talked he looked at Sally. She reminded him of the Psyche in the museum at Naples. Her features had the same dear purity of line, and though she had borne a child she had still a virginal aspect.

It was not till he had seen her two or three times that he induced her to speak. Then it was only to ask him if he had seen in Apia a man called Red. Two years had passed since his disappearance, but it was plain that she still thought of him incessantly.

It did not take Neilson long to discover that he was in love with her. It was only by an effort of will now that he prevented himself from going every day to the creek, and when he was not with Sally his thoughts were. At first, looking upon himself as a dying man, he asked only to look at her, and occasionally hear her speak, and his love gave him a wonderful happiness. He exulted in its purity. He wanted nothing from her but the opportunity to weave around her graceful person a web of beautiful fancies. But the open air, the equable temperature, the rest, the simple fare, began to have an unexpected effect on his health. His temperature did not soar at night to such alarming heights, he coughed less and began to put on weight; six months passed without his having a hæmorrhage; and on a sudden he saw the possibility that he might live. He had studied his disease carefully, and the hope dawned upon him that with great care he might arrest its course. It exhilarated him to look forward once more to the future. He made plans. It was evident that any active life was out of the question, but he could live on the islands, and the small income he had, insufficient elsewhere, would be ample to keep him. He could grow coconuts; that would give him an occupation; and he would send for his books and a piano; but his quick mind saw that in all this he was merely trying to conceal from himself the desire which obsessed him.

He wanted Sally. He loved not only her beauty, but that dim soul which he divined behind her suffering eyes. He would intoxicate her with his passion. In the end he would make her forget. And in an ecstasy of surrender he fancied himself giving her too the happiness which he had thought never to know again but had now so miraculously achieved.

He asked her to live with him. She refused. He had expected that and did not let it depress him, for he was sure that sooner or later she would yield. His love was irresistible. He told the old woman of his wishes and found somewhat to his surprise that she and the neighbours, long aware of them, were strongly urging Sally to accept his offer. After all, every native was glad to keep house for a white man, and Neilson according to the standards of the island was a rich one. The trader with whom he boarded went to her and told her not to be a fool; such an opportunity would not come again, and after so long she could not still believe that Red would ever return. The girl's resistance only increased Neilson's desire, and what had been a very pure love now became an agonising passion. He was determined that nothing should stand in his way. He gave Sally no peace. At last, worn out by his persistence and the persuasions, by turns pleading and angry, of everyone around her, she consented. But the day after when, exultant, he went to see her he found that in the night she had burnt down the hut in which she and Red had lived together. The old crone ran towards him full of angry abuse of Sally, but he waved her aside; it did not matter; they would build a bungalow on the place where the hut had stood. A European house would really be more convenient if he wanted to bring out a piano and a vast number of books.

And so, the little wooden house was built in which he had now lived for many years, and Sally became his wife. But after the first few weeks of rapture, during which he was satisfied with what she gave him he had known little happiness. She had yielded to him, through weariness, but she had only yielded what she set no store on. The soul which he had dimly glimpsed escaped him. He knew that she cared nothing for him. She still loved Red, and all the time she was waiting for his return. At a sign from him, Neilson knew that, notwithstanding his love, his tenderness, his sympathy, his generosity, she would leave him without a moment's hesitation. She would never give a thought to his distress. Anguish seized him and he battered at that impenetrable self of hers which sullenly resisted him. His love became bitter. He tried to melt her heart with kindness, but it remained as hard as before; he feigned indifference, but she did not notice it. Sometimes he lost his temper and abused her, and then she wept silently. Sometimes he thought she was nothing but a fraud, and that soul simply an invention of his own, and that he could not get into the sanctuary of her heart because there was no sanctuary there. His love became a prison from which he longed to escape, but he had not the strength merely to open the door—that was all it needed—and walk out into the open air. It was torture and at last he became numb and hopeless. In the end the fire burnt itself out and, when he saw her eyes rest for an instant on the slender bridge, it was no longer rage that filled his heart but impatience. For many years now they had lived together bound by the ties of habit and convenience, and it was with a smile that he looked back on his old passion. She was an old woman, for the women on the islands age quickly, and if he had no love for her any more he had tolerance. She left him alone. He was contented with his piano and his books.

His thoughts led him to a desire for words.

"When I look back now and reflect on that brief passionate love of Red and Sally, I think that perhaps they should thank the ruthless fate that separated them when their love seemed still to be at its height. They suffered, but they suffered in beauty. They were spared the real tragedy of love."

"I don't know exactly as I get you," said the skipper.

"The tragedy of love is not death or separation. How long do you think it would have been before one or other of them ceased to care? Oh, it is dreadfully bitter to look at a woman whom you have loved with all your heart and soul, so that you felt you could not bear to let her out of your sight and realise that you would not mind if you never saw her again. The tragedy of love is indifference."

But while he was speaking a very extraordinary thing happened. Though he had been addressing the skipper he had not been talking to him, he had been putting his thoughts into words for himself, and with his eyes fixed on the man in front of him he had not seen him. But now an image presented itself to them, an image not of the man he saw, but of another man. It was as though he were looking into one of those distorting mirrors that make you extraordinarily squat or outrageously elongate, but here exactly the opposite took place, and in the obese, ugly old man he caught the shadowy glimpse of a stripling. He gave him now a quick, searching scrutiny. Why had a haphazard stroll brought him just to this place? A sudden tremor of his heart made him slightly breathless. An absurd suspicion seized him. What had occurred to him was impossible, and yet it might be a fact.

"What is your name?" he asked abruptly.

The skipper's face puckered, and he gave a cunning chuckle. He looked then malicious and horribly vulgar.

"It's such a damned long time since I heard it that I almost forget it myself. But for thirty years now in the islands they've always called me Red."

His huge form shook as he gave a low, almost silent laugh. It was obscene. Neilson shuddered. Red was hugely amused, and from his bloodshot eye's tears ran down his cheeks.

Neilson gave a gasp, for at that moment a woman came in. She was a native, a woman of somewhat commanding presence, stout without being corpulent, dark, for the natives grow darker with age, with very grey hair. She wore a black Mother Hubbard, and its thinness showed her heavy breasts. The moment had come.

She made an observation to Neilson about some household matter, and he answered. He wondered if his voice sounded as unnatural to her as it did to himself. She gave the man who was sitting in the chair by the window an indifferent glance and went out of the room. The moment had come and gone.

Neilson for a moment could not speak. He was strangely shaken. Then he said:

"I'd be very glad if you'd stay and have a bit of dinner with me. Potluck."

"I don't think I will," said Red. "I must go after this fellow Gray. I'll give him his stuff and then I'll get away. I want to be back in Apia to-morrow."

"I'll send a boy along with you to show you the way."

"That'll be fine."

Red heaved himself out of his chair, while the Swede called one of the boys who worked on the plantation. He told him where the skipper wanted to go, and the boy stepped along the bridge. Red prepared to follow him.

"Don't fall in," said Neilson.

"Not on your life."

Neilson watched him make his way across and when he had disappeared among the coconuts he looked still. Then he sank heavily in his chair. Was that the man who had prevented him from being happy? Was that the man whom Sally had loved all these years and for whom she had waited so desperately? It was grotesque. A sudden fury seized him so that he had an instinct to spring up and smash everything around him. He had been cheated. They had seen each other at last and had not known it. He began to laugh, mirthlessly, and his laughter grew till it became hysterical. The Gods had played him a cruel trick. And he was old now.

At last Sally came in to tell him dinner was ready. He sat down in front of her and tried to eat. He wondered what she would say if he told her now that the fat old man sitting in the chair was the lover whom she remembered still with the passionate abandonment of her youth. Years ago, when he hated her because she made him so unhappy, he would have been glad to tell her. He wanted to hurt her then as she hurt him, because his hatred was only love. But now he did not care. He shrugged his shoulders listlessly.

"What did that man want?" she asked presently.

He did not answer at once. She was old too, a fat old native woman. He wondered why he had ever loved her so madly. He had laid at her feet all the treasures of his soul, and she had cared nothing for them. Waste, what waste! And now, when he looked at her, he felt only contempt. His patience was at last exhausted. He answered her question.

"He's the captain of a schooner. He's come from Apia."

"Yes."

"He brought me news from home. My eldest brother is very ill, and I must go back."

"Will you be gone long?"

He shrugged his shoulders.

V

THE POOL

When I was introduced to Lawson by Chaplin, the owner of the Hotel Metropole at Apia, I paid no particular attention to him. We were sitting in the lounge over an early cocktail, and I was listening with amusement to the gossip of the island.

Chaplin entertained me. He was by profession a mining engineer and perhaps it was characteristic of him that he had settled in a place where his professional attainments were of no possible value. It was, however, generally reported that he was an extremely clever mining engineer. He was a small man, neither fat nor thin, with black hair, scanty on the crown, turning grey, and a small, untidy moustache; his face, partly from the sun and partly from liquor, was very red. He was but a figurehead, for the hotel, though so grandly named but a frame building of two storeys was managed by his wife, a tall, gaunt Australian of five and forty, with an imposing presence and a determined air. The little man, excitable and often tipsy, was terrified of her, and the stranger soon heard of domestic quarrels in which she used her fist and her foot in order to keep him in subjection. She had been known after a night of drunkenness to confine him for twenty-four hours to his own room, and then he could be seen, afraid to leave his prison, talking somewhat pathetically from his verandah to people in the street below.

He was a character, and his reminiscences of a varied life, whether true or not, made him worth listening to, so that when Lawson strolled in I was inclined to resent the interruption. Although not midday, it was clear that he had had enough to drink, and it was without enthusiasm that I yielded to his persistence and accepted his offer of another cocktail. I knew already that Chaplin's head was weak. The next round, which in common politeness I should be forced to order would be enough to make him lively, and then Mrs. Chaplin would give me black looks.

Nor was there anything attractive in Lawson's appearance. He was a little thin man, with a long, sallow face and a narrow, weak chin, a prominent nose, large and bony, and great shaggy black eyebrows. They gave him a peculiar look. His eyes, very large and very dark, were magnificent. He was jolly, but his jollity did not seem to me sincere; it was on the surface, a mask which he wore to deceive the world, and I suspected that it concealed a mean nature. He was plainly anxious to be thought a "good sport" and he was hail-fellow-well-met; but, I do not know why, I felt that he was cunning and shifty. He talked a great deal in a raucous voice, and he and Chaplin capped one another's stories of beanos which had become legendary, stories of "wet" nights at the English Club, of shooting expeditions where an incredible amount of whisky had been consumed, and of jaunts to Sydney of which their pride was that they could remember nothing from the time they landed till the time they sailed. A pair of drunken swine. But even in their intoxication, for by now after four cocktails each, neither was sober, there was a great difference between Chaplin, rough and vulgar, and Lawson: Lawson might be drunk, but he was certainly a gentleman.

At last, he got out of his chair, a little unsteadily.

"Well, I'll be getting along home," he said. "See you before dinner."

"Missus all right?" said Chaplin.

"Yes."

He went out. There was a peculiar note in the monosyllable of his answer which made me look up.

"Good chap," said Chaplin flatly, as Lawson went out of the door into the sunshine. "One of the best. Pity he drinks."

This from Chaplin was an observation not without humour.

"And when he's drunk he wants to fight people."

"Is he often drunk?"

"Dead drunk, three or four days a week. It's the island done it, and Ethel."

"Who's Ethel?"

"Ethel's his wife. Married a half-caste. Old Brevald's daughter. Took her away from here. Only thing to do. But she couldn't stand it, and now they're back again. He'll hang himself one of these days, if he don't drink himself to death before. Good chap. Nasty when he's drunk."

Chaplin belched loudly.

"I'll go and put my head under the shower. I oughtn't to have had that last cocktail. It's always the last one that does you in."

He looked uncertainly at the staircase as he made up his mind to go to the cubby hole in which was the shower, and then with unnatural seriousness got up.

"Pay you to cultivate Lawson," he said. "A well-read chap. You'd be surprised when he's sober. Clever too. Worth talking to."

Chaplin had told me the whole story in these few speeches.

When I came in towards evening from a ride along the seashore Lawson was again in the hotel. He was heavily sunk in one of the cane chairs in the lounge and he looked at me with glassy eyes. It was plain that he had been drinking all the afternoon. He was torpid, and the look on his face was sullen and vindictive. His glance rested on me for a moment, but I could see that he did not recognise me. Two or three other men were sitting there, shaking dice, and they took no notice of him. His condition was evidently too usual to attract attention. I sat down and began to play.

"You're a damned sociable lot," said Lawson suddenly.

He got out of his chair and waddled with bent knees towards the door. I do not know whether the spectacle was more ridiculous than revolting. When he had gone one of the men sniggered.

"Lawson's fairly soused today," he said.

"If I couldn't carry my liquor better than that," said another, "I'd climb on the waggon and stay there."

Who would have thought that this wretched object was in his way a romantic figure or that his life had in it those elements of pity and terror which the theorist tells us are necessary to achieve the effect of tragedy?

I did not see him again for two or three days.

I was sitting one evening on the first floor of the hotel on a verandah that overlooked the street when Lawson came up and sank into a chair beside me. He was quite sober. He made a casual remark and then, when I had replied somewhat indifferently, added with a laugh which had in it an apologetic tone:

"I was devilish soused the other day."

I did not answer. There was really nothing to say. I pulled away at my pipe in the vain hope of keeping the mosquitoes away and looked at the natives going home from their work. They walked with long steps, slowly, with care and dignity, and the soft patter of their naked feet was strange to hear. Their dark hair, curling or straight, was often white with lime, and then they had a look of extraordinary distinction. They were tall and finely built. Then a gang of Solomon Islanders, indentured labourers, passed by, singing; they were shorter and slighter than the Samoans, coal black with great heads of fuzzy hair dyed red. Now and then a white man drove past in his buggy or rode into the hotel yard. In the lagoon two or three schooners reflected their grace in the tranquil water.

"I don't know what there is to do in a place like this except to get soused," said Lawson at last.

"Don't you like Samoa?" I asked casually, for something to say.

"It's pretty, isn't it?"

The word he chose seemed so inadequate to describe the unimaginable beauty of the island, that I smiled, and smiling I turned to look at him. I was startled by the expression in those fine sombre eyes of his, an expression of intolerable anguish; they betrayed a tragic depth of emotion of which I should never have thought him capable. But the expression passed away and he smiled. His smile was simple and a little naïve. It changed his face so that I wavered in my first feeling of aversion from him.

"I was all over the place when I first came out," he said.

He was silent for a moment.

"I went away for good about three years ago, but I came back." He hesitated. "My wife wanted to come back. She was born here, you know."

"Oh, yes."

He was silent again, and then hazarded a remark about Robert Louis Stevenson. He asked me if I had been up to Vailima. For some reason he was making an effort to be agreeable to me. He began to talk of Stevenson's books, and presently the conversation drifted to London.

"I suppose Covent Garden's still going strong," he said. "I think I miss the opera as much as anything here. Have you seen *Tristan and Isolde*?"

He asked me the question as though the answer were really important to him, and when I said, a little casually I daresay, that I had, he seemed pleased. He began to speak of Wagner, not as a musician, but as the plain man who received from him an emotional satisfaction that he could not analyse.

"I suppose Bayreuth was the place to go really," he said. "I never had the money, worse luck. But of course, one might do worse than Covent Garden, all the lights and the women dressed up to the nines, and the music. The first act of the *Walküre's* all right, isn't it? And the end of *Tristan*. Golly!"

His eyes were flashing now, and his face was lit up so that he hardly seemed the same man. There was a flush on his sallow, thin cheeks, and I forgot that his voice was harsh and unpleasant. There was even a certain charm about him.

"By George, I'd like to be in London tonight. Do you know the Pall Mall restaurant? I used to go there a lot. Piccadilly Circus with the shops all lit up, and the crowd. I think it's stunning to stand there and watch the buses and taxis streaming along as though they'd never stop. And I like the

Strand too. What are those lines about God and Charing Cross?"

I was taken aback.

"Thompson's, d'you mean?" I asked.

I quoted them.

"And when so sad, thou canst not sadder,
Cry, and upon thy so sore loss
Shall shine the traffic of Jacob's ladder
Pitched between Heaven and Charing Cross."

He gave a faint sigh.

"I've read *The Hound of Heaven*. It's a bit of all right."

"It's generally thought so," I murmured.

"You don't meet anybody here who's read anything. They think it's swank."

There was a wistful look on his face, and I thought I divined the feeling that made him come to me. I was a link with the world he regretted and a life that he would know no more. Because not so very long before I had been in the London which he loved, he looked upon me with awe and envy. He had not spoken for five minutes perhaps when he broke out with words that startled me by their intensity.

"I'm fed up," he said. "I'm fed up."

"Then why don't you clear out?" I asked.

His face grew sullen.

"My lungs are a bit dicky. I couldn't stand an English winter now."

At that moment another man joined us on the verandah and Lawson sank into a moody silence.

"It's about time for a drain," said the new-comer. "Who'll have a drop of Scotch with me? Lawson?"

Lawson seemed to arise from a distant world. He got up.

"Let's go down to the bar," he said.

When he left me I remained with a kindlier feeling towards him than I should have expected. He puzzled and interested me. And a few days later I met his wife. I knew they had been married for five or six years, and I was surprised to see that she was still extremely young. When he married her she could not have been more than sixteen. She was adorably pretty. She was no darker than a Spaniard, small and very beautifully made, with tiny hands and feet, and a slight, lithe figure. Her features were lovely; but I think what struck me most was the delicacy of her appearance; the half-caste as a rule have a certain coarseness, they seem a little roughly formed, but she had an exquisite daintiness which took your breath away. There was something extremely civilised about her, so that it surprised you to see her in those surroundings, and you thought of those famous beauties who had set all the world talking at the Court of the Emperor Napoleon III. Though she wore but a muslin frock and a straw hat she wore them with an elegance that suggested the woman of fashion. She must have been ravishing when Lawson first saw her.

He had but lately come out from England to manage the local branch of an English bank, and, reaching Samoa at the beginning of the dry season, he had taken a room at the hotel. He quickly made the acquaintance of all and sundry. The life of the island is pleasant and easy. He enjoyed the long idle talks in the lounge of the hotel and the gay evenings at the English Club when a group of fellows would play pool. He liked Apia straggling along the edge of the lagoon, with its stores and bungalows, and its native village. Then there were week-ends when he would ride over to the house of one planter or another and spend a couple of nights on the hills. He had never before known freedom or leisure. And he was intoxicated by the sunshine. When he rode through the bush his head reeled a little at the beauty that surrounded him. The country was indescribably fertile. In parts the forest was still virgin, a tangle of strange trees, luxuriant undergrowth, and vine; it gave the impression that was mysterious and troubling.

But the spot that entranced him was a pool a mile or two away from Apia to which in the evenings he often went to bathe. There was a little river that bubbled over the rocks in a swift stream, and then, after forming the deep pool, ran on, shallow and crystalline, past a ford made by great stones where the natives came sometimes to bathe or to wash their clothes. The coconut trees, with their frivolous elegance, grew thickly on the banks, all clad with trailing plants, and they were reflected in the green water. It was just such a scene as you might see in Devonshire among the hills, and yet with a difference, for it had a tropical richness, a passion, a scented languor which seemed to melt the heart. The water was fresh, but not cold; and it was delicious after the heat of the day. To bathe there refreshed not only the body but the soul.

At the hour when Lawson went, there was not a soul and he lingered for a long time, now floating idly in the water, now drying himself in the evening sun, enjoying the solitude and the friendly silence. He did not regret London then, nor the life that he had abandoned, for life as it seemed complete and exquisite.

It was here that he first saw Ethel.

Occupied till late by letters which had to be finished for the monthly sailing of the boat next day, he rode down one evening to the pool when the light was almost failing. He tied up his horse and sauntered to the bank. A girl was sitting there. She glanced round as he came and noiselessly slid into the water. She vanished like a naiad startled by the approach of a mortal. He was surprised and amused. He wondered where she had hidden herself. He swam downstream and presently saw her sitting on a rock. She looked at him with uncurious eyes. He called out a greeting in Samoan.

"Talofa."

She answered him, suddenly smiling, and then let herself into the water again. She swam easily and her hair spread out behind her. He watched her cross the pool and climb out on the bank. Like all the natives she bathed in a Mother Hubbard, and the water had made it cling to her slight body. She wrung out her hair, and as she stood there, unconcerned, she looked more than ever like a wild creature of the water or the woods. He saw now that she was half-caste. He swam towards her and, getting out, addressed her in English.

"You're having a late swim."

She shook back her hair and then let it spread over her shoulders in luxuriant curls.

"I like it when I'm alone," she said.

"So do I."

She laughed with the childlike frankness of the native. She slipped a dry Mother Hubbard over her head and, letting down the wet one, stepped out of it. She wrung it out and was ready to go. She paused a moment irresolutely and then sauntered off. The night fell suddenly.

Lawson went back to the hotel and, describing her to the men who were in the lounge shaking dice for drinks, soon discovered who she was. Her father was a Norwegian called Brevald who was often to be seen in the bar of the Hotel Metropole drinking rum and water. He was a little old man, knotted and gnarled like an ancient tree, who had come out to the islands forty years before as mate of a sailing vessel. He had been a blacksmith, a trader, a planter, and at one time fairly well-to-do; but, ruined by the great hurricane of the nineties, he had now nothing to live on but a small plantation of coconut trees. He had had four native wives and, as he told you with a cracked chuckle, more children than he could count. But some had died, and some had gone out into the world, so that now the only one left at home was Ethel.

"She's a peach," said Nelson, the supercargo of the *Moana*. "I've given her the glad eye once or twice, but I guess there's nothing doing."

"Old Brevald's not that sort of a fool, sonny," put in another, a man called Miller. "He wants a son-in-law who's prepared to keep him in comfort for the rest of his life."

It was distasteful to Lawson that they should speak of the girl in that fashion. He made a remark about the departing mail and so distracted their attention. But next evening he went again to the pool. Ethel was there; and the mystery of the sunset, the deep silence of the water, the lithe grace of the coconut trees, added to her beauty, giving it a profundity, a magic, which stirred the heart to unknown emotions. For some reason that time he had the whim not to speak to her. She took no notice of him. She did not even glance in his direction. She swam about the green pool. She dived, she rested on the bank, as though she were quite alone: he had a queer feeling that he was invisible. Scraps of poetry, half forgotten, floated across his memory, and vague recollections of the Greece he had negligently studied in his school days. When she had changed her wet clothes for dry ones and sauntered away he found a scarlet hibiscus where she had been. It was a flower that she had worn in her hair when she came to bathe and, having taken it out on getting into the water, had forgotten or not cared to put in again. He took it in his hands and looked at it with a singular emotion. He had an instinct to keep it, but his sentimentality irritated him, and he flung it away. It gave him quite a little pang to see it float down the stream.

He wondered what strangeness it was in her nature that urged her to go down to this hidden pool when there was no likelihood that anyone should be there. The natives of the islands are devoted to the water. They bathe, somewhere or other, every day, once always, and often twice; but they bathe in bands, laughing and joyous, a whole family together; and you often saw a group of girls, dappled by the sun shining through the trees, with the half-castes among them, splashing about the shallows of the stream. It looked as though there were in this pool some secret which attracted Ethel against her will.

Now the night had fallen, mysterious and silent, and he let himself down in the water softly, in order to make no sound, and swam lazily in the warm darkness. The water seemed fragrant still from her slender body. He rode back to the town under the starry sky. He felt at peace with the world.

Now he went every evening to the pool and every evening he saw Ethel. Presently he overcame her timidity. She became playful and friendly. They sat together on the rocks above the pool, where the water ran fast, and they lay side by side on the ledge that overlooked it, watching the gathering dusk envelop it with mystery. It was inevitable that their meetings should become known—in the South Seas everyone seems to know everyone's business—and he was subjected to much rude chaff by the men at the hotel. He smiled and let them talk. It was not even worthwhile to deny their coarse suggestions. His feelings were absolutely pure. He loved Ethel as a poet might love the moon. He thought of her not as a woman but as something not of this earth. She was the spirit of the pool.

One day at the hotel, passing through the bar, he saw that old Brevald, as ever in his shabby blue overalls, was standing there. Because he was Ethel's father he had a desire to speak to him, so he went in, nodded and, ordering his own drink, casually turned and invited the old man to have one with him. They chatted for a few minutes of local affairs, and Lawson was uneasily conscious that the Norwegian was scrutinising him with sly blue eyes. His manner was not agreeable. It was sycophantic, and yet behind the cringing air of an old man who had been worsted in his struggle with fate was a shadow of old truculence. Lawson remembered that he had once been captain of a schooner engaged in the slave trade, a blackbirder they call it in the Pacific, and he had a large hernia in the chest which was the result of a wound received in a scrap with Solomon Islanders. The bell rang for luncheon.

"Well, I must be off," said Lawson.

"Why don't you come along to my place one time?" said Brevald, in his wheezy voice. "It's not very grand, but you'll be welcome. You know Ethel."

"I'll come with pleasure."

"Sunday afternoon's the best time."

Brevald's bungalow, shabby and bedraggled, stood among the coconut trees of the plantation, a little away from the main road that ran up to Vailima. Immediately around it grew huge plantains. With their tattered leaves they had the tragic beauty of a lovely woman in rags. Everything was slovenly and neglected. Little black pigs, thin and high-backed, rooted about, and chickens clucked noisily as they picked at the refuse scattered here and there. Three or four natives were lounging about the verandah. When Lawson asked for Brevald the old man's cracked voice called out to him, and he found him in the sitting-room smoking an old briar pipe.

"Sit down and make yerself at home," he said. "Ethel's just titivating."

She came in. She wore a blouse and skirt, and her hair was done in the European fashion. Although she had not the wild, timid grace of the girl who came down every evening to the pool, she seemed now more usual and consequently more approachable. She shook hands with Lawson. It was the first time he had touched her hand.

"I hope you'll have a cup of tea with us," she said.

He knew she had been at a mission school, and he was amused, and at the same time touched, by the company manners she was putting on for his benefit. Tea was already set out on the table and in a minute old Brevald's fourth wife brought in the tea-pot. She was a handsome native, no longer very young, and she spoke but a few words of English. She smiled and smiled. Tea was rather a solemn meal, with a great deal of bread and butter and a variety of very sweet cakes, and the conversation was formal. Then a wrinkled old woman came in softly.

"That's Ethel's granny," said old Brevald, noisily spitting on the floor.

She sat on the edge of a chair, uncomfortably, so that you saw it was unusual for her and she would have been more at ease on the ground, and remained silently staring at Lawson with fixed, shining eyes. In the kitchen behind the bungalow someone began to play the concertina, and two or three voices were raised in a hymn. But they sang for the pleasure of the sounds rather than from piety.

When Lawson walked back to the hotel he was strangely happy. He was touched by the higgledy-piggledy way in which those people lived; and in the smiling good-nature of Mrs. Brevald, in the little Norwegian's fantastic career, and in the shining mysterious eyes of the old grandmother, he found something unusual and fascinating. It was a more natural life than any he had known, it was nearer to the friendly, fertile earth; civilisation repelled him at that moment, and by mere contact with these creatures of a more primitive nature he felt a greater freedom.

He saw himself rid of the hotel which already was beginning to irk him, settled in a little bungalow of his own, trim and white, in front of the sea so that he had before his eyes always the multicoloured variety of the lagoon. He loved the beautiful island. London and England meant nothing to him anymore, he was content to spend the rest of his days in that forgotten spot, rich in the best of the world's goods, love and happiness. He made up his mind that whatever the obstacles nothing should prevent him from marrying Ethel.

But there were no obstacles. He was always welcome at the Brevalds' house. The old man was ingratiating, and Mrs. Brevald smiled without ceasing. He had brief glimpses of natives who seemed somehow to belong to the establishment, and once he found a tall youth in a *lava-lava*, his body tattooed, his hair white with lime, sitting with Brevald, and was told he was Mrs. Brevald's brother's son; but for the most part they kept out of his way. Ethel was delightful with him. The light in her eyes when she saw him filled him with ecstasy. She was charming and naïve. He listened enraptured when she told him of the mission school at which she was educated, and of the sisters. He went with her to the cinema which was given once a fortnight and danced with her at the dance which followed it. They came from all parts of the island for this, since gaieties are few in Upolu; and you saw there all the society of the place, the white ladies keeping a good deal to themselves, the half-castes very elegant in American clothes, the natives, strings of dark girls in white

Mother Hubbard's and young men in unaccustomed ducks and white shoes. It was all very smart and gay. Ethel was pleased to show her friends the white admirer who did not leave her side. The rumour was soon spread that he meant to marry her, and her friends looked at her with envy. It was a great thing for a half-caste to get a white man to marry her, even the less regular relation was better than nothing, but one could never tell what it would lead to; and Lawson's position as manager of the bank made him one of the catches of the island. If he had not been so absorbed in Ethel he would have noticed that many eyes were fixed on him curiously, and he would have seen the glances of the white ladies and noticed how they put their heads together and gossiped.

Afterwards, when the men who lived at the hotel were having a whisky before turning in, Nelson burst out with:

"Say, they say Lawson's going to marry that girl."

"He's a damned fool then," said Miller.

Miller was a German-American who had changed his name from Müller, a big man, fat and bald-headed, with a round, clean-shaven face. He wore large gold-rimmed spectacles, which gave him a benign look, and his ducks were always clean and white. He was a heavy drinker, invariably ready to stay up all night with the "boys," but he never got drunk; he was jolly and affable, but very shrewd. Nothing interfered with his business; he represented a firm in San Francisco, jobbers of the goods sold in the islands, calico, machinery and what not; and his good-fellowship was part of his stock-in-trade.

"He don't know what he's up against," said Nelson. "Someone ought to put him wise."

"If you'll take my advice you won't interfere in what don't concern you," said Miller. "When a man's made up his mind to make a fool of himself, there's nothing like letting him."

"I'm all for having a good time with the girls out here, but when it comes to marrying them—this child ain't taking any, I'll tell the world."

Chaplin was there, and now he had his say.

"I've seen a lot of fellows do it, and it's no good."

"You ought to have a talk with him, Chaplin," said Nelson. "You know him better than anyone else does."

"My advice to Chaplin is to leave it alone," said Miller.

Even in those days Lawson was not popular and really no one took enough interest in him to bother. Mrs. Chaplin talked it over with two or three of the white ladies, but they contented themselves with saying that it was a pity; and when he told her definitely that he was going to be married it seemed too late to do anything.

For a year Lawson was happy. He took a bungalow at the point of the bay round which Apia is built, on the borders of a native village. It nestled charmingly among the coconut trees and faced the passionate blue of the Pacific. Ethel was lovely as she went about the little house, lithe and graceful like some young animal of the woods, and she was gay. They laughed a great deal. They talked nonsense. Sometimes one or two of the men at the hotel would come over and spend the evening, and often on a Sunday they would go for a day to some planter who had married a native; now and then one or other of the half-caste traders who had a store in Apia would give a party and they went to it. The half-castes treated Lawson quite differently now. His marriage had made him one of themselves and they called him Bertie. They put their arms through his and smacked him on the back. He liked to see Ethel at these gatherings. Her eyes shone and she laughed. It did him good to see her radiant happiness. Sometimes Ethel's relations would come to the bungalow, old Brevald of course, and her mother, but cousins too, vague native women in Mother Hubbard's and men and boys in *lava-lavas*, with their hair dyed red and their bodies elaborately tattooed. He would find them sitting there when he got back from the bank. He laughed indulgently.

"Don't let them eat us out of hearth and home," he said.

"They're my own family. I can't help doing something for them when they ask me."

He knew that when a white man marries a native or a half-caste he must expect her relations to look upon him as a gold mine. He took Ethel's face in his hands and kissed her red lips. Perhaps he could not expect her to understand that the salary which had amply sufficed for a bachelor must be managed with some care when it had to support a wife and a house. Then Ethel was delivered of a son.

It was when Lawson first held the child in his arms that a sudden pang shot through his heart. He had not expected it to be so dark. After all it had but a fourth part of native blood, and there was no reason really why it should not look just like an English baby; but, huddled together in his arms, sallow, its head covered already with black hair, with huge black eyes, it might have been a native child. Since his marriage he had been ignored by the white ladies of the colony. When he came across men in whose houses he had been accustomed to dine as a bachelor, they were a little self-conscious with him; and they sought to cover their embarrassment by an exaggerated cordiality.

"Mrs. Lawson well?" they would say. "You're a lucky fellow. Damned pretty girl."

But if they were with their wives and met him and Ethel they would feel it awkward when their wives gave Ethel a patronising nod. Lawson had laughed.

"They're as dull as ditchwater, the whole gang of them," he said. "It's not going to disturb my night's rest if they don't ask me to their dirty parties."

But now it irked him a little.

The little dark baby screwed up its face. That was his son. He thought of the half-caste children in Apia. They had an unhealthy look, sallow and pale, and they were odiously precocious. He had seen them on the boat going to school in New Zealand, and a school had to be chosen which took children with native blood in them; they were huddled together, brazen and yet timid, with traits which set them apart strangely from white people. They spoke the native language among themselves. And when they grew up the men accepted smaller salaries because of their native blood; girls might marry a white man, but boys had no chance; they must marry a half-caste like themselves or a native. Lawson made up his mind passionately that he would take his son away from the humiliation of such a life. At whatever cost he must get back to Europe. And when he went in to see Ethel, frail and lovely in her bed, surrounded by native women, his determination was strengthened. If he took her away among his own people she would belong more completely to him. He loved her so passionately, he wanted her to be one soul and one body with him; and he was conscious that here, with those deep roots attaching her to the native life, she would always keep something from him.

He went to work quietly, urged by an obscure instinct of secrecy, and wrote to a cousin who was partner in a shipping firm in Aberdeen, saying that his health (on account of which like so many more he had come out to the islands) was so much better, there seemed no reason why he should not return to Europe. He asked him to use what influence he could to get him a job, no matter how poorly paid, on Deeside, where the climate was particularly suitable to such as suffered from diseases of the lungs. It takes five or six weeks for letters to get from Aberdeen to Samoa, and several had to be exchanged. He had plenty of time to prepare Ethel. She was as delighted as a child. He was amused to see how she boasted to her friends that she was going to England; it was a step up for her; she would be quite English there; and she was excited at the interest the approaching departure gave her. When at length a cable came offering him a post in a bank in Kincardineshire she was beside herself with joy.

When, their long journey over, they were settled in the little Scots town with its granite houses Lawson realised how much it meant to him to live once more among his own people. He looked back on the three years he had spent in Apia as exile, and returned to the life that seemed the only normal one with a sigh of relief. It was good to play golf once more, and to fish—to fish properly, that was poor fun in the Pacific when you just threw in your line and pulled out one big sluggish fish after another from the crowded sea—and it was good to see a paper every day with that day's news, and to meet men and women of your own sort, people you could talk to; and it was good to eat meat that was not frozen and to drink milk that was not canned. They were thrown upon their own resources much more than in the Pacific, and he was glad to have Ethel exclusively to himself. After two years of marriage, he loved her more devotedly than ever, he could hardly bear her out of his sight, and the need in him grew urgent for a more intimate communion between them. But it was strange that after the first excitement of arrival she seemed to take less interest in the new life than he had expected. She did not accustom herself to her surroundings. She was a little lethargic. As the fine autumn darkened into winter she complained of the cold. She lay half the morning in bed and the rest of the day on a sofa, reading novels sometimes, but more often doing nothing. She looked pinched.

"Never mind, darling," he said. "You'll get used to it very soon. And wait till the summer comes. It can be almost as hot as in Apia."

He felt better and stronger than he had done for years.

The carelessness with which she managed her house had not mattered in Samoa, but here it was out of place. When anyone came he did not want the place to look untidy; and, laughing, chaffing Ethel a little, he set about putting things in order. Ethel watched him indolently. She spent long hours playing with her son. She talked to him in the baby language of her own country. To distract her, Lawson bestirred himself to make friends among the neighbours, and now and then they went to little parties where the ladies sang drawing-room ballads, and the men beamed in silent good nature. Ethel was shy. She seemed to sit apart. Sometimes Lawson, seized with a sudden anxiety, would ask her if she was happy.

"Yes, I'm quite happy," she answered.

But her eyes were veiled by some thought he could not guess. She seemed to withdraw into herself so that he was conscious that he knew no more of her than when he had first seen her bathing in the pool. He had an uneasy feeling that she was concealing something from him, and because he adored her it tortured him.

"You don't regret Apia, do you?" he asked her once.

"Oh, no—I think it's very nice here."

An obscure misgiving drove him to make disparaging remarks about the island and the people there. She smiled and did not answer. Very rarely she received a bundle of letters from Samoa and then she went about for a day or two with a set, pale face.

"Nothing would induce me ever to go back there," he said once. "It's no place for a white man."

But he grew conscious that sometimes, when he was away, Ethel cried. In Apia she had been talkative, chatting volubly about all the little details of their common life, the gossip of the place; but now she gradually became silent, and, though he increased his efforts to amuse her, she remained listless. It seemed to him that her recollections of the old life were drawing her away from him, and he was madly jealous of the island and of the sea, of Brevald, and all the dark-skinned people whom he remembered now with horror. When she spoke of Samoa he was bitter and satirical. One evening late in the spring when the birch trees were bursting into leaf, coming home from a round of golf, he found her not as usual lying on the sofa, but at the window, standing. She had evidently been waiting for his return. She addressed him the moment he came into the room. To his amazement she spoke in Samoan.

"I can't stand it. I can't live here anymore. I hate it. I hate it."

"For God's sake speak in a civilised language," he said irritably.

She went up to him and clasped her arms around his body awkwardly, with a gesture that had in it something barbaric.

"Let's go away from here. Let's go back to Samoa. If you make me stay here I shall die. I want to go home."

Her passion broke suddenly, and she burst into tears. His anger vanished and he drew her down on his knees. He explained to her that it was impossible for him to throw up his job, which after all meant his bread and butter. His place in Apia was long since filled. He had nothing to go back to there. He tried to put it to her reasonably, the inconveniences of life there, the humiliation to which they must be exposed, and the bitterness it must cause their son.

"Scotland's wonderful for education and that sort of thing. Schools are good and cheap, and he can go to the University at Aberdeen. I'll make a real Scot of him."

They had called him Andrew. Lawson wanted him to become a doctor. He would marry a white woman.

"I'm not ashamed of being half native," Ethel said sullenly.

"Of course not, darling. There's nothing to be ashamed of."

With her soft cheek against his he felt incredibly weak.

"You don't know how much I love you," he said. "I'd give anything in the world to be able to tell you what I've got in my heart."

He sought her lips.

The summer came. The highland valley was green and fragrant, and the hills were gay with the heather. One sunny day followed another in that sheltered spot, and the shade of the birch trees was grateful after the glare of the high road. Ethel spoke no more of Samoa and Lawson grew less nervous. He thought that she was resigned to her surroundings, and he felt that his love for her was so passionate that it could leave no room in her heart for any longing. One day the local doctor stopped him in the street.

"I say, Lawson, your missus ought to be careful how she bathes in our highland streams. It's not like the Pacific, you know."

Lawson was surprised and did not have the presence of mind to conceal the fact.

"I didn't know she was bathing."

The doctor laughed.

"A good many people have seen her. It makes them talk a bit, you know, because it seems a rum place to choose, the pool up above the bridge, and bathing isn't allowed there, but there's no harm in that. I don't know how she can stand the water."

Lawson knew the pool the doctor spoke of, and suddenly it occurred to him that in a way it was just like that pool at Upolu where Ethel had been in the habit of bathing every evening. A clear highland stream ran down a sinuous course, rocky, splashing gaily, and then formed a deep, smooth pool, with a little sandy beach. Trees overshadowed it thickly, not coconut trees, but beeches, and the sun played fitfully through the leaves on the sparkling water. It gave him a shock. With his imagination he saw Ethel go there every day and undress on the bank and slip into the water, cold, colder than that of the pool she loved at home, and for a moment regain the feeling of the past. He saw her once more as the strange, wild spirit of the stream, and it seemed to him fantastically that the running water called her. That afternoon he went along to the river. He made his way cautiously among the trees and the grassy path deadened the sound of his steps. Presently he came to a spot from which he could see the pool. Ethel was sitting on the bank, looking down at the water. She sat quite still. It seemed as though the water drew her irresistibly. He wondered what strange thoughts wandered through her head. At last, she got up and for a minute or two she was hidden from his gaze; then he saw her again, wearing a Mother Hubbard, and with her little bare feet she stepped delicately over the mossy bank. She came to the water's edge, and softly, without a splash, let herself down. She swam about quietly, and there was something not quite of a human being in the way she swam. He did not know why it affected him so queerly. He waited till she clambered out. She stood for a moment with the wet folds of her dress clinging to her body, so that its shape was outlined, and then, passing her hands slowly over her breasts, gave a little sigh of delight. Then she disappeared. Lawson turned away and walked back to the village. He had a bitter pain in his heart, for he knew that she was still a stranger to him and his hungry love was destined ever to remain unsatisfied.

He did not make any mention of what he had seen. He ignored the incident completely, but he looked at her curiously, trying to divine what was in her mind. He redoubled the tenderness with which he used her. He sought to make her forget the deep longing of her soul by the passion of his love.

Then one day, when he came home, he was astonished to find her not in the house.

"Where's Mrs. Lawson?" he asked the maid.

"She went into Aberdeen, Sir, with the baby," the maid answered, a little surprised at the question. "She said she would not be back till the last train."

"Oh, all right."

He was vexed that Ethel had said nothing to him about the excursion, but he was not disturbed, since of late she had been in now and again to Aberdeen, and he was glad that she should look at the shops and perhaps visit a cinema. He went to meet the last train, but when she did not come he grew suddenly frightened. He went up to the bedroom and saw at once that her toilet things were no longer in their place. He opened the wardrobe and the drawers. They were half empty. She had bolted.

He was seized with a passion of anger. It was too late that night to telephone to Aberdeen and make enquiries, but he knew already all that his enquiries might have taught him. With fiendish cunning she had chosen a time when they were making up their periodical accounts at the bank and there was no chance that he could follow her. He was imprisoned by his work. He took up a paper and saw that there was a boat sailing for Australia next morning. She must be now well on the way to London. He could not prevent the sobs that were wrung painfully from him.

"I've done everything in the world for her," he cried, "and she had the heart to treat me like this. How cruel, how monstrously cruel!"

After two days of misery, he received a letter from her. It was written in her school-girl hand. She had always written with difficulty:

Dear Bertie:
I couldn't stand it anymore. I'm going back home. Good-bye.

Ethel.

She did not say a single word of regret. She did not even ask him to come too. Lawson was prostrated. He found out where the ship made its first stop and, though he knew very well she would not come, sent a cable beseeching her to return. He waited with pitiful anxiety. He wanted her to send him just one word of love; she did not even answer. He passed through one violent phase after another. At one moment he told himself that he was well rid of her, and at the next that he would force her to return by withholding money. He was lonely and wretched. He wanted his boy, and he wanted her. He knew that whatever he pretended to himself, there was only one thing to do and that was to follow her. He could never live without her now. All his plans for the future were like a house of cards and he scattered them with angry impatience. He did not care whether he threw away his chances for the future, for nothing in the world mattered but that he should get Ethel back again. As soon as he could he went into Aberdeen and told the manager of his bank that he meant to leave at once. The manager remonstrated. The short notice was inconvenient. Lawson would not listen to reason. He was determined to be free before the next boat sailed; and it was not until he was on board of her, having sold everything he possessed, that in some measure he regained his calm. Till then to those who had come in contact with him he seemed hardly sane. His last action in England was to cable to Ethel at Apia that he was joining her.

He sent another cable from Sydney, and when at last with the dawn his boat crossed the bar at Apia, and he saw once more the white house's straggling along the bay he felt an immense relief. The doctor came on board and the agent. They were both old acquaintances and he felt kindly towards their familiar faces. He had a drink or two with them for old times' sake, and also because he was desperately nervous. He was not sure if Ethel would be glad to see him. When he got into the launch and approached the wharf he scanned anxiously the little crowd that waited. She was not there, and his heart sank, but then he saw Brevald, in his old blue clothes, and his heart warmed towards him.

"Where's Ethel?" he said, as he jumped on shore.

"She's down at the bungalow. She's living with us."

Lawson was dismayed, but he put on a jovial air.

"Well, have you got room for me? I daresay it'll take a week or two to fix ourselves up."

"Oh, yes, I guess we can make room for you."

After passing through the custom-house they went to the hotel and there Lawson was greeted by several of his old friends. There were a good many rounds of drinks before it seemed possible to get away and when they did go out at last to Brevald's house they were both rather gay. He clasped Ethel in his arms. He had forgotten all his bitter thoughts in the joy of beholding her once more. His mother-in-law was pleased to see him, and so was the old, wrinkled beldame, her mother; natives and half-castes came in, and they all sat round, beaming on him. Brevald had a bottle of whisky and everyone who came was given a nip. Lawson sat with his little dark-skinned boy on his knees, they had taken his English clothes off him, and he was stark, with Ethel by his side in a Mother Hubbard. He felt like a returning prodigal. In the afternoon he went down to the hotel again and when he got back he was more than gay, he was drunk. Ethel and her mother knew that white men got drunk now and then, it was what you expected of them, and they laughed good-naturedly as they helped him to bed.

But in a day or two he set about looking for a job. He knew that he could not hope for such a position as that which he had thrown away to go to England; but with his training he could not fail to be useful to one of the trading firms, and perhaps in the end he would not lose by the change.

"After all, you can't make money in a bank," he said. "Trade's the thing."

He had hopes that he would soon make himself so indispensable that he would get someone to take him into partnership, and there was no reason why in a few years he should not be a rich man.

"As soon as I'm fixed up we'll find ourselves a shack," he told Ethel. "We can't go on living here."

Brevald's bungalow was so small that they were all piled on one another, and there was no chance of ever being alone. There was neither peace nor privacy.

"Well, there's no hurry. We shall be all right here till we find just what we want."

It took him a week to get settled and then he entered the firm of a man called Bain. But when he talked to Ethel about moving she said she wanted to stay where she was till her baby was born, for she was expecting another child. Lawson tried to argue with her.

"If you don't like it," she said, "go and live at the hotel."

He grew suddenly pale.

"Ethel, how can you suggest that!"

She shrugged her shoulders.

"What's the good of having a house of our own when we can live here."

He yielded.

When Lawson, after his work, went back to the bungalow he found it crowded with natives. They lay about smoking, sleeping, drinking *kava*; and they talked incessantly. The place was grubby and untidy. His child crawled about, playing with native children, and it heard nothing spoken but Samoan. He fell into the habit of dropping into the hotel on his way home to have a few cocktails, for he could only face the evening and the crowd of friendly natives when he was fortified with liquor. And all the time, though he loved her more passionately than ever, he felt that Ethel was slipping away from him. When the baby was born he suggested that they should get into a house of their own, but Ethel refused. Her stay in Scotland seemed to have thrown her back on her own people, now that she was once more among them, with a passionate zest, and she turned to her native ways with abandon. Lawson began to drink more. Every Saturday night he went to the English Club and got blind drunk.

He had the peculiarity that as he grew drunk he grew quarrelsome and once he had a violent dispute with Bain, his employer. Bain dismissed him, and he had to look out for another job. He was idle for two or three weeks and during these, sooner than sit in the bungalow, he lounged about in the hotel or at the English Club and drank. It was more out of pity than anything else that Miller, the German-American, took him into his office; but he was a businessman and though Lawson's financial skill made him valuable, the circumstances were such that he could hardly refuse a smaller salary than he had had before, and Miller did not hesitate to offer it to him. Ethel and Brevald blamed him for taking it, since Pedersen, the half-caste, offered him more. But he resented bitterly the thought of being under the orders of a half-caste. When Ethel nagged him he burst out furiously:

"I'll see myself dead before I work for a nigger."

"You may have to," she said.

And in six months he found himself forced to this final humiliation. The passion for liquor had been gaining on him, he was often heavy with drink, and he did his work badly. Miller warned him once or twice and Lawson was not the man to accept remonstrance easily. One day in the midst of an altercation he put on his hat and walked out. But by now his reputation was well known and he could find no one to engage him. For a while he idled, and then he had an attack of *delirium tremens*. When he recovered, shameful and weak, he could no longer resist the constant pressure, and he went to Pedersen and asked him for a job. Pedersen was glad to have a white man in his store and Lawson's skill at figures made him useful.

From that time his degeneration was rapid. The white people gave him the cold shoulder. They were only prevented from cutting him completely by disdainful pity and by a certain dread of his angry violence when he was drunk. He became extremely susceptible and was always on the lookout for affront.

He lived entirely among the natives and half-castes, but he had no longer the prestige of the white man. They felt his loathing for them, and they resented his attitude of superiority. He was one of themselves now and they did not see why he should put on airs. Brevald, who had been ingratiating and obsequious, now treated him with contempt. Ethel had made a bad bargain. There were disgraceful scenes and once or twice the two men came to blows. When there was a quarrel Ethel took the part of her family. They found he was better drunk than sober, for when he was drunk he would lie on the bed or on the floor, sleeping heavily.

Then he became aware that something was being hidden from him.

When he got back to the bungalow for the wretched, half native supper which was his evening meal, often Ethel was not in. If he asked where she was Brevald told him she had gone to spend the evening with one or other of her friends. Once he followed her to the house Brevald had mentioned and found she was not there. On her return he asked her where she had been, and she told him her father had made a mistake; she had been to so-and-so's. But he knew that she was lying. She was in her best clothes; her eyes were shining, and she looked lovely.

"Don't try any monkey tricks on me, my girl," he said, "or I'll break every bone in your body."

"You drunken beast," she said, scornfully.

He fancied that Mrs. Brevald, and the old grandmother looked at him maliciously and he ascribed Brevald's good-humour with him, so unusual those days, to his satisfaction at having something up his sleeve against his son-in-law. And then, his suspicions aroused, he imagined that the white men gave him curious glances. When he came into the lounge of the hotel the sudden silence which fell upon the company convinced him that he had been the subject of the conversation. Something was going on and everyone knew it but himself. He was seized with furious jealousy. He believed that Ethel was carrying on with one of the white men, and he looked at one after the other with scrutinising eyes; but there was nothing to give him even a hint. He was helpless. Because he could find no one on whom definitely to fix his suspicions, he went about like a raving maniac, looking for someone on whom to vent his wrath. Chance caused him in the end to hit upon the man who of all others least deserved to suffer from his violence. One afternoon, when he was sitting in the hotel by himself, moodily, Chaplin came in and sat down beside him. Perhaps Chaplin was the only man on the island who had any sympathy for him. They ordered drinks and chatted a few minutes about the races that were shortly to be run. Then Chaplain said:

"I guess we shall all have to fork out money for new dresses."

Lawson sniggered. Since Mrs. Chaplin held the purse-strings if she wanted a new frock for the occasion she would certainly not ask her husband for the money.

"How is your missus?" asked Chaplin, desiring to be friendly.

"What the hell's that got to do with you?" said Lawson, knitting his dark brows.

"I was only asking a civil question."

"Well, keep your civil questions to yourself."

Chaplin was not a patient man; his long residence in the tropics, the whisky bottle, and his domestic affairs had given him a temper hardly more under control than Lawson's.

"Look here, my boy, when you're in my hotel you behave like a gentleman, or you'll find yourself in the street before you can say knife."

Lawson's lowering face grew dark and red.

"Let me just tell you once for all and you can pass it on to the others," he said, panting with rage. "If any of you fellows come messing round with my wife he'd better look out."

"Who do you think wants to mess around with your wife?"

"I'm not such a fool as you think. I can see a stone wall in front of me as well as most men, and I warn you straight, that's all. I'm not going to put up with any hanky-panky, not on your life."

"Look here, you'd better clear out of here, and come back when you're sober."

"I shall clear out when I choose and not a minute before," said Lawson.

It was an unfortunate boast, for Chaplin in the course of his experience as a hotel-keeper had acquired a peculiar skill in dealing with gentlemen whose room he preferred to their company, and the words were hardly out of Lawson's mouth before he found himself caught by the collar and arm and hustled not without force into the street. He stumbled down the steps into the blinding glare of the sun.

It was in consequence of this that he had his first violent scene with Ethel. Smarting with humiliation and unwilling to go back to the hotel, he went home that afternoon earlier than usual. He found Ethel dressing to go out. As a rule, she lay about in a Mother Hubbard, barefoot, with a flower in her dark hair; but now, in white silk stockings and high-heeled shoes, she was doing up a pink muslin dress which was the newest she had.

"You're making yourself very smart," he said. "Where are you going?"

"I'm going to the Crossley's."

"I'll come with you."

"Why?" she asked coolly.

"I don't want you to gad about by yourself all the time."

"You're not asked."

"I don't care a damn about that. You're not going without me."

"You'd better lie down till I'm ready."

She thought he was drunk and if he once settled himself on the bed would quickly drop off to sleep. He sat down on a chair and began to smoke a cigarette. She watched him with increasing irritation: When she was ready he got up. It happened by an unusual chance that there was no one in the bungalow. Brevald was working on the plantation and his wife had gone into Apia. Ethel faced him.

"I'm not going with you. You're drunk."

"That's a lie. You're not going without me."

She shrugged her shoulders and tried to pass him, but he caught her by the arm and held her.

"Let me go, you devil," she said, breaking into Samoan.

"Why do you want to go without me? Haven't I told you I'm not going to put up with any monkey tricks?"

She clenched her fist and hit him in the face. He lost all control of himself. All his love, all his hatred, welled up in him and he was beside himself.

"I'll teach you," he shouted. "I'll teach you."

He seized a riding-whip which happened to be under his hand and struck her with it. She screamed, and the scream maddened him so that he went on striking her, again and again. Her shrieks rang through the bungalow, and he cursed her as he hit. Then he flung her on the bed. She lay there sobbing with pain and terror. He threw the whip away from him and rushed out of the room. Ethel heard him go and she stopped crying. She looked round cautiously, then she raised herself. She was sore, but she had not been badly hurt, and she looked at her dress to see if it was damaged. The native women are not unused to blows. What he had done did not outrage her. When she looked at herself in the glass and arranged her hair, her eyes were shining. There was a strange look in them. Perhaps then she was nearer loving him than she had ever been before.

But Lawson, driven forth blindly, stumbled through the plantation and suddenly exhausted, weak as a child, flung himself on the ground at the foot of a tree. He was miserable and ashamed. He thought of Ethel, and in the yielding tenderness of his love all his bones seemed to grow soft within him. He thought of the past, and of his hopes, and he was aghast at what he had done. He wanted her more than ever. He wanted to take her in his arms. He must go to her at once.

He got up. He was so weak that he staggered as he walked. He went into the house, and she was sitting in their cramped bedroom in front of her looking-glass.

"Oh, Ethel, forgive me. I'm so awfully ashamed of myself. I didn't know what I was doing."

He fell on his knees before her and timidly stroked the skirt of her dress.

"I can't bear to think of what I did. It's awful. I think I was mad. There's no one in the world I love as I love you. I'd do anything to save you from pain and I've hurt you. I can never forgive myself, but for God's sake say you forgive me."

He heard her shrieks still. It was unendurable. She looked at him silently. He tried to take her hands, and the tears streamed from his eyes. In his humiliation he hid his face in her lap and his frail body shook with sobs. An expression of utter contempt came over her face. She had the native woman's disdain of a man who abased himself before a woman. A weak creature! And for a moment she had been on the point of thinking there was something in him. He grovelled at her feet like a cur. She gave him a little scornful kick.

"Get out," she said. "I hate you."

He tried to hold her, but she pushed him aside. She stood up. She began to take off her dress. She kicked off her shoes and slid the stockings off her feet, then she slipped on her old Mother Hubbard.

"Where are you going?"

"What's that got to do with you? I'm going down to the pool."

"Let me come too," he said.

He asked as though he were a child.

"Can't you even leave me that?"

He hid his face in his hands, crying miserably, while she, her eyes hard and cold, stepped past him and went out.

From that time she entirely despised him; and though, herded together in the small bungalow, Lawson and Ethel with her two children, Brevald, his wife and her mother, and the vague relations and hangers-on who were always in and about, they had to live cheek by jowl, Lawson, ceasing to be of any account, was hardly noticed. He left in the morning after breakfast and came back only to have supper. He gave up the struggle, and when for want of money he could not go to the English Club he spent the evening playing hearts with old Brevald and the natives. Except when he was drunk he was cowed and listless. Ethel treated him like a dog. She submitted at times to his fits of wild passion, and she was frightened by the gusts of hatred with which they were followed; but when, afterwards, he was cringing and lachrymose she had such a contempt for him that she could have spat in his face. Sometimes he was violent, but now she was prepared for him, and when he hit her she kicked and scratched and bit. They had horrible battles in which he had not always the best of it. Very soon it was known all over Apia that they got on badly. There was little sympathy for Lawson, and at the hotel the general surprise was that old Brevald did not kick him out of the place.

"Brevald's a pretty ugly customer," said one of the men. "I shouldn't be surprised if he put a bullet into Lawson's carcass one of these days."

Ethel still went in the evenings to bathe in the silent pool. It seemed to have an attraction for her that was not quite human, just that attraction you might imagine that a mermaid who had won a soul would have for the cool salt waves of the sea; and sometimes Lawson went also. I do not know what urged him to go, for Ethel was obviously irritated by his presence; perhaps it was because in that spot he hoped to regain the clean rapture which had filled his heart when first he saw her; perhaps only, with the madness of those who love them that love them not, from the feeling that his obstinacy could force love. One day he strolled down there with a feeling that was rare with him now. He felt suddenly at peace with the world. The evening was drawing in and the dusk seemed to cling to the leaves of the coconut trees like a little thin cloud. A faint breeze stirred them noiselessly. A crescent moon hung just over their tops. He made his way to the bank. He saw Ethel in the water floating on her back. Her hair streamed out all round her, and she was holding in her hand a large hibiscus. He stopped a moment to admire her; she was like Ophelia.

"Hulloa, Ethel," he cried joyfully.

She made a sudden movement and dropped the red flower. It floated idly away. She swam a stroke or two till she knew there was ground within her depth and then stood up.

"Go away," she said. "Go away."

He laughed.

"Don't be selfish. There's plenty of room for both of us."

"Why can't you leave me alone? I want to be by myself."

"Hang it all, I want to bathe," he answered, good-humouredly.

"Go down to the bridge. I don't want you here."

"I'm sorry for that," he said, smiling still.

He was not in the least angry, and he hardly noticed that she was in a passion. He began to take off his coat.

"Go away," she shrieked. "I won't have you here. Can't you even leave me this? Go away."

"Don't be silly, darling."

She bent down and picked up a sharp stone and flung it quickly at him. He had no time to duck. It hit him on the temple. With a cry he put his hand to his head and when he took it away it was wet with blood. Ethel stood still, panting with rage. He turned very pale, and without a word, taking up his coat, went away. Ethel let herself fall back into the water and the stream carried her slowly down to the ford.

The stone had made a jagged wound and for some days Lawson went about with a bandaged head. He had invented a likely story to account for the accident when the fellows at the club asked him about it, but he had no occasion to use it. No one referred to the matter. He saw them cast surreptitious glances at his head, but not a word was said. The silence could only mean that they knew how he came by his wound. He was certain now that Ethel had a lover, and they all knew who it was. But there was not the smallest indication to guide him. He never saw Ethel with anyone; no one showed a wish to be with her or treated him in a manner that seemed strange. Wild rage seized him and having no one to vent it on he drank more and more heavily. A little while before I came to the island he had had another attack of *delirium tremens*.

I met Ethel at the house of a man called Caster, who lived two or three miles from Apia with a native wife. I had been playing tennis with him and when we were tired he suggested a cup of tea. We went into the house and in the untidy living-room found Ethel chatting with Mrs. Caster.

"Hulloa, Ethel," he said, "I didn't know you were here."

I could not help looking at her with curiosity. I tried to see what there was in her to have excited in Lawson such a devastating passion. But who can explain these things? It was true that she was lovely; she reminded one of the red hibiscus, the common flower of the hedgerow in Samoa, with its grace and its languor and its passion; but what surprised me most, taking into consideration the story I knew even then a good deal of, was her freshness and simplicity. She was quiet and a little shy. There was nothing coarse or loud about her; she had not the exuberance common to the half-caste; and it was almost impossible to believe that she could be the virago that the horrible scenes between husband and wife, which were now common knowledge, indicated. In her pretty pink frock and high-heeled shoes she looked quite European. You could hardly have guessed at that dark background of native life in which she felt herself so much more at home. I did not imagine that she was at all intelligent, and I should not have been surprised if a man, after living with her for some time, had found the passion which had drawn him to her sink into boredom. It suggested itself to me that in her elusiveness, like a thought that presents itself to consciousness and vanishes before it can be captured by words, lay her peculiar charm; but perhaps that was merely fancy, and if I had known nothing about her I should have seen in her only a pretty little half-caste like another.

She talked to me of the various things which they talk of to the stranger in Samoa, of the journey, and whether I had slid down the water rock at Papaseea and if I meant to stay in a native village. She talked to me of Scotland, and perhaps I noticed in her a tendency to enlarge on the sumptuousness of her establishment there. She asked me naïvely if I knew Mrs. This and Mrs. That with whom she had been acquainted when she lived in the north.

Then Miller, the fat German-American, came in. He shook hands all round very cordially and sat down, asking in his loud, cheerful voice for a whisky and soda. He was very fat, and he sweated profusely. He took off his gold-rimmed spectacles and wiped them; you saw then that his little eyes, benevolent behind the large round glasses, were shrewd and cunning; the party had been somewhat dull till he came, but he was a good story-teller and a jovial fellow. Soon he had the two women, Ethel and my friend's wife, laughing delightedly at his sallies. He had a reputation on the island of a lady's man, and you could see how this fat, gross fellow, old and ugly, had yet the possibility of fascination. His humour was on a level with the understanding of his company, an affair of vitality and assurance, and his Western accent gave a peculiar point to what he said. At last, he turned to me:

"Well, if we want to get back for dinner we'd better be getting. I'll take you along in my machine if you like."

I thanked him and got up. He shook hands with the others, went out of the room, massive and strong in his walk, and climbed into his car.

"Pretty little thing, Lawson's wife," I said, as we drove along.

"Too bad the way he treats her. Knocks her about. Gets my dander up when I hear of a man hitting a woman."

We went on a little. Then he said:

"He was a darned fool to marry her. I said so at the time. If he hadn't, he'd have had the whip hand over her. He's yaller, that's what he is, yaller."

The year was drawing to its end and the time approached when I was to leave Samoa. My boat was scheduled to sail for Sydney on the fourth of January. Christmas Day had been celebrated at the hotel with suitable ceremonies, but it was looked upon as no more than a rehearsal for New Year, and the men who were accustomed to foregather in the lounge determined on New Year's Eve to make a night of it. There was an uproarious dinner, after which the party sauntered down to the English Club, a simple little frame house, to play pool. There was a great deal of talking, laughing, and betting, but some very poor play, except on the part of Miller, who had drunk as much as any of them, all far younger than he, but had kept unimpaired the keenness of his eye and the sureness of his hand. He pocketed the young men's money with humour and urbanity. After an hour of this I grew tired and went out. I crossed the road and came on to the beach. Three coconut trees grew there, like three moon maidens waiting for their lovers to ride out of the sea, and I sat at the foot of one of them, watching the lagoon and the nightly assemblage of the stars.

I do not know where Lawson had been during the evening, but between ten and eleven he came along to the club. He shambled down the dusty, empty road, feeling dull and bored, and when he reached the club, before going into the billiard-room, went into the bar to have a drink by himself. He had a shyness now about joining the company of white men when there were a lot of them together and needed a stiff dose of whisky to give him confidence. He was standing with the glass in his hand when Miller came in to him. He was in his shirt sleeves and still held his cue. He gave the bar-tender a glance.

"Get out, Jack," he said.

The bar-tender, a native in a white jacket and a red *lava-lava*, without a word slid out of the small room.

"Look here, I've been wanting to have a few words with you, Lawson," said the big American.

"Well, that's one of the few things you can have free, gratis, and for nothing on this damned island."

Miller fixed his gold spectacles more firmly on his nose and held Lawson with his cold determined eyes.

"See here, young fellow, I understand you've been knocking Mrs. Lawson about again. I'm not going to stand for that. If you don't stop it right now I'll break every bone of your dirty little body."

Then Lawson knew what he had been trying to find out so long. It was Miller. The appearance of the man, fat, bald-headed, with his round bare face and double chin and the gold spectacles, his age, his benign, shrewd look, like that of a renegade priest, and the thought of Ethel, so slim and virginal, filled him with a sudden horror. Whatever his faults Lawson was no coward, and without a word he hit out violently at Miller. Miller quickly warded the blow with the hand that held the cue, and then with a great swing of his right arm brought his fist down on Lawson's ear. Lawson was four inches shorter than the American and he was slightly built, frail and weakened not only by illness and the enervating tropics, but by drink. He fell like a log and lay half dazed at the foot of the bar. Miller took off his spectacles and wiped them with his handkerchief.

"I guess you know what to expect now. You've had your warning, and you'd better take it."

He took up his cue and went back into the billiard-room. There was so much noise there that no one knew what had happened. Lawson picked himself up. He put his hand to his ear, which was singing still. Then he slunk out of the club.

I saw a man cross the road, a patch of white against the darkness of the night but did not know who it was. He came down to the beach, passed me sitting at the foot of the tree, and looked down. I saw then that it was Lawson, but since he was doubtless drunk, did not speak. He went on, walked irresolutely two or three steps, and turned back. He came up to me and bending down stared in my face.

"I thought it was you," he said.

He sat down and took out his pipe.

"It was hot and noisy in the club," I volunteered.

"Why are you sitting here?"

"I was waiting about for the midnight mass at the Cathedral."

"If you like I'll come with you."

Lawson was quite sober. We sat for a while smoking in silence. Now and then in the lagoon was the splash of some big fish, and a little way out towards the opening in the reef was the light of a schooner.

"You're sailing next week, aren't you?" he said.

"Yes."

"It would be jolly to go home once more. But I could never stand it now. The cold, you know."

"It's odd to think that in England now they're shivering round the fire," I said.

There was not even a breath of wind. The balminess of the night was like a spell. I wore nothing but a thin shirt and a suit of ducks. I enjoyed the exquisite languor of the night and stretched my limbs voluptuously.

"This isn't the sort of New Year's Eve that persuades one to make good resolutions for the future," I smiled.

He made no answer, but I do not know what train of thought my casual remark had suggested in him, for presently he began to speak. He spoke in a low voice, without any expression, but his accents were educated, and it was a relief to hear him after the twang and the vulgar intonations which for some time had wounded my ears.

"I've made an awful hash of things. That's obvious, isn't it? I'm right down at the bottom of the pit and there's no getting out for me. '*Black as the pit from pole to pole.*'" I felt him smile as he made the quotation. "And the strange thing is that I don't see how I went wrong."

I held my breath, for to me there is nothing more awe-inspiring than when a man discovers to you the nakedness of his soul. Then you see that no one is so trivial or debased but that in him is a spark of something to excite compassion.

"It wouldn't be so rotten if I could see that it was all my own fault. It's true I drink, but I shouldn't have taken to that if things had gone differently. I wasn't really fond of liquor. I suppose I ought not to have married Ethel. If I'd kept her it would be all right. But I did love her so."

His voice faltered.

"She's not a bad lot, you know, not really. It's just rotten luck. We might have been as happy as lords. When she bolted I suppose I ought to have let her go, but I couldn't do that—I was dead stuck on her then; and there was the kid."

"Are you fond of the kid?" I asked.

"I was. There are two, you know. But they don't mean so much to me now. You'd take them for natives anywhere. I have to talk to them in Samoan."

"Is it too late for you to start fresh? Couldn't you make a dash for it and leave the place?"

"I haven't the strength. I'm done for."

"Are you still in love with your wife?"

"Not now. Not now." He repeated the two words with a kind of horror in his voice. "I haven't even got that now. I'm down and out."

The bells of the Cathedral were ringing.

"If you really want to come to the midnight mass we'd better go along," I said.

"Come on."

We got up and walked along the road. The Cathedral, all white, stood facing the sea not without impressiveness, and beside it the Protestant chapels had the look of meeting-houses. In the road were two or three cars, and a great number of traps, and traps were put up against the walls at the side. People had come from all parts of the island for the service, and through the great open doors we saw that the place was crowded. The high altar was all ablaze with light. There were a few whites and a good many half-castes, but the great majority were natives. All the men wore trousers, for the Church has decided that the *lava-lava* is indecent. We found chairs at the back, near the open door, and sat down. Presently, following Lawson's eyes, I saw Ethel come in with a party of half-castes. They were all very much dressed up, the men in high, stiff collars and shiny boots, the women in large, gay hats. Ethel nodded and smiled to her friends as she passed up the aisle. The service began.

When it was over Lawson and I stood on one side for a while to watch the crowd stream out, then he held out his hand.

"Good-night," he said. "I hope you'll have a pleasant journey home."

"Oh, but I shall see you before I go."

He sniggered.

"The question is if you'll see me drunk or sober."

He turned and left me. I had a recollection of those very large black eyes, shining wildly under the shaggy brows. I paused irresolutely. I did not feel sleepy, and I thought I would at all events go along to the club for an hour before turning in. When I got there I found the billiard-room empty, but half-a-dozen men were sitting round a table in the lounge, playing poker. Miller looked up as I came in.

"Sit down and take a hand," he said.

"All right."

I bought some chips and began to play. Of course, it is the most fascinating game in the world and my hour lengthened out to two, and then to three. The native bar-tender, cheery and wide-awake notwithstanding the time, was at our elbow to supply us with drinks and from somewhere or other he produced a ham and a loaf of bread. We played on. Most of the party had drunk more than was good for them and the play was high and reckless. I played modestly, neither wishing to win nor anxious to lose, but I watched Miller with a fascinated interest. He drank glass for glass with the rest of the company but remained cool and level-headed. His pile of chips increased in size, and he had a neat little paper in front of him on which he had marked various sums lent to players in distress. He beamed amiably at the young men whose money he was taking. He kept up interminably his stream of jest and anecdote, but he never missed a draw, he never let an expression of the face pass him. At last, the dawn crept into the windows, gently, with a sort of deprecating shyness, as though it had no business there, and then it was day.

"Well," said Miller, "I reckon we've seen the old year out in style. Now let's have a round of jackpots and me for my mosquito net. I'm fifty, remember, I can't keep these late hours."

The morning was beautiful and fresh when we stood on the verandah, and the lagoon was like a sheet of multicoloured glass. Someone suggested a dip before going to bed, but none cared to bathe in the lagoon, sticky and treacherous to the feet. Miller had his car at the door, and he offered to take us down to the pool. We jumped in and drove along the deserted road. When we reached the pool it seemed as though the day had hardly risen there yet. Under the trees the water was all in shadow and the night had the effect of lurking still. We were in great spirits. We had no towels or any costume and in my prudence I wondered how we were going to dry ourselves. None of us had much on and it did not take us long to snatch off our clothes. Nelson, the little supercargo, was stripped first.

"I'm going down to the bottom," he said.

He dived and in a moment another man dived too, but shallow, and was out of the water before him. Then Nelson came up and scrambled to the side.

"I say, get me out," he said.

"What's up?"

Something was evidently the matter. His face was terrified. Two fellows gave him their hands and he slithered up.

"I say, there's a man down there."

"Don't be a fool. You're drunk."

"Well, if there isn't I'm in for D. T's. But I tell you there's a man down there. It just scared me out of my wits."

Miller looked at him for a moment. The little man was all white. He was actually trembling.

"Come on, Caster," said Miller to the big Australian, "we'd better go down and see."

"He was standing up," said Nelson, "all dressed. I saw him. He tried to catch hold of me."

"Hold your row," said Miller. "Are you ready?"

They dived in. We waited on the bank, silent. It really seemed as though they were under water longer than any men could breathe. Then Caster came up, and immediately after him, red in the face as though he were going to have a fit, Miller. They were pulling something behind them. Another man jumped in to help them, and the three together dragged their burden to the side. They shoved it up. Then we saw that it was Lawson, with a great stone tied up in his coat and bound to his feet.

"He was set on making a good job of it," said Miller, as he wiped the water from his shortsighted eyes.

VI

HONOLULU

The wise traveller travels only in imagination. An old Frenchman (he was really a Savoyard) once wrote a book called *Voyage autour de ma Chambre*. I have not read it and do not even know what it is about, but the title stimulates my fancy. In such a journey I could circumnavigate the globe. An eikon by the chimneypiece can take me to Russia with its great forests of birch and its white, domed churches. The Volga is wide, and at the end of a straggling village, in the wine-shop, bearded men in rough sheepskin coats sit drinking. I stand on the little hill from which Napoleon first saw Moscow and I look upon the vastness of the city. I will go down and see the people whom I know more intimately than so many of my friends, Alyosha, and Vronsky, and a dozen more. But my eyes fall on a piece of porcelain, and I smell the acrid odours of China. I am born in a chair along a narrow causeway between the padi fields or else I skirt a tree-clad mountain. My bearers chat gaily as they trudge along in the bright morning and every now and then, distant and mysterious, I hear the deep sound of a monastery bell. In the streets of Peking there is a motley crowd, and it scatters to allow passage to a string of camels, stepping delicately, that bring skins and strange drugs from the stony deserts of Mongolia. In England, in London, there are certain afternoons in winter when the clouds hang heavy and low and the light is so bleak that your heart sinks, but then you can look out of your window, and you see the coconut trees crowded upon the beach of a coral island. The sand is silvery and when you walk along in the sunshine it is so dazzling that you can hardly bear to look at it. Overhead the mynah birds are making a great to-do, and the surf beats ceaselessly against the reef. Those are the best journeys, the journeys that you take at your own fireside, for then you lose none of your illusions.

But there are people who take salt in their coffee. They say it gives it a tang, a savour, which is peculiar and fascinating. In the same way there are certain places, surrounded by a halo of romance, to which the inevitable disillusionment which you must experience on seeing them gives a singular spice. You had expected something wholly beautiful, and you get an impression which is infinitely more complicated than any that beauty can give you. It is like the weakness in the character of a great man which may make him less admirable but certainly makes him more interesting.

Nothing had prepared me for Honolulu. It is so far away from Europe, it is reached after so long a journey from San Francisco, so strange and so charming associations are attached to the name, that at first I could hardly believe my eyes. I do not know that I had formed in my mind any very exact picture of what I expected, but what I found caused me a great surprise. It is a typical western city. Shacks are cheek by jowl with stone mansions; dilapidated frame houses stand next door to smart stores with plate glass windows; electric cars rumble noisily along the streets; and motors, Fords, Buicks, Packards, line the pavement. The shops are filled with all the necessities of American civilisation. Every third house is a bank and every fifth the agency of a steamship company.

Along the streets crowd an unimaginable assortment of people. The Americans, ignoring the climate, wear black coats and high, starched collars, straw hats, soft hats, and bowlers. The Kanakas, pale brown, with crisp hair, have nothing on but a shirt and a pair of trousers; but the half-breeds are very smart with flaring ties and patent-leather boots. The Japanese, with their obsequious smile, are neat and trim in white duck, while their women walk a step or two behind them, in native dress, with a baby on their backs. The Japanese children, in bright coloured frocks, their little heads shaven, look like quaint dolls. Then there are the Chinese. The men, fat and prosperous, wear their American clothes oddly, but the women are enchanting with their tightly-dressed black hair, so neat that you feel it can never be disarranged, and they are very clean in their tunics and trousers, white, or powder blue, or black. Lastly there are the Filipinos, the men in huge straw hats, the women in bright yellow muslin with great puffed sleeves.

It is the meeting-place of East and West. The very new rubs shoulders with the immeasurably old. And if you have not found the romance you expected you have come upon something singularly intriguing. All these strange people live close to each other, with different languages and different thoughts; they believe in different gods, and they have different values; two passions alone they share, love and hunger. And somehow as you watch them you have an impression of extraordinary vitality. Though the air is so soft and the sky so blue, you have, I know not why, a feeling of something hotly passionate that beats like a throbbing pulse through the crowd. Though the native policeman at the corner, standing on a platform, with a white club to direct the traffic, gives the scene an air of respectability, you cannot but feel that it is a respectability only of the surface; a little below there is darkness and mystery. It gives you just that thrill, with a little catch at the heart, that you have when at night in the forest the silence trembles on a sudden with the low, insistent beating of a drum. You are all expectant of I know not what.

If I have dwelt on the incongruity of Honolulu, it is because just this, to my mind, gives its point to the story I want to tell. It is a story of primitive superstition, and it startles me that anything of the sort should survive in a civilisation which, if not very distinguished, is certainly very elaborate. I cannot get over the fact that such incredible things should happen, or at least be thought to happen, right in the middle, so to speak, of telephones, tram-cars, and daily papers. And the friend who showed me Honolulu had the same incongruity which I felt from the beginning was its most striking characteristic.

He was an American named Winter, and I had brought a letter of introduction to him from an acquaintance in New York. He was a man between forty and fifty, with scanty black hair, grey at the temples, and a sharp-featured, thin face. His eyes had a twinkle in them and his large horn spectacles gave him a demureness which was not a little diverting. He was tall rather than otherwise and very spare. He was born in Honolulu and his father had a large store which sold hosiery and all such goods, from tennis racquets to tarpaulins, as a man of fashion could require. It was a prosperous business, and I could well understand the indignation of Winter *père* when his son, refusing to go into it, had announced his determination to be an actor. My friend spent twenty years on the stage, sometimes in New York, but more often on the road, for his gifts were small; but at last, being no fool, he came to the conclusion that it was better to sell sock-suspenders in Honolulu than to play small parts in Cleveland, Ohio. He left the stage and went into the business. I think after the hazardous existence he had lived so long, he thoroughly enjoyed the luxury of driving a large car and living in a beautiful house near the golf-course, and I am quite sure, since he was a man of parts, he managed the business competently. But he could not bring himself entirely to break his connection with the arts and since he might no longer act he began to paint. He took me to his studio and showed me his work. It was not at all bad, but not what I should have expected from him. He painted nothing but still life, very small pictures, perhaps eight by ten; and he painted very delicately, with the utmost finish. He had evidently a passion for detail. His fruit pieces reminded you of the fruit in a picture by Ghirlandajo. While you marvelled a little at his patience, you could not help being impressed by his dexterity. I imagine that he failed as an actor because his effects, carefully studied, were neither bold nor broad enough to get across the footlights.

I was entertained by the proprietary, yet ironical air with which he showed me the city. He thought in his heart that there was none in the United States to equal it, but he saw quite clearly that his attitude was comic. He drove me round to the various buildings and swelled with satisfaction when I expressed a proper admiration for their architecture. He showed me the houses of rich men.

"That's the Stubbs' house," he said. "It cost a hundred thousand dollars to build. The Stubbs are one of our best families. Old man Stubbs came here as a missionary more than seventy years ago."

He hesitated a little and looked at me with twinkling eyes through his big round spectacles.

"All our best families are missionary families," he said. "You're not very much in Honolulu unless your father or your grandfather converted the heathen."

"Is that so?"

"Do you know your Bible?"

"Fairly," I answered.

"There is a text which says: The fathers have eaten sour grapes and the children's teeth are set on edge. I guess it runs differently in Honolulu. The fathers brought Christianity to the Kanaka and the children jumped his land."

"Heaven helps those who help themselves," I murmured.

"It surely does. By the time the natives of this island had embraced Christianity they had nothing else they could afford to embrace. The kings gave the missionaries land as a mark of esteem, and the missionaries bought land by way of laying up treasure in heaven. It surely was a good investment. One missionary left the business—I think one may call it a business without offence—and became a land agent, but that is an exception. Mostly it was their sons who looked after the commercial side of the concern. Oh, it's a fine thing to have a father who came here fifty years ago to spread the faith."

But he looked at his watch.

"Gee, it's stopped. That means it's time to have a cocktail."

We sped along an excellent road, bordered with red hibiscus, and came back into the town.

"Have you been to the Union Saloon?"

"Not yet."

"We'll go there."

I knew it was the most famous spot in Honolulu and I entered it with a lively curiosity. You get to it by a narrow passage from King Street, and in the passage are offices, so that thirsty souls may be supposed bound for one of these just as well as for the saloon. It is a large square room, with three entrances, and opposite the bar, which runs the length of it, two corners have been partitioned off into little cubicles. Legend states that they were built so that King Kalakaua might drink there without being seen by his subjects, and it is pleasant to think that in one or other of these he may have sat over his bottle, a coal-black potentate, with Robert Louis Stevenson. There is a portrait of him, in oils, in a rich gold frame; but there are also two prints of Queen Victoria. On the walls, besides, are old line engravings of the eighteenth century, one of which, and heaven knows how it got there, is after a theatrical picture by De Wilde; and there are oleographs from the Christmas supplements of the *Graphic* and the *Illustrated London News* of twenty years ago. Then there are advertisements of whisky, gin, champagne, and beer, and photographs of baseball teams and of native orchestras.

The place seemed to belong not to the modern, hustling world that I had left in the bright street outside, but to one that was dying. It had the savour of the day before yesterday. Dingy and dimly lit, it had a vaguely mysterious air, and you could imagine that it would be a fit scene for shady transactions. It suggested a more lurid time, when ruthless men carried their lives in their hands, and violent deeds diapered the monotony of life.

When I went in the saloon was fairly full. A group of businessmen stood together at the bar, discussing affairs, and in a corner two Kanakas were drinking. Two or three men who might have been store-keepers were shaking dice. The rest of the company plainly followed the sea; they were captains of tramps, first mates, and engineers. Behind the bar, busily making the Honolulu cocktail for which the place was famous, served two large half-castes, in white, fat, clean-shaven and dark skinned, with thick, curly hair and large bright eyes.

Winter seemed to know more than half the company, and when we made our way to the bar a little fat man in spectacles, who was standing by himself, offered him a drink.

"No, you have one with me, Captain," said Winter.

He turned to me.

"I want you to know Captain Butler."

The little man shook hands with me. We began to talk, but, my attention distracted by my surroundings, I took small notice of him, and after we had each ordered a cocktail we separated. When we had got into the motor again and were driving away, Winter said to me:

"I'm glad we ran up against Butler. I wanted you to meet him. What did you think of him?"

"I don't know that I thought very much of him at all," I answered.

"Do you believe in the supernatural?"

"I don't exactly know that I do," I smiled.

"A very queer thing happened to him a year or two ago. You ought to have him tell you about it."

"What sort of thing?"

Winter did not answer my question.

"I have no explanation of it myself," he said. "But there's no doubt about the facts. Are you interested in things like that?"

"Things like what?"

"Spells and magic and all that."

"I've never met anyone who wasn't."

Winter paused for a moment.

"I guess I won't tell you myself. You ought to hear it from his own lips so that you can judge. How are you fixed up for tonight?"

"I've got nothing on at all."

"Well, I'll get hold of him between now and then and see if we can't go down to his ship."

Winter told me something about him. Captain Butler had spent all his life on the Pacific. He had been in much better circumstances than he was now, because he had been first officer and then captain of a passenger-boat plying along the coast of California, but he had lost his ship, and a number of passengers had been drowned.

"Drink, I guess," said Winter.

Of course, there had been an enquiry, which had cost him his certificate, and then he drifted further afield. For some years he had knocked about the South Seas, but he was now in command of a small schooner which sailed between Honolulu and the various islands of the group. It belonged to a Chinese to whom the fact that his skipper had no certificate meant only that he could be had for lower wages, and to have a white man in charge was always an advantage.

And now that I had heard this about him I took the trouble to remember more exactly what he was like. I recalled his round spectacles and the round blue eyes behind them, and so gradually reconstructed him before my mind. He was a little man, without angles, plump, with a round face like the full moon and a little fat round nose. He had fair short hair, and he was red-faced and clean shaven. He had plump hands, dimpled on the knuckles, and short fat legs. He was a jolly soul, and the tragic experience he had gone through seemed to have left him unscarred. Though he must have been thirty-four or thirty-five he looked much younger. But after all I had given him but a superficial attention, and now that I knew of this catastrophe, which had obviously ruined his life, I promised myself that when I saw him again I would take more careful note of him. It is very curious to observe the differences of emotional response that you find in different people. Some can go through terrific battles, the fear of imminent death and unimaginable horrors, and preserve their soul unscathed, while with others the trembling of the moon on a solitary sea or the song of a bird in a thicket will cause a convulsion great enough to transform their entire being. Is it due to strength or weakness, want of imagination or instability of character? I do not know. When I called up in my fancy that scene of shipwreck, with the shrieks of the drowning and the terror, and then later, the ordeal of the enquiry, the bitter grief of those who sorrowed for the lost, and the harsh things he must have read of himself in the papers, the shame and the disgrace, it came to me with a shock to remember that Captain Butler had talked with the frank obscenity of a schoolboy of the Hawaiian girls and of Ewelei, the Red Light district, and of his successful adventures. He laughed readily, and one would have thought he could never laugh again. I remembered his shining, white teeth; they were his best feature. He began to interest me, and thinking of him and of his gay insouciance I forgot the particular story, to hear which I was to see him again. I wanted to see him rather to find out if I could a little more what sort of man he was.

Winter made the necessary arrangements and after dinner we went down to the waterfront. The ship's boat was waiting for us, and we rowed out. The schooner was anchored some way across the harbour, not far from the breakwater. We came alongside, and I heard the sound of a ukalele. We clambered up the ladder.

"I guess he's in the cabin," said Winter, leading the way.

It was a small cabin, bedraggled and dirty, with a table against one side and a broad bench all round upon which slept, I supposed, such passengers as were ill-advised enough to travel in such a ship. A petroleum lamp gave a dim light. The ukalele was being played by a native girl and Butler was lolling on the seat, half lying, with his head on her shoulder and an arm round her waist.

"Don't let us disturb you, Captain," said Winter, facetiously.

"Come right in," said Butler, getting up and shaking hands with us. "What'll you have?"

It was a warm night, and through the open door you saw countless stars in a heaven that was still almost blue. Captain Butler wore a sleeveless under-shirt, showing his fat white arms, and a pair of incredibly dirty trousers. His feet were bare, but on his curly head he wore a very old, a very shapeless felt hat.

"Let me introduce you to my girl. Ain't she a peach?"

We shook hands with a very pretty person. She was a good deal taller than the captain, and even the Mother Hubbard, which the missionaries of a past generation had, in the interests of decency, forced on the unwilling natives, could not conceal the beauty of her form. One could not but suspect that age would burden her with a certain corpulence, but now she was graceful and alert. Her brown skin had an exquisite translucency, and her eyes were magnificent. Her black hair, very thick and rich, was coiled round her head in a massive plait. When she smiled in a greeting that was charmingly natural, she showed teeth that were small, even, and white. She was certainly a most attractive creature. It was easy to see that the captain was madly in love with her. He could not take his eyes off her; he wanted to touch her all the time. That was very easy to understand; but what seemed to me stranger was that the girl was apparently in love with him. There was a light in her eyes that was unmistakable, and her lips were slightly parted as though in a sigh of desire. It was thrilling. It was even a little moving, and I could not help feeling somewhat in the way. What had a stranger to do with this love-sick pair? I wished that Winter had not brought me. And it seemed to me that the dingy cabin was transfigured and now it seemed a fit and proper scene for such an extremity of passion. I thought I should never forget that schooner in the harbour of Honolulu, crowded with shipping, and yet, under the immensity of the starry sky, remote from all the world. I liked to think of those lovers sailing off together in the night over the empty spaces of the Pacific from one green, hilly island to another. A faint breeze of romance softly fanned my cheek.

And yet Butler was the last man in the world with whom you would have associated romance, and it was hard to see what there was in him to arouse love. In the clothes he wore now he looked podgier than ever, and his round spectacles gave his round face the look of a prim cherub. He suggested rather a curate who had gone to the dogs. His conversation was peppered with the quaintest Americanisms, and it is because I despair of reproducing these that, at whatever loss of vividness, I mean to narrate the story he told me a little later in my own words. Moreover, he was unable to frame a sentence without an oath, though a good-natured one, and his speech, albeit offensive only to prudish ears, in print would seem coarse. He was a mirth-loving man, and perhaps that accounted not a little for his successful amours; since women, for the most part frivolous creatures, are excessively bored by the seriousness with which men treat them, and they can seldom resist the buffoon who makes them laugh. Their sense of humour is crude. Diana of Ephesus is always prepared to fling prudence to the winds for the red-nosed comedian who sits on his hat. I realised that Captain Butler had charm. If I had not known the tragic story of the shipwreck I should have thought he had never had a care in his life.

Our host had rung the bell on our entrance and now a Chinese cook came in with more glasses and several bottles of soda. The whisky and the captain's empty glass stood already on the table. But when I saw the Chinese I positively started, for he was certainly the ugliest man I had ever seen. He was very short, but thick-set, and he had a bad limp. He wore a singlet and a pair of trousers that had been white, but were now filthy, and, perched on a shock of bristly, grey hair, an old tweed deer-stalker. It would have been grotesque on any Chinese, but on him it was outrageous. His broad, square face was very flat as though it had been bashed in by a mighty fist, and it was deeply pitted with smallpox; but the most revolting thing in him was a very pronounced harelip which had never been operated on, so that his upper lip, cleft, went up in an angle to his nose, and in the opening was a huge yellow fang. It was horrible. He came in with the end of a cigarette at the corner of his mouth, and this, I do not know why, gave him a devilish expression.

He poured out the whisky and opened a bottle of soda.

"Don't drown it, John," said the captain.

He said nothing but handed a glass to each of us. Then he went out.

"I saw you lookin' at my Chink," said Butler, with a grin on his fat, shining face.

"I should hate to meet him on a dark night," I said.

"He sure is homely," said the captain, and for some reason he seemed to say it with a peculiar satisfaction. "But he's fine for one thing, I'll tell the world; you just have to have a drink every time you look at him."

But my eyes fell on a calabash that hung against the wall over the table, and I got up to look at it. I had been hunting for an old one and this was better than any I had seen outside the museum.

"It was given me by a chief over on one of the islands," said the captain, watching me. "I done him a good turn and he wanted to give me something good."

"He certainly did," I answered.

I was wondering whether I could discreetly make Captain Butler an offer for it, I could not imagine that he set any store on such an article, when, as though he read my thoughts, he said:

"I wouldn't sell that for ten thousand dollars."

"I guess not," said Winter. "It would be a crime to sell it."

"Why?" I asked.

"That comes into the story," returned Winter. "Doesn't it, Captain?"

"It surely does."

"Let's hear it then."

"The night's young yet," he answered.

The night distinctly lost its youth before he satisfied my curiosity, and meanwhile we drank a great deal too much whisky while Captain Butler narrated his experiences of San Francisco in the old days and of the South Seas. At last, the girl fell asleep. She lay curled up on the seat, with her face on her brown arm, and her bosom rose and fell gently with her breathing. In sleep she looked sullen, but darkly beautiful.

He had found her on one of the islands in the group among which, whenever there was cargo to be got, he wandered with his crazy old schooner. The Kanakas have little love for work, and the laborious Chinese, the cunning Japs, have taken the trade out of their hands. Her father had a strip of land on which he grew taro and bananas, and he had a boat in which he went fishing. He was vaguely related to the mate of the schooner, and it was he who took Captain Butler up to the shabby little frame house to spend an idle evening. They took a bottle of whisky with them and the ukalele. The captain was not a shy man and when he saw a pretty girl he made love to her. He could speak the native language fluently and it was not long before he had overcome the girl's timidity. They spent the evening singing and dancing, and by the end of it she was sitting by his side and he had his arm round her waist. It happened that they were delayed on the island for several days and the captain, at no time a man to hurry, made no effort to shorten his stay. He was very comfortable in the snug little harbour and life was long. He had a swim round his ship in the morning and another in the evening. There was a chandler's shop on the waterfront where sailormen could get a drink of whisky, and he spent the best part of the day there, playing cribbage with the half-caste who owned it. At night the mate and he went up to the house where the pretty girl lived, and they sang a song or two and told stories. It was the girl's father who suggested that he should take her away with him. They discussed the matter in a friendly fashion, while the girl, nestling against the captain, urged him by the pressure of her hands and her soft, smiling glances. He had taken a fancy to her, and he was a domestic man. He was a little dull sometimes at sea and it would be very pleasant to have a pretty little creature like that about the old ship. He was of a practical turn too, and he recognised that it would be useful to have someone around to darn his socks and look after his linen. He was tired of having his things washed by a Chink who tore everything to pieces; the natives washed much better, and now and then when the captain went ashore at Honolulu he liked to cut a dash in a smart duck suit. It was only a matter of arranging a price. The father wanted two hundred and fifty dollars, and the captain, never a thrifty man, could not put his hand on such a sum. But he was a generous one, and with the girl's soft face against his, he was not inclined to haggle. He offered to give a hundred and fifty dollars there and then and another hundred in three months. There was a good deal of argument, and the parties could not come to any agreement that night, but the idea had fired the captain, and he could not sleep as well as usual. He kept dreaming of the lovely girl and each time he awoke it was with the pressure of her soft, sensual lips on his. He cursed himself in the morning because a bad night at poker the last time he was at Honolulu had left him so short of ready money. And if the night before he had been in love with the girl, this morning he was crazy about her.

"See here, Bananas," he said to the mate, "I've got to have that girl. You go and tell the old man I'll bring the dough up tonight and she can get fixed up. I figure we'll be ready to sail at dawn."

I have no idea why the mate was known by that eccentric name. He was called Wheeler, but though he had that English surname there was not a drop of white blood in him. He was a tall man, and well-made though inclined to stoutness, but much darker than is usual in Hawaii. He was no longer young, and his crisply curling, thick hair was grey. His upper front teeth were cased in gold. He was very proud of them. He had a marked squint, and this gave him a saturnine expression. The captain, who was fond of a joke, found in it a constant source of humour and hesitated the less to rally him on the defect because he realised that the mate was sensitive about it. Bananas, unlike most of the natives, was a taciturn fellow and Captain Butler would have disliked him if it had been possible for a man of his good nature to dislike anyone. He liked to be at sea with someone he could talk to, he was a chatty, sociable creature, and it was enough to drive a missionary to drink to live there day after day with a chap who never opened his mouth. He did his best to wake the mate up, that is to say, he chaffed him without mercy, but it was poor fun to laugh by oneself, and he came to the conclusion that, drunk or sober, Bananas was no fit companion for a white man. But he was a good seaman, and the captain was shrewd enough to know the value of a mate he could trust. It was not rare for him to come aboard, when they were sailing, fit for nothing but to fall into his bunk, and it was worth something to know that he could stay there till he had slept his liquor off, since Bananas could be relied on. But he was an unsociable devil, and it would be a treat to have someone he could talk to. That girl would be fine. Besides, he wouldn't be so likely to get drunk when he went ashore if he knew there was a little girl waiting for him when he came on board again.

He went to his friend the chandler and over a peg of gin asked him for a loan. There were one or two useful things a ship's captain could do for a ship's chandler, and after a quarter of an hour's conversation in low tones (there is no object in letting all and sundry know your business), the captain crammed a wad of notes in his hip-pocket, and that night, when he went back to his ship, the girl went with him.

What Captain Butler, seeking for reasons to do what he had already made up his mind to, had anticipated, actually came to pass. He did not give up drinking, but he ceased to drink to excess. An evening with the boys, when he had been away from town two or three weeks, was pleasant enough, but it was pleasant too to get back to his little girl; he thought of her, sleeping so softly, and how, when he got into his cabin and leaned over her, she would open her eyes lazily and stretch out her arms for him: it was as good as a full hand. He found he was saving money, and since he was a generous man he did the right thing by the little girl: he gave her some silver-backed brushes for her long hair, and a gold chain, and a reconstructed ruby for her finger. Gee, but it was good to be alive.

A year went by, a whole year, and he was not tired of her yet. He was not a man who analysed his feelings, but this was so surprising that it forced itself upon his attention. There must be something very wonderful about that girl. He couldn't help seeing that he was more wrapped up in her than ever, and sometimes the thought entered his mind that it might not be a bad thing if he married her.

Then, one day the mate did not come in to dinner or to tea. Butler did not bother himself about his absence at the first meal, but at the second he asked the Chinese cook:

"Where's the mate? He no come tea?"

"No wantchee," said the Chink.

"He ain't sick?"

"No savvy."

Next day Bananas turned up again, but he was more sullen than ever, and after dinner the captain asked the girl what was the matter with him. She smiled and shrugged her pretty shoulders. She told the captain that Bananas had taken a fancy to her, and he was sore because she had told him off. The captain was a good-humoured man, and he was not of a jealous nature; it struck him as exceeding funny that Bananas should be in love. A man who had a squint like that had a precious poor chance. When tea came round he chaffed him gaily. He pretended to speak in the air, so that the mate should not be certain that he knew anything, but he dealt him some pretty shrewd blows. The girl did not think him as funny as he thought himself, and afterwards she begged him to say nothing more. He was surprised at her seriousness. She told him he did not know her people. When their passion was aroused they were capable of anything. She was a little frightened. This was so absurd to him that he laughed heartily.

"If he comes bothering round you, you just threaten to tell me. That'll fix him."

"Better fire him, I think."

"Not on your sweet life. I know a good sailor when I see one. But if he don't leave you alone I'll give him the worst licking he's ever had."

Perhaps the girl had a wisdom unusual in her sex. She knew that it was useless to argue with a man when his mind was made up, for it only increased his stubbornness, and she held her peace. And now on the shabby schooner, threading her way across the silent sea, among those lovely islands, was enacted a dark, tense drama of which the fat little captain remained entirely ignorant. The girl's resistance fired Bananas so that he ceased to be a man but was simply blind desire. He did not make love to her gently or gaily, but with a black and savage ferocity. Her contempt now was changed to hatred and when he besought her she answered him with bitter, angry taunts. But the struggle went on silently, and when the captain asked her after a little while whether Bananas was bothering her, she lied.

But one night, when they were in Honolulu, he came on board only just in time. They were sailing at dawn. Bananas had been ashore, drinking some native spirit, and he was drunk. The captain, rowing up, heard sounds that surprised him. He scrambled up the ladder. He saw Bananas, beside himself, trying to wrench open the cabin door. He was shouting at the girl. He swore he would kill her if she did not let him in.

"What in hell are you up to?" cried Butler.

The mate let go the handle, gave the captain a look of savage hate, and without a word turned away.

"Stop here. What are you doing with that door?"

The mate still did not answer. He looked at him with sullen, bootless rage.

"I'll teach you not to pull any of your queer stuff with me, you dirty, cross-eyed nigger," said the captain.

He was a good foot shorter than the mate and no match for him, but he was used to dealing with native crews, and he had his knuckle-duster handy. Perhaps it was not an instrument that a gentleman would use, but then Captain Butler was not a gentleman. Nor was he in the habit of dealing with gentlemen. Before Bananas knew what the captain was at, his right arm had shot out and his fist, with its ring of steel, caught him fair and square on the jaw. He fell like a bull under the pole-axe.

"That'll learn him," said the captain.

Bananas did not stir. The girl unlocked the cabin door and came out.

"Is he dead?"

"He ain't."

He called a couple of men and told them to carry the mate to his bunk. He rubbed his hands with satisfaction and his round blue eyes gleamed behind his spectacles. But the girl was strangely silent. She put her arms round him as though to protect him from invisible harm.

It was two or three days before Bananas was on his feet again, and when he came out of his cabin his face was torn and swollen. Through the darkness of his skin, you saw the livid bruise. Butler saw him slinking along the deck and called him. The mate went to him without a word.

"See here, Bananas," he said to him, fixing his spectacles on his slippery nose, for it was very hot. "I ain't going to fire you for this, but you know now that when I hit, I hit hard. Don't forget it and don't let me have any more funny business."

Then he held out his hand and gave the mate that good-humoured, flashing smile of his which was his greatest charm. The mate took the outstretched hand and twitched his swollen lips into a devilish grin. The incident in the captain's mind was so completely finished that when the three of them sat at dinner he chaffed Bananas on his appearance. He was eating with difficulty and, his swollen face still more distorted by pain, he looked truly a repulsive object.

That evening, when he was sitting on the upper deck, smoking his pipe, a shiver passed through the captain.

"I don't know what I should be shiverin' for on a night like this," he grumbled. "Maybe I've gotten a dose of fever. I've been feelin' a bit queer all day."

When he went to bed he took some quinine, and next morning he felt better, but a little washed out, as though he were recovering from a debauch.

"I guess my liver's out of order," he said, and he took a pill.

He had not much appetite that day and towards evening he began to feel very unwell. He tried the next remedy he knew, which was to drink two or three hot whiskies, but that did not seem to help him much, and when in the morning he surveyed himself in the glass he thought he was not looking quite the thing.

"If I ain't right by the time we get back to Honolulu I'll just give Dr. Denby a call. He'll sure fix me up."

He could not eat. He felt a great lassitude in all his limbs. He slept soundly enough, but he awoke with no sense of refreshment; on the contrary he felt a peculiar exhaustion. And the energetic little man, who could not bear the thought of lying in bed, had to make an effort to force himself out of his bunk. After a few days he found it impossible to resist the languor that oppressed him, and he made up his mind not to get up.

"Bananas can look after the ship," he said. "He has before now."

He laughed a little to himself as he thought how often he had lain speechless in his bunk after a night with the boys. That was before he had his girl. He smiled at her and pressed her hand. She was puzzled and anxious. He saw that she was concerned about him and tried to reassure her. He had never had a day's illness in his life and in a week at the outside he would be as right as rain.

"I wish you'd fired Bananas," she said. "I've got a feeling that he's at the bottom of this."

"Damned good thing I didn't, or there'd be no one to sail the ship. I know a good sailor when I see one." His blue eyes, rather pale now, with the whites all yellow, twinkled. "You don't think he's trying to poison me, little girl?"

She did not answer, but she had one or two talks with the Chinese cook, and she took great care with the captain's food.

But he ate little enough now, and it was only with the greatest difficulty that she persuaded him to drink a cup of soup two or three times a day. It was clear that he was very ill, he was losing weight quickly, and his chubby face was pale and drawn. He suffered no pain, but merely grew every day weaker and more languid. He was wasting away. The round trip on this occasion lasted about four weeks and by the time they came to Honolulu the captain was a little anxious about himself. He had not been out of his bed for more than a fortnight and really he felt too weak to get up and go to the doctor. He sent a message asking him to come on board. The doctor examined him but could find nothing to account for his condition. His temperature was normal.

"See here, Captain," he said, "I'll be perfectly frank with you. I don't know what's the matter with you, and just seeing you like this don't give me a chance. You come into the hospital so that we can keep you under observation. There's nothing organically wrong with you, I know that, and my impression is that a few weeks in hospital ought to put you to rights."

"I ain't going to leave my ship."

Chinese owners were queer customers, he said; if he left his ship because he was sick, his owner might fire him, and he couldn't afford to lose his job. So long as he stayed where he was his contract safe-guarded him, and he had a first-rate mate. Besides, he couldn't leave his girl. No man could want a better nurse; if anyone could pull him through she would. Every man had to die once, and he only wished to be left in peace. He would not listen to the doctor's expostulations and finally the doctor gave in.

"I'll write you a prescription," he said doubtfully, "and see if it does you any good. You'd better stay in bed for a while."

"There ain't much fear of my getting up, doc," answered the captain. "I feel as weak as a cat."

But he believed in the doctor's prescription as little as did the doctor himself, and when he was alone amused himself by lighting his cigar with it. He had to get amusement out of something, for his cigar tasted like nothing on earth, and he smoked only to persuade himself that he was not too ill to. That evening a couple of friends of his, masters of tramp steamers, hearing he was sick came to see him. They discussed his case over a bottle of whisky and a box of Philippine cigars. One of them remembered how a mate of his had been taken queer just like that and not a doctor in the United States had been able to cure him. He had seen in the paper an advertisement of a patent medicine and thought there'd be no harm in trying it. That man was as strong as ever he'd been in his life after two bottles. But his illness had given Captain Butler a lucidity which was new and strange, and while they talked he seemed to read their minds. They thought he was dying. And when they left him he was afraid.

The girl saw his weakness. This was her opportunity. She had been urging him to let a native doctor see him, and he had stoutly refused; but now she entreated him. He listened with harassed eyes. He wavered. It was very funny that the American doctor could not tell what was the matter with him. But he did not want her to think that he was scared. If he let a damned nigger come along and look at him, it was to comfort *her*. He told her to do what she liked.

The native doctor came the next night. The captain was lying alone, half awake, and the cabin was dimly lit by an oil lamp. The door was softly opened, and the girl came in on tip-toe. She held the door open, and someone slipped in silently behind her. The captain smiled at this mystery, but he was so weak now, the smile was no more than a glimmer in his eyes.

The doctor was a little, old man, very thin and very wrinkled, with a completely bald head, and the face of a monkey. He was bowed and gnarled like an old tree. He looked hardly human, but his eyes were very bright, and in the half darkness, they seemed to glow with a reddish light. He was dressed filthily in a pair of ragged dungarees, and the upper part of his body was naked. He sat down on his haunches and for ten minutes looked at the captain. Then he felt the palms of his hands and the soles of his feet. The girl watched him with frightened eyes. No word was spoken. Then he asked for something that the captain had worn. The girl gave him the old felt hat which the captain used constantly and taking it, he sat down again on the floor, clasping it firmly with both hands; and rocking backwards and forwards slowly he muttered some gibberish in a very low tone.

At last, he gave a little sigh and dropped the hat. He took an old pipe out of his trouser pocket and lit it. The girl went over to him and sat by his side. He whispered something to her, and she started violently. For a few minutes they talked in hurried undertones, and then they stood up. She gave him money and opened the door for him. He slid out as silently as he had come in. Then she went over to the captain and leaned over him so that she could speak into his ear.

"It's an enemy praying you to death."

"Don't talk fool stuff, girlie," he said impatiently.

"It's truth. It's God's truth. That's why the American doctor couldn't do anything. Our people can do that. I've seen it done. I thought you were safe because you were a white man."

"I haven't an enemy."

"Bananas."

"What's he want to pray me to death for?"

"You ought to have fired him before he had a chance."

"I guess if I ain't got nothing more the matter with me than Bananas' hoodoo I shall be sitting up and taking nourishment in a very few days."

She was silent for a while, and she looked at him intently.

"Don't you know you're dying?" she said to him at last.

That was what the two skippers had thought, but they hadn't said it. A shiver passed across the captain's wan face.

"The doctor says there ain't nothing really the matter with me. I've only to lie quiet for a bit and I shall be all right."

She put her lips to his ear as if she were afraid that the air itself might hear.

"You're dying, dying, dying. You'll pass out with the old moon."

"That's something to know."

"You'll pass out with the old moon unless Bananas dies before."

He was not a timid man, and he had recovered already from the shock her words, and still more her vehement, silent manner, had given him. Once more a smile flickered in his eyes.

"I guess I'll take my chance, girlie."

"There's twelve days before the new moon."

There was something in her tone that gave him an idea.

"See here, my girl, this is all bunk. I don't believe a word of it. But I don't want you to try any of your monkey tricks with Bananas. He ain't a beauty, but he's a first-rate mate."

He would have said a good deal more, but he was tired out. He suddenly felt very weak and faint. It was always at that hour that he felt worse. He closed his eyes. The girl watched him for a minute and then slipped out of the cabin. The moon, nearly full, made a silver pathway over the dark sea. It shone from an unclouded sky. She looked at it with terror, for she knew that with its death the man she loved would die. His life was in her hands. She could save him, she alone could save him, but the enemy was cunning, and she must be cunning too. She felt that someone was looking at her, and without turning, by the sudden fear that seized her, knew that from the shadow the burning eyes of the mate were fixed upon her. She did not know what he could do; if he could read her thoughts she was defeated already, and with a desperate effort she emptied her mind of all content. His death alone could save her lover, and she could bring his death about. She knew that if he could be brought to look into a calabash in which was water so that a reflection of him was made, and the reflection were broken by hurtling the water, he would die as though he had been struck by lightning; for the reflection was his soul. But none knew better than he the danger, and he could be made to look only by a guile which had lulled his least suspicion. He must never think that he had an enemy who was on the watch to cause his destruction. She knew what she had to do. But the time was short, the time was terribly short. Presently she realised that the mate had gone. She breathed more freely.

Two days later they sailed, and there were ten now before the new moon. Captain Butler was terrible to see. He was nothing but skin and bone, and he could not move without help. He could hardly speak. But she dared do nothing yet. She knew that she must be patient. The mate was cunning, cunning. They went to one of the smaller islands of the group and discharged cargo, and now there were only seven days more. The moment had come to start. She brought some things out of the cabin she shared with the captain and made them into a bundle. She put the bundle in the deck cabin where she and Bananas ate their meals, and at dinnertime, when she went in, he turned quickly, and she saw that he had been looking at it. Neither of them spoke, but she knew what he suspected. She was making her preparations to leave the ship. He looked at her mockingly. Gradually, as though to prevent the captain from knowing what she was about, she brought everything she owned into the cabin, and some of the captain's clothes, and made them all into bundles. At last Bananas could keep silence no longer. He pointed to a suit of ducks.

"What are you going to do with that?" he asked.

She shrugged her shoulders.

"I'm going back to my island."

He gave a laugh that distorted his grim face. The captain was dying, and she meant to get away with all she could lay hands on.

"What'll you do if I say you can't take those things? They're the captains."

"They're no use to you," she said.

There was a calabash hanging on the wall. It was the very calabash I had seen when I came into the cabin and which we had talked about. She took it down. It was all dusty, so she poured water into it from the water-bottle and rinsed it with her fingers.

"What are you doing with that?"

"I can sell it for fifty dollars," she said.

"If you want to take it you'll have to pay me."

"What d'you want?"

"You know what I want."

She allowed a fleeting smile to play on her lips. She flashed a quick look at him and quickly turned away. He gave a gasp of desire. She raised her shoulders in a little shrug. With a savage bound he sprang upon her and seized her in his arms. Then she laughed. She put her arms, her soft, round arms, about his neck, and surrendered herself to him voluptuously.

When the morning came she roused him out of a deep sleep. The early rays of the sun slanted into the cabin. He pressed her to his heart. Then he told her that the captain could not last more than a day or two, and the owner wouldn't so easily find another white man to command the ship. If Bananas offered to take less money he would get the job, and the girl could stay with him. He looked at her with love-sick eyes. She nestled up against him. She kissed his lips, in the foreign way, in the way the captain had taught her to kiss. And she promised to stay. Bananas was drunk with happiness.

It was now or never.

She got up and went to the table to arrange her hair. There was no mirror, and she looked into the calabash, seeking her reflection. She tidied her beautiful hair. Then she beckoned to Bananas to come to her. She pointed to the calabash.

"There's something in the bottom of it," she said.

Instinctively, without suspecting anything, Bananas looked full into the water. His face was reflected in it. In a flash she beat upon it violently, with both her hands, so that they pounded on the bottom and the water splashed up. The reflection was broken in pieces. The bananas started back with a sudden hoarse cry, and he looked at the girl. She was standing there with a look of triumphant hatred on her face. A horror came into his eyes. His heavy features were twisted in agony, and with a thud, as though he had taken a violent poison, he crumpled up on to the ground. A great shudder passed through his body, and he was still. She leaned over him callously. She put her hand on his heart and then she pulled down his lower eye-lid. He was quite dead.

She went into the cabin in which lay Captain Butler. There was a faint colour in his cheeks and he looked at her in a startled way.

"What's happened?" he whispered.

They were the first words he had spoken for forty-eight hours.

"Nothing's happened," she said.

"I feel all funny."

Then his eyes closed, and he fell asleep. He slept for a day and a night, and when he awoke he asked for food. In a fortnight he was well.

It was past midnight when Winter and I rowed back to shore, and we had drunk innumerable whiskies and sodas.

"What do you think of it all?" asked Winter.

"What a question! If you mean, have I any explanation to suggest, I haven't."

"The captain believes every word of it."

"That's obvious; but you know that's not the part that interests me most, whether it's true or not, and what it all means; the part that interests me is that such things should happen to such people. I wonder what there is in that commonplace little man to arouse such a passion in that lovely creature. As I watched her, asleep there, while he was telling the story I had some fantastic idea about the power of love being able to work miracles."

"But that's not the girl," said Winter.

"What on earth do you mean?"

"Didn't you notice the cook?"

"Of course I did. He's the ugliest man I ever saw."

"That's why Butler took him. The girl ran away with the Chinese cook last year. This is a new one. He's only had her there about two months."

"Well, I'm hanged."

"He thinks this cook is safe. But I wouldn't be too sure in his place. There's something about a Chink, when he lays himself out to please a woman she can't resist him."

VII

RAIN

It was nearly bed-time and when they awoke the next morning land would be in sight. Dr. Macphail lit his pipe and, leaning over the rail, searched the heavens for the Southern Cross. After two years at the front and a wound that had taken longer to heal than it should, he was glad to settle down quietly at Apia for twelve months at least, and he felt already better for the journey. Since some of the passengers were leaving the ship next day at Pago-Pago they had had a little dance that evening and in his ears hammered still the harsh notes of the mechanical piano. But the deck was quiet at last. A little way off he saw his wife in a long chair talking with the Davidsons, and he strolled over to her. When he sat down under the light and took off his hat you saw that he had very red hair, with a bald patch on the crown, and the red, freckled skin which accompanies red hair; he was a man of forty, thin, with a pinched face, precise and rather pedantic; and he spoke with a Scots accent in a very low, quiet voice.

Between the Macphails and the Davidsons, who were missionaries, there had arisen the intimacy of shipboard, which is due to propinquity rather than to any community of taste. Their chief tie was the disapproval they shared of the men who spent their days and nights in the smoking-room playing poker or bridge and drinking. Mrs. Macphail was not a little flattered to think that she and her husband were the only people on board with whom the Davidsons were willing to associate, and even the doctor, shy but no fool, half unconsciously acknowledged the compliment. It was only because he was of an argumentative mind that in their cabin at night he permitted himself to carp.

"Mrs. Davidson was saying she didn't know how they'd have got through the journey if it hadn't been for us," said Mrs. Macphail, as she neatly brushed out her transformation. "She said we were really the only people on the ship they cared to know."

"I shouldn't have thought a missionary was such a big bug that he could afford to put on frills."

"It's not frills. I quite understand what she means. It wouldn't have been very nice for the Davidsons to have to mix with all that rough lot in the smoking-room."

"The founder of their religion wasn't so exclusive," said Dr Macphail with a chuckle.

"I've asked you over and over again not to joke about religion," answered his wife. "I shouldn't like to have a nature like yours, Alec. You never look for the best in people."

He gave her a sidelong glance with his pale, blue eyes, but did not reply. After many years of married life, he had learned that it was more conducive to peace to leave his wife with the last word. He was undressed before she was, and climbing into the upper bunk he settled down to read himself to sleep.

When he came on deck next morning they were close to land. He looked at it with greedy eyes. There was a thin strip of silver beach rising quickly to hills covered to the top with luxuriant vegetation. The coconut trees, thick and green, came nearly to the water's edge, and among them you saw the grass houses of the Samoans; and here and there, gleaming white, a little church. Mrs. Davidson came and stood beside him. She was dressed in black and wore round her neck a gold chain, from which dangled a small cross. She was a little woman, with brown, dull hair very elaborately arranged, and she had prominent blue eyes behind invisible *pince-nez*. Her face was long, like a sheep's but she gave no impression of foolishness, rather of extreme alertness; she had the quick movements of a bird. The most remarkable thing about her was her voice, high, metallic, and without inflection; it fell on the ear with a hard monotony, irritating to the nerves like the pitiless clamour of the pneumatic drill.

"This must seem like home to you," said Dr Macphail, with his thin, difficult smile.

"Ours are low islands, you know, not like these. Coral. These are volcanic. We've got another ten days' journey to reach them."

"In these parts that's almost like being in the next street at home," said Dr. Macphail facetiously.

"Well, that's rather an exaggerated way of putting it, but one does look at distances differently in the South Seas. So far you're right."

Dr Macphail sighed faintly.

"I'm glad we're not stationed here," she went on. "They say this is a terribly difficult place to work in. The steamers' touching makes the people unsettled; and then there's the naval station; that's bad for the natives. In our district we don't have difficulties like that to contend with. There are one or two traders, of course, but we take care to make them behave, and if they don't we make the place so hot for them they're glad to go."

Fixing the glasses on her nose she looked at the green island with a ruthless stare.

"It's almost a hopeless task for the missionaries here. I can never be sufficiently thankful to God that we are at least spared that."

Davidson's district consisted of a group of islands to the North of Samoa; they were widely separated, and he had frequently to go long distances by canoe. At these times his wife remained at their headquarters and managed the mission. Dr Macphail felt his heart sink when he considered the efficiency with which she certainly managed it. She spoke of the depravity of the natives in a voice which nothing could hush, but with a vehemently unctuous horror. Her sense of delicacy was singular. Early in their acquaintance she had said to him:

"You know, their marriage customs when we first settled in the islands were so shocking that I couldn't possibly describe them to you. But I'll tell Mrs. Macphail, and she'll tell you."

Then he had seen his wife and Mrs. Davidson, their deck-chairs close together, in earnest conversation for about two hours. As he walked past them backwards and forwards for the sake of exercise, he had heard Mrs. Davidson's agitated whisper, like the distant flow of a mountain torrent, and he saw by his wife's open mouth and pale face that she was enjoying an alarming experience. At night in their cabin, she repeated to him with bated breath all she had heard.

"Well, what did I say to you?" cried Mrs. Davidson, exultant, next morning. "Did you ever hear anything more dreadful? You don't wonder that I couldn't tell you myself, do you? Even though you are a doctor."

Mrs. Davidson scanned his face. She had a dramatic eagerness to see that she had achieved the desired effect.

"Can you wonder that when we first went there our hearts sank? You'll hardly believe me when I tell you it was impossible to find a single good girl in any of the villages."

She used the word *good* in a severely technical manner.

"Mr. Davidson and I talked it over, and we made up our minds the first thing to do was to put down the dancing. The natives were crazy about dancing."

"I was not averse to it myself when I was a young man," said Dr Macphail.

"I guessed as much when I heard you ask Mrs. Macphail to have a turn with you last night. I don't think there's any real harm if a man dances with his wife, but I was relieved that she wouldn't. Under the circumstances I thought it better that we should keep ourselves to ourselves."

"Under what circumstances?"

Mrs. Davidson gave him a quick look through her *pince-nez* but did not answer his question.

"But among white people it's not quite the same," she went on, "though I must say I agree with Mr. Davidson, who says he can't understand how a husband can stand by and see his wife in another man's arms, and as far as I'm concerned I've never danced a step since I married. But the native dancing is quite another matter. It's not only immoral in itself, but it distinctly leads to immorality. However, I'm thankful to God that we stamped it out, and I don't think I'm wrong in saying that no one has danced in our district for eight years."

But now they came to the mouth of the harbour and Mrs. Macphail joined them. The ship turned sharply and steamed slowly in. It was a great land-locked harbour big enough to hold a fleet of battleships; and all around it rose, high and steep, the green hills. Near the entrance, getting such breeze as blew from the sea, stood the governor's house in a garden. The Stars and Stripes dangled languidly from a flagstaff. They passed two or three trim bungalows, and a tennis court, and then they came to the quay with its warehouses. Mrs. Davidson pointed out the schooner, moored two or three hundred yards from the side, which was to take them to Apia. There was a crowd of eager, noisy, and good-humoured natives come from all parts of the island, some from curiosity, others to barter with the travellers on their way to Sydney; and they brought pineapples and huge bunches of bananas, *tapa* cloths, necklaces of shells or sharks' teeth, *kava*-bowls, and models of war canoes. American sailors, neat and trim, clean-shaven and frank of face, sauntered among them, and there was a little group of officials. While their luggage was being landed the Macphails and Mrs. Davidson watched the crowd. Dr Macphail looked at the yaws from which most of the children and the young boys seemed to suffer, disfiguring sores like torpid ulcers, and his professional eyes glistened when he saw for the first time in his experience cases of elephantiasis, men going about with a huge, heavy arm, or dragging along a grossly disfigured leg. Men and women wore the *lava-lava*.

"It's a very indecent costume," said Mrs. Davidson. "Mr. Davidson thinks it should be prohibited by law. How can you expect people to be moral when they wear nothing but a strip of red cotton round their loins?"

"It's suitable enough to the climate," said the doctor, wiping the sweat off his head.

Now that they were on land the heat, though it was so early in the morning, was already oppressive. Closed in by its hills, not a breath of air came into Pago-Pago.

"In our islands," Mrs. Davidson went on in her high-pitched tones, "we've practically eradicated the *lava-lava*. A few old men still continue to wear it, but that's all. The women have all taken to the Mother Hubbard and the men wear trousers and singlets. At the very beginning of our stay Mr. Davidson said in one of his reports: the inhabitants of these islands will never be thoroughly Christianised till every boy of more than ten years is made to wear a pair of trousers."

But Mrs. Davidson had given two or three of her birdlike glances at heavy grey clouds that came floating over the mouth of the harbour. A few drops began to fall.

"We'd better take shelter," she said.

They made their way with all the crowd to a great shed of corrugated iron, and the rain began to fall in torrents. They stood there for some time and then were joined by Mr. Davidson. He had been polite enough to the Macphails during the journey, but he had not his wife's sociability, and had spent much of his time reading. He was a silent, rather sullen man, and you felt that his affability was a duty that he imposed upon himself Christianly; he was by nature reserved and even morose. His appearance was singular. He was very tall and thin, with long limbs loosely jointed; hollow cheeks and curiously high cheek-bones; he had so cadaverous an air that it surprised you to notice how full and sensual were his lips. He wore his hair very long. His dark eyes, set deep in their sockets, were large and tragic; and his hands with their big, long fingers, were finely shaped; they gave him a look of great strength. But the most striking thing about him was the feeling he gave you of suppressed fire. It was impressive and vaguely troubling. He was not a man with whom any intimacy was possible.

He brought now unwelcome news. There was an epidemic of measles, a serious and often fatal disease among the Kanakas, on the island, and a case had developed among the crew of the schooner which was to take them on their journey. The sick man had been brought ashore and put in hospital on the quarantine station, but telegraphic instructions had been sent from Apia to say that the schooner would not be allowed to enter the harbour till it was certain no other member of the crew was affected.

"It means we shall have to stay here for ten days at least."

"But I'm urgently needed at Apia," said Dr Macphail.

"That can't be helped. If no more cases develop on board, the schooner will be allowed to sail with white passengers, but all native traffic is prohibited for three months."

"Is there a hotel here?" asked Mrs. Macphail.

Davidson gave a low chuckle.

"There's not."

"What shall we do then?"

"I've been talking to the governor. There's a trader along the front who has rooms that he rents, and my proposition is that as soon as the rain lets up we should go along there and see what we can do. Don't expect comfort. You've just got to be thankful if we get a bed to sleep on and a roof over our heads."

But the rain showed no sign of stopping, and at length with umbrellas and waterproofs they set out. There was no town, but merely a group of official buildings, a store or two, and at the back, among the coconut trees and plantains, a few native dwellings. The house they sought was about five minutes' walk from the wharf. It was a frame house of two storeys, with broad verandahs on both floors and a roof of corrugated iron. The owner was a half-caste named Horn, with a native wife surrounded by little brown children, and on the ground-floor he had a store where he sold canned goods and cottons. The rooms he showed them were almost bare of furniture. In the Macphails' there was nothing but a poor, worn bed with a ragged mosquito net, a rickety chair, and a washstand. They looked round with dismay. The rain poured down without ceasing.

"I'm not going to unpack more than we actually need," said Mrs. Macphail.

Mrs. Davidson came into the room as she was unlocking a portmanteau. She was very brisk and alert. The cheerless surroundings had no effect on her.

"If you'll take my advice you'll get a needle and cotton and start right in to mend the mosquito net," she said, "or you'll not be able to get a wink of sleep tonight."

"Will they be very bad?" asked Dr Macphail.

"This is the season for them. When you're asked to a party at Government House at Apia you'll notice that all the ladies are given a pillow-slip to put their—their lower extremities in."

"I wish the rain would stop for a moment," said Mrs. Macphail. "I could try to make the place comfortable with more heart if the sun were shining."

"Oh, if you wait for that, you'll wait a long time. Pago-Pago is about the rainiest place in the Pacific. You see, the hills, and that bay, they attract the water, and one expects rain at this time of year anyway."

She looked from Macphail to his wife, standing helplessly in different parts of the room, like lost souls, and she pursed her lips. She saw that she must take them in hand. Feckless people like that made her impatient, but her hands itched to put everything in the order which came so naturally to her.

"Here, you give me a needle and cotton and I'll mend that net of yours, while you go on with your unpacking. Dinners at one. Dr Macphail, you'd better go down to the wharf and see that your heavy luggage has been put in a dry place. You know what these natives are, they're quite capable of storing it where the rain will beat in on it all the time."

The doctor put on his waterproof again and went downstairs. At the door Mr. Horn was standing in conversation with the quartermaster of the ship they had just arrived in and a second-class passenger whom Dr Macphail had seen several times on board. The quartermaster, a little, shrivelled man, extremely dirty, nodded to him as he passed.

"This is a bad job about the measles, doc," he said. "I see you've fixed yourself up already."

Dr Macphail thought he was rather familiar, but he was a timid man, and he did not take offence easily.

"Yes, we've got a room upstairs."

"Miss Thompson was sailing with you to Apia, so I've brought her along here."

The quartermaster pointed with his thumb to the woman standing by his side. She was twenty-seven perhaps, plump, and in a coarse fashion pretty. She wore a white dress and a large white hat. Her fat calves in white cotton stockings bulged over the tops of long white boots in glacé kid. She gave Macphail an ingratiating smile.

"The feller's tryin' to soak me a dollar and a half a day for the meanest sized room," she said in a hoarse voice.

"I tell you she's a friend of mine, Jo," said the quartermaster. "She can't pay more than a dollar, and you've sure got to take her for that."

The trader was fat and smooth and quietly smiling.

"Well, if you put it like that, Mr. Swan, I'll see what I can do about it. I'll talk to Mrs. Horn and if we think we can make a reduction we will."

"Don't try to pull that stuff with me," said Miss Thompson. "We'll settle this right now. You get a dollar a day for the room and not one bean more."

Dr Macphail smiled. He admired the effrontery with which she bargained. He was the sort of man who always paid what he was asked. He preferred to be over-charged than to haggle. The trader sighed.

"Well, to oblige Mr. Swan I'll take it."

"That's the goods," said Miss Thompson. "Come right in and have a shot of hooch. I've got some really good rye in that grip if you'll bring it along, Mr. Swan. You come along too, doctor."

"Oh, I don't think I will, thank you," he answered. "I'm just going down to see that our luggage is all right."

He stepped out into the rain. It swept in from the opening of the harbour in sheets and the opposite shore was all blurred. He passed two or three natives clad in nothing but the *lava-lava*, with huge umbrellas over them. They walked finely, with leisurely movements, very upright; and they smiled and greeted him in a strange tongue as they went by.

It was nearly dinner-time when he got back, and their meal was laid in the trader's parlour. It was a room designed not to live in but for purposes of prestige, and it had a musty, melancholy air. A suite of stamped plush was arranged neatly round the walls, and from the middle of the ceiling, protected from the flies by yellow tissue paper, hung a gilt chandelier. Davidson did not come.

"I know he went to call on the governor," said Mrs. Davidson, "and I guess he's kept him to dinner."

A little native girl brought them a dish of Hamburger steak, and after a while the trader came up to see that they had everything they wanted.

"I see we have a fellow lodger, Mr. Horn," said Dr Macphail.

"She's taken a room, that's all," answered the trader. "She's getting her own board."

He looked at the two ladies with an obsequious air.

"I put her downstairs so she shouldn't be in the way. She won't be any trouble to you."

"Is it someone who was on the boat?" asked Mrs. Macphail.

"Yes, ma'am, she was in the second cabin. She was going to Apia. She has a position as cashier waiting for her."

"Oh!"

When the trader was gone Macphail said:

"I shouldn't think she'd find it exactly cheerful having her meals in her room."

"If she was in the second cabin I guess she'd rather," answered Mrs. Davidson. "I don't exactly know who it can be."

"I happened to be there when the quartermaster brought her along. Her name's Thompson."

"It's not the woman who was dancing with the quartermaster last night?" asked Mrs. Davidson.

"That's who it must be," said Mrs. Macphail. "I wondered at the time what she was. She looked rather fast to me."

"Not good style at all," said Mrs. Davidson.

They began to talk of other things and after dinner, tired with their early rise, they separated and slept. When they awoke, though the sky was still grey and the clouds hung low, it was not raining, and they went for a walk on the high road which the Americans had built along the bay.

On their return they found that Davidson had just come in.

"We may be here for a fortnight," he said irritably. "I've argued it out with the governor, but he says there is nothing to be done."

"Mr. Davidson's just longing to get back to his work," said his wife, with an anxious glance at him.

"We've been away for a year," he said, walking up and down the verandah. "The mission has been in charge of native missionaries and I'm terribly nervous that they've let things slide. They're good men, I'm not saying a word against them, God-fearing, devout, and truly Christian men—their Christianity would put many so-called Christians at home to the blush—but they're pitifully lacking in energy. They can make a stand once, they can make a stand twice, but they can't make a stand all the time. If you leave a mission in charge of a native missionary, no matter how trustworthy he seems, in course of time you'll find he's let abuses creep in."

Mr. Davidson stood still. With his tall, spare form, and his great eyes flashing out of his pale face, he was an impressive figure. His sincerity was obvious in the fire of his gestures and in his deep, ringing voice.

"I expect to have my work cut out for me. I shall act and I shall act promptly. If the tree is rotten it shall be cut down and cast into the flames."

And in the evening after the high tea, which was their last meal, while they sat in the stiff parlour, the ladies working and

Dr Macphail smoking his pipe, the missionary told them of his work in the islands.

"When we went there they had no sense of sin at all," he said. "They broke the commandments one after the other and never knew they were doing wrong. And I think that was the most difficult part of my work, to instil into the natives the sense of sin."

The Macphails knew already that Davidson had worked in the Solomons for five years before he met his wife. She had been a missionary in China, and they had become acquainted in Boston, where they were both spending part of their leave to attend a missionary congress. On their marriage they had been appointed to the islands in which they had laboured ever since.

In the course of all the conversations they had had with Mr. Davidson one thing had shone out clearly and that was the man's unflinching courage. He was a medical missionary, and he was liable to be called at any time to one or other of the islands in the group. Even the whaleboat is not so very safe a conveyance in the stormy Pacific of the wet season, but often he would be sent for in a canoe, and then the danger was great. In cases of illness or accident he never hesitated. A dozen times he had spent the whole night baling for his life, and more than once Mrs. Davidson had given him up for lost.

"I'd beg him not to go sometimes," she said, "or at least to wait till the weather was more settled, but he'd never listen. He's obstinate, and when he's once made up his mind, nothing can move him."

"How can I ask the natives to put their trust in the Lord if I am afraid to do so myself?" cried Davidson. "And I'm not, I'm not. They know that if they send for me in their trouble I'll come if it's humanly possible. And do you think the Lord is going to abandon me when I am on his business? The wind blows at his bidding and the waves toss and rage at his word."

Dr Macphail was a timid man. He had never been able to get used to the hurtling of the shells over the trenches, and when he was operating in an advanced dressing-station the sweat poured from his brow and dimmed his spectacles in the effort he made to control his unsteady hand. He shuddered' a little as he looked at the missionary.

"I wish I could say that I've never been afraid," he said.

"I wish you could say that you believed in God," retorted the other.

But for some reason, that evening the missionary's thoughts travelled back to the early days he and his wife had spent on the islands.

"Sometimes Mrs. Davidson and I would look at one another and the tears would stream down our cheeks. We worked without ceasing, day and night, and we seemed to make no progress. I don't know what I should have done without her then. When I felt my heart sink, when I was very near despair, she gave me courage and hope."

Mrs. Davidson looked down at her work, and a slight colour rose to her thin cheeks. Her hands trembled a little. She did not trust herself to speak.

"We had no one to help us. We were alone, thousands of miles from any of our own people, surrounded by darkness. When I was broken and weary she would put her work aside and take the Bible and read to me till peace came and settled upon me like sleep upon the eyelids of a child, and when at last she closed the book she'd say: 'We'll save them in spite of themselves.' And I felt strong again in the Lord, and I answered: 'Yes, with God's help I'll save them. I must save them.'"

He came over to the table and stood in front of it as though it were a lectern.

"You see, they were so naturally depraved that they couldn't be brought to see their wickedness. We had to make sins out of what they thought were natural actions. We had to make it a sin, not only to commit adultery and to lie and thieve, but to expose their bodies, and to dance and not to come to church. I made it a sin for a girl to show her bosom and a sin for a man not to wear trousers."

"How?" asked Dr Macphail, not without surprise.

"I instituted fines. Obviously the only way to make people realise that an action is sinful is to punish them if they commit it. I fined them if they didn't come to church, and I fined them if they danced. I fined them if they were improperly dressed. I had a tariff, and every sin had to be paid for either in money or work. And at last, I made them understand."

"But did they never refuse to pay?"

"How could they?" asked the missionary.

"It would be a brave man who tried to stand up against Mr. Davidson," said his wife, tightening her lips.

Dr Macphail looked at Davidson with troubled eyes. What he heard shocked him, but he hesitated to express his disapproval.

"You must remember that in the last resort I could expel them from their church membership."

"Did they mind that?"

Davidson smiled a little and gently rubbed his hands.

"They couldn't sell their copra. When the men fished they got no share of the catch. It meant something very like starvation. Yes, they minded quite a lot."

"Tell him about Fred Ohlson," said Mrs. Davidson.

The missionary fixed his fiery eyes on Dr Macphail.

"Fred Ohlson was a Danish trader who had been in the islands a good many years. He was a pretty rich man as traders go and he wasn't very pleased when we came. You see, he'd had things very much his own way. He paid the natives what he liked for their copra, and he paid in goods and whiskey. He had a native wife, but he was flagrantly unfaithful to her. He was a drunkard. I gave him a chance to mend his ways, but he wouldn't take it. He laughed at me."

Davidson's voice fell to a deep bass as he said the last words, and he was silent for a minute or two. The silence was heavy with menace.

"In two years, he was a ruined man. He'd lost everything he'd saved in a quarter of a century. I broke him, and at last he was forced to come to me like a beggar and beseech me to give him a passage back to Sydney."

"I wish you could have seen him when he came to see Mr. Davidson," said the missionary's wife. "He had been a fine, powerful man, with a lot of fat on him, and he had a great big voice, but now he was half the size, and he was shaking all over. He'd suddenly become an old man."

With abstracted gaze Davidson looked out into the night. The rain was falling again.

Suddenly from below came a sound, and Davidson turned and looked questioningly at his wife. It was the sound of a gramophone, harsh and loud, wheezing out a syncopated tune.

"What's that?" he asked.

Mrs. Davidson fixed her *pince-nez* more firmly on her nose.

"One of the second-class passengers has a room in the house. I guess it comes from there."

They listened in silence, and presently they heard the sound of dancing. Then the music stopped, and they heard the popping of corks and voices raised in animated conversation.

"I daresay she's giving a farewell party to her friends on board," said Dr Macphail. "The ship sails at twelve, doesn't it?"

Davidson made no remark, but he looked at his watch.

"Are you ready?" he asked his wife.

She got up and folded her work.

"Yes, I guess I am," she answered.

"It's early to go to bed yet, isn't it?" said the doctor.

"We have a good deal of reading to do," explained Mrs. Davidson. "Wherever we are, we read a chapter of the Bible before retiring for the night and we study it with the commentaries, you know, and discuss it thoroughly. It's a wonderful training for the mind."

The two couples bade one another good night. Dr and Mrs. Macphail were left alone. For two or three minutes they did not speak.

"I think I'll go and fetch the cards," the doctor said at last.

Mrs. Macphail looked at him doubtfully. Her conversation with the Davidsons had left her a little uneasy, but she did not like to say that she thought they had better not play cards when the Davidsons might come in at any moment. Dr

Macphail brought them, and she watched him, though with a vague sense of guilt, while he laid out his patience. Below the sound of revelry continued.

It was fine enough next day, and the Macphails, condemned to spend a fortnight of idleness at Pago-Pago, set about making the best of things. They went down to the quay and got out of their boxes a number of books. The doctor called on the chief surgeon of the naval hospital and went round the beds with him. They left cards on the governor. They passed Miss Thompson on the road. The doctor took off his hat, and she gave him a "Good morning, doc.," in a loud, cheerful voice. She was dressed as on the day before, in a white frock, and her shiny white boots with their high heels, her fat legs bulging over the tops of them, were strange things on that exotic scene.

"I don't think she's very suitably dressed, I must say," said Mrs. Macphail. "She looks extremely common to me."

When they got back to their house, she was on the verandah playing with one of the trader's dark children.

"Say a word to her," Dr Macphail whispered to his wife. "She's all alone here, and it seems rather unkind to ignore her."

Mrs. Macphail was shy, but she was in the habit of doing what her husband bade her.

"I think we're fellow lodgers here," she said, rather foolishly.

"Terrible, ain't it, bein' cooped up in a one-horse burg like this?" answered Miss Thompson. "And they tell me I'm lucky to have gotten a room. I don't see myself livin' in a native house, and that's what some have to do. I don't know why they don't have a hotel."

They exchanged a few more words. Miss Thompson, loud-voiced and garrulous, was evidently quite willing to gossip, but Mrs. Macphail had a poor stock of small talk and presently she said:

"Well, I think we must go upstairs."

In the evening when they sat down to their high-tea Davidson on coming in said:

"I see that woman downstairs has a couple of sailors sitting there. I wonder how she's gotten acquainted with them."

"She can't be very particular," said Mrs. Davidson.

They were all rather tired after the idle, aimless day.

"If there's going to be a fortnight of this I don't know what we shall feel like at the end of it," said Dr Macphail.

"The only thing to do is to portion out the day to different activities," answered the missionary. "I shall set aside a certain number of hours to study and a certain number to exercise, rain or fine—in the wet season you can't afford to pay any attention to the rain—and a certain number to recreation."

Dr Macphail looked at his companion with misgiving. Davidson's programme oppressed him. They were eating Hamburger steak again. It seemed the only dish the cook knew how to make. Then below the gramophone began. Davidson started nervously when he heard it but said nothing. Men's voices floated up. Miss Thompson's guests were joining in a well-known song and presently they heard her voice too, hoarse and loud. There was a good deal of shouting and laughing. The four people upstairs, trying to make conversation, listened despite themselves to the clink of glasses and the scrape of chairs. More people had evidently come. Miss Thompson was giving a party.

"I wonder how she gets them all in," said Mrs. Macphail, suddenly breaking into a medical conversation between the missionary and her husband.

It showed whither her thoughts were wandering. The twitch of Davidson's face proved that, though he spoke of scientific things, his mind was busy in the same direction. Suddenly, while the doctor was giving some experience of practice on the Flanders front, rather prosily, he sprang to his feet with a cry.

"What's the matter, Alfred?" asked Mrs. Davidson.

"Of course! It never occurred to me. She's out of Iwelei."

"She can't be."

"She came on board at Honolulu. It's obvious. And she's carrying on her trade here. Here."

He uttered the last word with a passion of indignation.

"What's Iwelei?" asked Mrs. Macphail.

He turned his gloomy eyes on her and his voice trembled with horror.

"The plague spot of Honolulu. The Red-Light district. It was a blot on our civilisation."

Iwelei was on the edge of the city. You went downside streets by the harbour, in the darkness, across a rickety bridge, till you came to a deserted road, all ruts and holes, and then suddenly you came out into the light. There was parking room for motors on each side of the road, and there were saloons, tawdry and bright, each one noisy with its mechanical piano, and there were barbers' shops and tobacconists. There was a stir in the air and a sense of expectant gaiety. You turned down a narrow alley, either to the right or to the left, for the road divided Iwelei into two parts, and you found yourself in the district. There were rows of little bungalows, trim and neatly painted in green, and the pathway between them was broad and straight. It was laid out like a garden-city. In its respectable regularity, its order and spruceness, it gave an impression of sardonic horror; for never can the search for love have been so systematised and ordered. The pathways were lit by a rare lamp, but they would have been dark except for the lights that came from the open windows of the bungalows. Men wandered about, looking at the women who sat at their windows, reading or sewing, for the most part taking no notice of the passers-by; and like the women they were of all nationalities. There were Americans, sailors from the ships in port, enlisted men off the gunboats, sombrely drunk and soldiers from the regiments, white and black, quartered on the island; there were Japanese, walking in twos and threes; Hawaiians, Chinese in long robes, and Filipinos in preposterous hats. They were silent and as it were oppressed. Desire is sad.

"It was the most crying scandal of the Pacific," exclaimed Davidson vehemently. "The missionaries had been agitating against it for years, and at last the local press took it up. The police refused to stir. You know their argument. They say that vice is inevitable and consequently the best thing is to localise and control it. The truth is, they were paid. Paid. They were paid by the saloon-keepers, paid by the bullies, paid by the women themselves. At last, they were forced to move."

"I read about it in the papers that came on board in Honolulu," said Dr Macphail.

"Iwelei, with its sin and shame, ceased to exist on the very day we arrived. The whole population was brought before the justices. I don't know why I didn't understand at once what that woman was."

"Now you come to speak of it," said Mrs. Macphail, "I remember seeing her come on board only a few minutes before the boat sailed. I remember thinking at the time she was cutting it rather fine."

"How dare she come here!" cried Davidson indignantly. "I'm not going to allow it."

He strode towards the door.

"What are you going to do?" asked Macphail.

"What do you expect me to do? I'm going to stop it. I'm not going to have this house turned into—into...."

He sought for a word that should not offend the ladies' ears. His eyes were flashing, and his pale face was paler still in his emotion.

"It sounds as though there were three or four men down there," said the doctor. "Don't you think it's rather rash to go in just now?"

The missionary gave him a contemptuous look and without a word flung out of the room.

"You know Mr. Davidson very little if you think the fear of personal danger can stop him in the performance of his duty," said his wife.

She sat with her hands nervously clasped, a spot of colour on her high cheek bones, listening to what was about to happen below. They all listened. They heard him clatter down the wooden stairs and throw open the door. The singing stopped suddenly, but the gramophone continued to bray out its vulgar tune. They heard Davidson's voice and then the noise of something heavy falling. The music stopped. He had hurled the gramophone on the floor. Then again they heard Davidson's voice, they could not make out the words, then

Miss Thompson's, loud and shrill, then a confused clamour as though several people were shouting together at the top of their lungs. Mrs. Davidson gave a little gasp, and she clenched her hands more tightly. Dr Macphail looked uncertainly from her to his wife. He did not want to go down, but he wondered if they expected him to. Then there was something that sounded like a scuffle. The noise now was more distinct. It might be that Davidson was being thrown out of the room. The door was slammed. There was a moment's silence, and they heard Davidson come up the stairs again. He went to his room.

"I think I'll go to him," said Mrs. Davidson.

She got up and went out.

"If you want me, just call," said Mrs. Macphail, and then when the other was gone: "I hope he isn't hurt."

"Why couldn't he mind his own business?" said Dr Macphail.

They sat in silence for a minute or two and then they both started, for the gramophone began to play once more, defiantly, and mocking voices shouted hoarsely the words of an obscene song.

Next day Mrs. Davidson was pale and tired. She complained of headache, and she looked old and wizened. She told Mrs. Macphail that the missionary had not slept at all; he had passed the night in a state of frightful agitation and at five had got up and gone out. A glass of beer had been thrown over him and his clothes were stained and stinking. But a sombre fire glowed in Mrs. Davidson's eyes when she spoke of Miss Thompson.

"She'll bitterly rue the day when she flouted Mr. Davidson," she said. "Mr. Davidson has a wonderful heart and no one who is in trouble has ever gone to him without being comforted, but he has no mercy for sin, and when his righteous wrath is excited he's terrible."

"Why, what will he do?" asked Mrs. Macphail.

"I don't know, but I wouldn't stand in that creature's shoes for anything in the world."

Mrs. Macphail shuddered. There was something positively alarming in the triumphant assurance of the little woman's manner. They were going out together that morning, and they went down the stairs side by side. Miss Thompson's door was open, and they saw her in a bedraggled dressing-gown, cooking something in a chafing-dish.

"Good morning," she called. "Is Mr. Davidson better this morning?"

They passed her in silence, with their noses in the air, as if she did not exist. They flushed, however, when she burst into a shout of derisive laughter. Mrs. Davidson turned on her suddenly.

"Don't you dare to speak to me," she screamed. "If you insult me I shall have you turned out of here."

"Say, did I ask Mr. Davidson to visit with me?"

"Don't answer her," whispered Mrs. Macphail hurriedly.

They walked on till they were out of earshot.

"She's brazen, brazen," burst from Mrs. Davidson.

Her anger almost suffocated her.

And on their way home they met her strolling towards the quay. She had all her finery on. Her great white hat with its vulgar, showy flowers was an affront. She called out cheerily to them as she went by, and a couple of American sailors who were standing there grinned as the ladies set their faces to an icy stare. They got in just before the rain began to fall again.

"I guess she'll get her fine clothes spoilt," said Mrs. Davidson with a bitter sneer.

Davidson did not come in till they were halfway through dinner. He was wet through, but he would not change. He sat, morose and silent, refusing to eat more than a mouthful, and he stared at the slanting rain. When Mrs. Davidson told him of their two encounters with Miss Thompson he did not answer. His deepening frown alone showed that he had heard.

"Don't you think we ought to make Mr. Horn turn her out of here?" asked Mrs. Davidson. "We can't allow her to insult us."

"There doesn't seem to be any other place for her to go," said Macphail.

"She can live with one of the natives."

"In weather like this a native hut must be a rather uncomfortable place to live in."

"I lived in one for years," said the missionary.

When the little native girl brought in the fried bananas which formed the sweet they had every day, Davidson turned to her.

"Ask Miss Thompson when it would be convenient for me to see her," he said.

The girl nodded shyly and went out.

"What do you want to see her for, Alfred?" asked his wife.

"It's my duty to see her. I won't act till I've given her every chance."

"You don't know what she is. She'll insult you."

"Let her insult me. Let her spit on me. She has an immortal soul, and I must do all that is in my power to save it."

Mrs. Davidson's ears rang still with the harlot's mocking laughter.

"She's gone too far."

"Too far for the mercy of God?" His eyes lit up suddenly and his voice grew mellow and soft. "Never. The sinner may be deeper in sin than the depth of hell itself, but the love of the Lord Jesus can reach him still."

The girl came back with the message.

"Miss Thompson's compliments and as long as Rev. Davidson don't come in business hours she'll be glad to see him any time."

The party received it in stony silence, and Dr Macphail quickly effaced from his lips the smile which had come upon them. He knew his wife would be vexed with him if he found Miss Thompson's effrontery amusing.

They finished the meal in silence. When it was over the two ladies got up and took their work, Mrs. Macphail was making another of the innumerable comforters which she had turned out since the beginning of the war, and the doctor lit his pipe. But Davidson remained in his chair and with abstracted eyes stared at the table. At last, he got up and without a word went out of the room. They heard him go down and they heard Miss Thompson's defiant "Come in" when he knocked at the door. He remained with her for an hour. And Dr Macphail watched the rain. It was beginning to get on his nerves. It was not like our soft English rain that drops gently on the earth; it was unmerciful and somehow terrible; you felt in it the malignancy of the primitive powers of nature. It did not pour, it flowed. It was like a deluge from heaven, and it rattled on the roof of corrugated iron with a steady persistence that was maddening. It seemed to have a fury of its own. And sometimes you felt that you must scream if it did not stop, and then suddenly you felt powerless, as though your bones had suddenly become soft; and you were miserable and hopeless.

Macphail turned his head when the missionary came back. The two women looked up.

"I've given her every chance. I have exhorted her to repent. She is an evil woman."

He paused, and Dr Macphail saw his eyes darken and his pale face grow hard and stern.

"Now I shall take the whips with which the Lord Jesus drove the usurers and the money changers out of the Temple of the Highest."

He walked up and down the room. His mouth was close set, and his black brows were frowning.

"If she fled to the uttermost parts of the earth I should pursue her."

With a sudden movement he turned round and strode out of the room. They heard him go downstairs again.

"What is he going to do?" asked Mrs. Macphail.

"I don't know." Mrs. Davidson took off her *pince-nez* and wiped them. "When he is on the Lord's work I never ask him questions."

She sighed a little.

"What is the matter?"

"He'll wear himself out. He doesn't know what it is to spare himself."

Dr Macphail learnt the first results of the missionary's activity from the half-caste trader in whose house they lodged. He stopped the doctor when he passed the store and came out to speak to him on the stoop. His fat face was worried.

"The Rev. Davidson has been at me for letting Miss Thompson have a room here," he said, "but I didn't know what she was when I rented it to her. When people come and ask if I can rent them a room all I want to know is if they've the money to pay for it. And she paid me for hers a week in advance."

Dr Macphail did not want to commit himself.

"When all's said and done it's your house. We're very much obliged to you for taking us in at all."

Horn looked at him doubtfully. He was not certain yet how definitely Macphail stood on the missionary's side.

"The missionaries are in with one another," he said, hesitatingly. "If they get it in for a trader he may just as well shut up his store and quit."

"Did he want you to turn her out?"

"No, he said so long as she behaved herself he couldn't ask me to do that. He said he wanted to be just to me. I promised she shouldn't have no more visitors. I've just been and told her."

"How did she take it?"

"She gave me Hell."

The trader squirmed in his old ducks. He had found Miss Thompson a rough customer.

"Oh, well, I daresay she'll get out. I don't suppose she wants to stay here if she can't have anyone in."

"There's nowhere she can go, only a native house, and no native will take her now, not now that the missionaries have got their knife in her."

Dr Macphail looked at the falling rain.

"Well, I don't suppose it's any good waiting for it to clear up."

In the evening when they sat in the parlour Davidson talked to them of his early days at college. He had had no means and had worked his way through by doing odd jobs during the vacations. There was silence downstairs. Miss Thompson was sitting in her little room alone. But suddenly the gramophone began to play. She had set it on in defiance, to cheat her loneliness, but there was no one to sing, and it had a melancholy note. It was like a cry for help. Davidson took no notice. He was in the middle of a long anecdote and without change of expression went on. The gramophone continued. Miss Thompson put on one reel after another. It looked as though the silence of the night were getting on her nerves. It was breathless and sultry. When the Macphails went to bed they could not sleep. They lay side by side with their eyes wide open, listening to the cruel singing of the mosquitoes outside their curtain.

"What's that?" whispered Mrs. Macphail at last.

They heard a voice, Davidson's voice, through the wooden partition. It went on with a monotonous, earnest insistence. He was praying aloud. He was praying for the soul of Miss Thompson.

Two or three days went by. Now when they passed Miss Thompson on the road she did not greet them with ironic cordiality or smile; she passed with her nose in the air, a sulky look on her painted face, frowning, as though she did not see them. The trader told Macphail that she had tried to get lodging elsewhere but had failed. In the evening, she played through the various reels of her gramophone, but the pretence of mirth was obvious now. The ragtime had a cracked, heart-broken rhythm as though it were a one-step of despair. When she began to play on Sunday Davidson sent Horn to beg her to stop at once since it was the Lord's day. The reel was taken off and the house was silent except for the steady pattering of the rain on the iron roof.

"I think she's getting a bit worked up," said the trader next day to Macphail. "She don't know what Mr. Davidson's up to, and it makes her scared."

Macphail had caught a glimpse of her that morning and it struck him that her arrogant expression had changed. There was in her face a hunted look. The half-caste gave him a sidelong glance.

"I suppose you don't know what Mr. Davidson is doing about it?" he hazarded.

"No, I don't."

It was singular that Horn should ask him that question, for he also had the idea that the missionary was mysteriously at work. He had an impression that he was weaving a net around the woman, carefully, systematically, and suddenly, when everything was ready would pull the strings tight.

"He told me to tell her," said the trader, "that if at any time she wanted him she only had to send, and he'd come."

"What did she say when you told her that?"

"She didn't say nothing. I didn't stop. I just said what he said I was to and then I beat it. I thought she might be going to start weepin'."

"I have no doubt the loneliness is getting on her nerves," said the doctor. "And the rain—that's enough to make anyone jumpy," he continued irritably. "Doesn't it ever stop in this confounded place?"

"It goes on pretty steady in the rainy season. We have three hundred inches in the year. You see, it's the shape of the bay. It seems to attract the rain from all over the Pacific."

"Damn the shape of the bay," said the doctor.

He scratched his mosquito bites. He felt very short-tempered. When the rain stopped and the sun shone, it was like a hothouse, seething, humid, sultry, breathless, and you had a strange feeling that everything was growing with a savage violence. The natives, blithe and childlike by reputation, seemed then, with their tattooing and their dyed hair, to have something sinister in their appearance; and when they pattered along at your heels with their naked feet you looked back instinctively. You felt they might at any moment come behind you swiftly and thrust a long knife between your shoulder blades. You could not tell what dark thoughts lurked behind their wide-set eyes. They had a little the look of ancient Egyptians painted on a temple wall, and there was about them the terror of what is immeasurably old.

The missionary came and went. He was busy, but the Macphails did not know what he was doing. Horn told the doctor that he saw the governor every day, and once Davidson mentioned him.

"He looks as if he had plenty of determination," he said, "but when you come down to brass tacks he has no backbone."

"I suppose that means he won't do exactly what you want," suggested the doctor facetiously.

The missionary did not smile.

"I want him to do what's right. It shouldn't be necessary to persuade a man to do that."

"But there may be differences of opinion about what is right."

"If a man had a gangrenous foot would you have patience with anyone who hesitated to amputate it?"

"Gangrene is a matter of fact."

"And Evil?"

What Davidson had done soon appeared. The four of them had just finished their midday meal, and they had not yet separated for the siesta which the heat imposed on the ladies and on the doctor. Davidson had little patience with the slothful habit. The door was suddenly flung open, and Miss Thompson came in. She looked round the room and then went up to Davidson.

"You low-down skunk, what have you been saying about me to the governor?"

She was spluttering with rage. There was a moment's pause. Then the missionary drew forward a chair.

"Won't you be seated, Miss Thompson? I've been hoping to have another talk with you."

"You poor low-life bastard."

She burst into a torrent of insult, foul and insolent. Davidson kept his grave eyes on her.

"I'm indifferent to the abuse you think fit to heap on me, Miss Thompson," he said, "but I must beg you to remember that ladies are present."

Tears by now were struggling with her anger. Her face was red and swollen as though she were choking.

"What has happened?" asked Dr Macphail.

"A feller's just been in here and he says I gotter beat it on the next boat."

Was there a gleam in the missionary's eyes? His face remained impassive.

"You could hardly expect the governor to let you stay here under the circumstances."

"You done it," she shrieked. "You can't kid me. You done it."

"I don't want to deceive you. I urged the governor to take the only possible step consistent with his obligations."

"Why couldn't you leave me be? I wasn't doin' you no harm."

"You may be sure that if you had I should be the last man to resent it."

"Do you think I want to stay on in this poor imitation of a burg? I don't look no busher, do I?"

"In that case I don't see what cause of complaint you have," he answered.

She gave an inarticulate cry of rage and flung out of the room. There was a short silence.

"It's a relief to know that the governor has acted at last," said Davidson finally. "He's a weak man and he shilly-shallied. He said she was only here for a fortnight anyway and if she went on to Apia that was under British jurisdiction and had nothing to do with him."

The missionary sprang to his feet and strode across the room.

"It's terrible the way the men who are in authority seek to evade their responsibility. They speak as though evil that was out of sight ceased to be evil. The very existence of that woman is a scandal, and it does not help matters to shift it to another of the islands. In the end I had to speak straight from the shoulder."

Davidson's brow lowered, and he protruded his firm chin. He looked fierce and determined.

"What do you mean by that?"

"Our mission is not entirely without influence at Washington. I pointed out to the governor that it wouldn't do him any good if there was a complaint about the way he managed things here."

"When has she got to go?" asked the doctor, after a pause.

"The San Francisco boat is due here from Sydney next Tuesday. She's to sail on that."

That was in five days' time. It was next day, when he was coming back from the hospital where for want of something better to do Macphail spent most of his mornings, that the half-caste stopped him as he was going upstairs.

"Excuse me, Dr Macphail, Miss Thompson's sick. Will you have a look at her."

"Certainly."

Horn led him to her room. She was sitting in a chair idly, neither reading nor sewing, staring in front of her. She wore her white dress and the large hat with the flowers on it. Macphail noticed that her skin was yellow and muddy under her powder, and her eyes were heavy.

"I'm sorry to hear you're not well," he said.

"Oh, I ain't sick really. I just said that, because I just had to see you. I've got to clear on a boat that's going to 'Frisco."

She looked at him and he saw that her eyes were suddenly startled. She opened and clenched her hands spasmodically. The trader stood at the door, listening.

"So, I understand," said the doctor.

She gave a little gulp.

"I guess it ain't very convenient for me to go to 'Frisco just now. I went to see the governor yesterday afternoon, but I couldn't get to him. I saw the secretary, and he told me I'd got to take that boat and that was all there was to it. I just had to see the governor, so I waited outside his house this morning, and when he come out I spoke to him. He didn't want to speak to me, I'll say, but I wouldn't let him shake me off, and at last he said he hadn't no objection to my staying here till the next boat to Sydney if the Rev. Davidson will stand for it."

She stopped and looked at Dr Macphail anxiously.

"I don't know exactly what I can do," he said.

"Well, I thought maybe you wouldn't mind asking him. I swear to God I won't start anything here if he'll just only let me stay. I won't go out of the house if that'll suit him. It's no more'n a fortnight."

"I'll ask him."

"He won't stand for it," said Horn. "He'll have you out on Tuesday, so you may as well make up your mind to it."

"Tell him I can get work in Sydney, straight stuff, I mean. 'Tain't asking very much."

"I'll do what I can."

"And come and tell me right away, will you? I can't set down to a thing till I get the dope one way or the other."

It was not an errand that much pleased the doctor, and, characteristically perhaps, he went about it indirectly. He told his wife what Miss Thompson had said to him and asked her to speak to Mrs. Davidson. The missionary's attitude seemed rather arbitrary, and it could do no harm if the girl were allowed to stay in Pago-Pago another fortnight. But he was not prepared for the result of his diplomacy. The missionary came to him straightway.

"Mrs. Davidson tells me that Thompson has been speaking to you."

Dr Macphail, thus directly tackled, had the shy man's resentment at being forced out into the open. He felt his temper rising, and he flushed.

"I don't see that it can make any difference if she goes to Sydney rather than to San Francisco, and so long as she promises to behave while she's here it's dashed hard to persecute her."

The missionary fixed him with his stern eyes.

"Why is she unwilling to go back to San Francisco?"

"I didn't enquire," answered the doctor with some asperity. "And I think one does better to mind one's own business."

Perhaps it was not a very tactful answer.

"The governor has ordered her to be deported by the first boat that leaves the island. He's only done his duty, and I will not interfere. Her presence is a peril here."

"I think you're very harsh and tyrannical."

The two ladies looked up at the doctor with some alarm, but they need not have feared a quarrel, for the missionary smiled gently.

"I'm terribly sorry you should think that of me, Dr Macphail. Believe me, my heart bleeds for that unfortunate woman, but I'm only trying to do my duty."

The doctor made no answer. He looked out of the window sullenly. For once it was not raining and across the bay you saw nestling among the trees the huts of a native village.

"I think I'll take advantage of the rain stopping to go out," he said.

"Please don't bear me malice because I can't accede to your wish," said Davidson, with a melancholy smile. "I respect you very much, doctor, and I should be sorry if you thought ill of me."

"I have no doubt you have a sufficiently good opinion of yourself to bear mine with equanimity," he retorted.

"That's one on me," chuckled Davidson.

When Dr Macphail, vexed with himself because he had been uncivil to no purpose, went downstairs, Miss Thompson was waiting for him with her door ajar.

"Well," she said, "have you spoken to him?"

"Yes, I'm sorry, he won't do anything," he answered, not looking at her in his embarrassment.

But then he gave her a quick glance, for a sob broke from her. He saw that her face was white with fear. It gave him a shock of dismay. And suddenly he had an idea.

"But don't give up hope yet. I think it's a shame the way they're treating you and I'm going to see the governor myself."

"Now?"

He nodded. Her face brightened.

"Say, that's really good of you. I'm sure he'll let me stay if you speak for me. I just won't do a thing I didn't ought all the time I'm here."

Dr Macphail hardly knew why he had made up his mind to appeal to the governor. He was perfectly indifferent to Miss Thompson's affairs, but the missionary had irritated him, and with him temper was a smouldering thing. He found the governor at home. He was a large, handsome man, a sailor, with a grey toothbrush moustache; and he wore a spotless uniform of white drill.

"I've come to see you about a woman who's lodging in the same house as we are," he said. "Her name's Thompson."

"I guess I've heard nearly enough about her, Dr Macphail," said the governor, smiling. "I've given her the order to get out next Tuesday and that's all I can do."

"I wanted to ask you if you couldn't stretch a point and let her stay here till the boat comes in from San Francisco so that she can go to Sydney. I will guarantee her good behaviour."

The governor continued to smile, but his eyes grew small and serious.

"I'd be very glad to oblige you, Dr Macphail, but I've given the order, and it must stand."

The doctor put the case as reasonably as he could, but now the governor ceased to smile at all. He listened sullenly, with averted gaze. Macphail saw that he was making no impression.

"I'm sorry to cause any lady inconvenience, but she'll have to sail on Tuesday and that's all there is to it."

"But what difference can it make?"

"Pardon me, doctor, but I don't feel called upon to explain my official actions except to the proper authorities."

Macphail looked at him shrewdly. He remembered Davidson's hint that he had used threats, and in the governor's attitude he read a singular embarrassment.

"Davidson's a damned busybody," he said hotly.

"Between ourselves, Dr Macphail, I don't say that I have formed a very favourable opinion of Mr. Davidson, but I am bound to confess that he was within his rights in pointing out to me the danger that the presence of a woman of Miss Thompson's character was to a place like this where a number of enlisted men are stationed among a native population."

He got up and Dr Macphail was obliged to do so too.

"I must ask you to excuse me. I have an engagement. Please give my respects to Mrs. Macphail."

The doctor left him crest-fallen. He knew that Miss Thompson would be waiting for him and unwilling to tell her himself that he had failed, he went into the house by the back door and sneaked up the stairs as though he had something to hide.

At supper he was silent and ill-at-ease, but the missionary was jovial and animated. Dr Macphail thought his eyes rested on him now and then with triumphant good-humour. It struck him suddenly that Davidson knew of his visit to the governor and of its ill success. But how on earth could he have heard of it? There was something sinister about the power of that man. After supper he saw Horn on the verandah and, as though to have a casual word with him, went out.

"She wants to know if you've seen the governor," the trader whispered.

"Yes. He wouldn't do anything. I'm awfully sorry, I can't do anything more."

"I knew he wouldn't. They daren't go against the missionaries."

"What are you talking about?" said Davidson affably, coming out to join them.

"I was just saying there was no chance of your getting over to Apia for at least another week," said the trader glibly.

He left them, and the two men returned into the parlour. Mr. Davidson devoted one hour after each meal to recreation. Presently a timid knock was heard at the door.

"Come in," said Mrs. Davidson, in her sharp voice.

The door was not opened. She got up and opened it. They saw Miss Thompson standing at the threshold. But the change in her appearance was extraordinary. This was no longer the flaunting hussy who had jeered at them in the road, but a broken, frightened woman. Her hair, as a rule so elaborately arranged, was tumbling untidily over her neck. She wore bedroom slippers and a skirt and blouse. They were unfresh and bedraggled. She stood at the door with the tears streaming down her face and did not dare to enter.

"What do you want?" said Mrs. Davidson harshly.

"May I speak to Mr. Davidson?" she said in a choking voice.

The missionary rose and went towards her.

"Come right in, Miss Thompson," he said in cordial tones. "What can I do for you?"

She entered the room.

"Say, I'm sorry for what I said to you the other day an' for—for everythin' else. I guess I was a bit lit up. I beg pardon."

"Oh, it was nothing. I guess my back's broad enough to bear a few hard words."

She stepped towards him with a movement that was horribly cringing.

"You've got me beat. I'm all in. You won't make me go back to 'Frisco?"

His genial manner vanished, and his voice grew on a sudden hard and stern.

"Why don't you want to go back there?"

She cowered before him.

"I guess my people live there. I don't want them to see me like this. I'll go anywhere else you say."

"Why don't you want to go back to San Francisco?"

"I've told you."

He leaned forward, staring at her, and his great, shining eyes seemed to try to bore into her soul. He gave a sudden gasp.

"The penitentiary."

She screamed, and then she fell at his feet, clasping his legs.

"Don't send me back there. I swear to you before God I'll be a good woman. I'll give all this up."

She burst into a torrent of confused supplication and the tears coursed down her painted cheeks. He leaned over her and, lifting her face, forced her to look at him.

"Is that it, the penitentiary?"

"I beat it before they could get me," she gasped. "If the bulls grab me it's three years for mine."

He let go his hold of her and she fell in a heap on the floor, sobbing bitterly. Dr Macphail stood up.

"This alters the whole thing," he said. "You can't make her go back when you know this. Give her another chance. She wants to turn over a new leaf."

"I'm going to give her the finest chance she's ever had. If she repents let her accept her punishment."

She misunderstood the words and looked up. There was a gleam of hope in her heavy eyes.

"You'll let me go?"

"No. You shall sail for San Francisco on Tuesday."

She gave a groan of horror and then burst into low, hoarse shrieks which sounded hardly human, and she beat her head passionately on the ground. Dr Macphail sprang to her and lifted her up.

"Come on, you mustn't do that. You'd better go to your room and lie down. I'll get you something."

He raised her to her feet and partly dragging her, partly carrying her, got her downstairs. He was furious with Mrs. Davidson and with his wife because they made no effort to help. The half-caste was standing on the landing and with his assistance he managed to get her on the bed. She was moaning and crying. She was almost insensible. He gave her a hypodermic injection. He was hot and exhausted when he went upstairs again.

"I've got her to lie down."

The two women and Davidson were in the same positions as when he had left them. They could not have moved or spoken since he went.

"I was waiting for you," said Davidson, in a strange, distant voice. "I want you all to pray with me for the soul of our erring sister."

He took the Bible off a shelf and sat down at the table at which they had supped. It had not been cleared, and he pushed the tea-pot out of the way. In a powerful voice, resonant and deep, he read to them the chapter in which is narrated the meeting of Jesus Christ with the woman taken in adultery.

"Now kneel with me and let us pray for the soul of our dear sister, Sadie Thompson."

He burst into a long, passionate prayer in which he implored God to have mercy on the sinful woman. Mrs. Macphail and Mrs. Davidson knelt with covered eyes. The doctor, taken by surprise, awkward and sheepish, knelt too. The missionary's prayer had a savage eloquence. He was extraordinarily moved, and as he spoke the tears ran down his cheeks. Outside, the pitiless rain fell, fell steadily, with a fierce malignity that was all too human.

At last, he stopped. He paused for a moment and said:

"We will now repeat the Lord's prayer."

They said it and then; following him, they rose from their knees. Mrs. Davidson's face was pale and restful. She was comforted and at peace, but the Macphails felt suddenly bashful. They did not know which way to look.

"I'll just go down and see how she is now," said Dr Macphail.

When he knocked at her door it was opened for him by Horn. Miss Thompson was in a rocking-chair, sobbing quietly.

"What are you doing there?" exclaimed Macphail. "I told you to lie down."

"I can't lie down. I want to see Mr. Davidson."

"My poor child, what do you think is the good of it? You'll never move him."

"He said he'd come if I sent for him."

Macphail motioned to the trader.

"Go and fetch him."

He waited with her in silence while the trader went upstairs. Davidson came in.

"Excuse me for asking you to come here," she said, looking at him sombrely.

"I was expecting you to send for me. I knew the Lord would answer my prayer."

They stared at one another for a moment and then she looked away. She kept her eyes averted when she spoke.

"I've been a bad woman. I want to repent."

"Thank God! thank God! He has heard our prayers."

He turned to the two men.

"Leave me alone with her. Tell Mrs. Davidson that our prayers have been answered."

They went out and closed the door behind them.

"Gee whizz," said the trader.

That night Dr Macphail could not get to sleep till late, and when he heard the missionary come upstairs he looked at his watch. It was two o'clock. But even then he did not go to bed at once, for through the wooden partition that separated their rooms he heard him praying aloud, till he himself, exhausted, fell asleep.

When he saw him next morning he was surprised at his appearance. He was paler than ever, tired, but his eyes shone with an inhuman fire. It looked as though he were filled with an overwhelming joy.

"I want you to go down presently and see Sadie," he said. "I can't hope that her body is better, but her soul—her soul is transformed."

The doctor was feeling wan and nervous.

"You were with her very late last night," he said.

"Yes, she couldn't bear to have me leave her."

"You look as pleased as Punch," the doctor said irritably.

Davidson's eyes shone with ecstasy.

"A great mercy has been vouchsafed me. Last night I was privileged to bring a lost soul to the loving arms of Jesus."

Miss Thompson was again in the rocking-chair. The bed had not been made. The room was in disorder. She had not troubled to dress herself, but wore a dirty dressing-gown, and her hair was tied in a sluttish knot. She had given her face a dab with a wet towel, but it was all swollen and creased with crying. She looked a drab.

She raised her eyes dully when the doctor came in. She was cowed and broken.

"Where's Mr. Davidson?" she asked.

"He'll come presently if you want him," answered Macphail acidly. "I came here to see how you were."

"Oh, I guess I'm O. K. You needn't worry about that."

"Have you had anything to eat?"

"Horn brought me some coffee."

She looked anxiously at the door.

"D'you think he'll come down soon? I feel as if it wasn't so terrible when he's with me."

"Are you still going on Tuesday?"

"Yes, he says I've got to go. Please tell him to come right along. You can't do me any good. He's the only one as can help me now."

"Very well," said Dr Macphail.

During the next three days the missionary spent almost all his time with Sadie Thompson. He joined the others only to have his meals. Dr Macphail noticed that he hardly ate.

"He's wearing himself out," said Mrs. Davidson pitifully. "He'll have a breakdown if he doesn't take care, but he won't spare himself."

She herself was white and pale. She told Mrs. Macphail that she had no sleep. When the missionary came upstairs from Miss Thompson he prayed till he was exhausted, but even then he did not sleep for long. After an hour or two he got up and dressed himself and went for a tramp along the bay. He had strange dreams.

"This morning, he told me that he'd been dreaming about the mountains of Nebraska," said Mrs. Davidson.

"That's curious," said Dr Macphail.

He remembered seeing them from the windows of the train when he crossed America. They were like huge mole-hills, rounded and smooth, and they rose from the plain abruptly. Dr Macphail remembered how it struck him that they were like a woman's breasts.

Davidson's restlessness was intolerable even to himself. But he was buoyed up by a wonderful exhilaration. He was tearing out by the roots the last vestiges of sin that lurked in the hidden corners of that poor woman's heart. He read with her and prayed with her.

"It's wonderful," he said to them one day at supper. "It's a true rebirth. Her soul, which was black as night, is now pure and white like the new-fallen snow. I am humble and afraid. Her remorse for all her sins is beautiful. I am not worthy to touch the hem of her garment."

"Have you the heart to send her back to San Francisco?" said the doctor. "Three years in an American prison. I should have thought you might have saved her from that."

"Ah, but don't you see? It's necessary. Do you think my heart doesn't bleed for her? I love her as I love my wife and my sister. All the time that she is in prison I shall suffer all the pain that she suffers."

"Bunkum," cried the doctor impatiently.

"You don't understand because you're blind. She's sinned, and she must suffer. I know what she'll endure. She'll be starved and tortured and humiliated. I want her to accept the punishment of man as a sacrifice to God. I want her to accept it joyfully. She has an opportunity which is offered to very few of us. God is very good and very merciful."

Davidson's voice trembled with excitement. He could hardly articulate the words that tumbled passionately from his lips.

"All day I pray with her and when I leave her I pray again, I pray with all my might and main, so that Jesus may grant her this great mercy. I want to put in her heart the passionate desire to be punished so that at the end, even if I offered to let her go, she would refuse. I want her to feel that the bitter punishment of prison is the thank-offering that she places at the feet of our Blessed Lord, who gave his life for her."

The days passed slowly. The whole household, intent on the wretched, tortured woman downstairs, lived in a state of unnatural excitement. She was like a victim that was being prepared for the savage rites of a bloody idolatry. Her terror numbed her. She could not bear to let Davidson out of her sight; it was only when he was with her that she had courage, and she hung upon him with a slavish dependence. She cried a great deal, and she read the Bible, and prayed. Sometimes she was exhausted and apathetic. Then she did indeed look forward to her ordeal, for it seemed to offer an escape, direct and concrete, from the anguish she was enduring. She could not bear much longer the vague terrors which now assailed her. With her sins she had put aside all personal vanity, and she slopped about her room, unkempt and dishevelled, in her tawdry dressing-gown. She had not taken off her night-dress for four days, nor put on stockings. Her room was littered and untidy. Meanwhile the rain fell with a cruel persistence. You felt that the heavens must at last be empty of water, but still it poured down, straight and heavy, with a maddening iteration, on the iron roof. Everything was damp and clammy. There was mildew on the walls and on the boots that stood on the floor. Through the sleepless nights the mosquitoes droned their angry chant.

"If it would only stop raining for a single day it wouldn't be so bad," said Dr Macphail.

They all looked forward to the Tuesday when the boat for San Francisco was to arrive from Sydney. The strain was intolerable. So far as Dr Macphail was concerned, his pity and his resentment were alike extinguished by his desire to be rid of the unfortunate woman. The inevitable must be accepted. He felt he would breathe more freely when the ship had sailed. Sadie Thompson was to be escorted on board by a clerk in the governor's office. This person called on the Monday evening and told Miss Thompson to be prepared at eleven in the morning. Davidson was with her.

"I'll see that everything is ready. I mean to come on board with her myself."

Miss Thompson did not speak.

When Dr Macphail blew out his candle and crawled cautiously under his mosquito curtains, he gave a sigh of relief.

"Well, thank God that's over. By this time to-morrow she'll be gone."

"Mrs. Davidson will be glad too. She says he's wearing himself to a shadow," said Mrs. Macphail. "She's a different woman."

"Who?"

"Sadie. I should never have thought it possible. It makes one humble."

Dr Macphail did not answer, and presently he fell asleep. He was tired out, and he slept more soundly than usual.

He was awakened in the morning by a hand placed on his arm, and, starting up, saw Horn by the side of his bed. The trader put his finger on his mouth to prevent any exclamation from Dr Macphail and beckoned to him to come. As a rule, he wore shabby ducks, but now he was barefoot and wore only the *lava-lava* of the natives. He looked suddenly savage, and Dr Macphail, getting out of bed, saw that he was heavily tattooed. Horn made him a sign to come on to the verandah. Dr Macphail got out of bed and followed the trader out.

"Don't make a noise," he whispered. "You're wanted. Put on a coat and some shoes. Quick."

Dr Macphail's first thought was that something had happened to Miss Thompson.

"What is it? Shall I bring my instruments?"

"Hurry, please, hurry."

Dr Macphail crept back into the bedroom, put on a waterproof over his pyjamas and a pair of rubber-soled shoes. He rejoined the trader, and together they tiptoed down the stairs. The door leading out to the road was open and at it were standing half a dozen natives.

"What is it?" repeated the doctor.

"Come along with me," said Horn.

He walked out and the doctor followed him. The natives came after them in a little bunch. They crossed the road and came on to the beach. The doctor saw a group of natives standing round some object at the water's edge. They hurried along, a couple of dozen yards perhaps, and the natives opened out as the doctor came up. The trader pushed him forwards. Then he saw, lying half in the water and half out, a dreadful object, the body of Davidson. Dr Macphail bent down—he was not a man to lose his head in an emergency—and turned the body over. The throat was cut from ear to ear, and in the right hand was still the razor with which the deed was done.

"He's quite cold," said the doctor. "He must have been dead some time."

"One of the boys saw him lying there on his way to work just now and came and told me. Do you think he did it himself?"

"Yes. Someone ought to go for the police."

Horn said something in the native tongue, and two youths started off.

"We must leave him here till they come," said the doctor.

"They mustn't take him into my house. I won't have him in my house."

"You'll do what the authorities say," replied the doctor sharply. "In point of fact I expect they'll take him to the mortuary."

They stood waiting where they were. The trader took a cigarette from a fold in his *lava-lava* and gave one to Dr Macphail. They smoked while they stared at the corpse. Dr Macphail could not understand.

"Why do you think he did it?" asked Horn.

The doctor shrugged his shoulders. In a little while native police came along, under the charge of a marine, with a stretcher, and immediately afterwards a couple of naval officers and a naval doctor. They managed everything in a businesslike manner.

"What about the wife?" said one of the officers.

"Now that you've come I'll go back to the house and get some things on. I'll see that it's broken to her. She'd better not see him till he's been fixed up a little."

"I guess that's right," said the naval doctor.

When Dr Macphail went back he found his wife nearly dressed.

"Mrs. Davidson's in a dreadful state about her husband," she said to him as soon as he appeared. "He hasn't been to bed all night. She heard him leave Miss Thompson's room at two, but he went out. If he's been walking about since then he'll be absolutely dead."

Dr Macphail told her what had happened and asked her to break the news to Mrs. Davidson.

"But why did he do it?" she asked, horror-stricken.

"I don't know."

"But I can't. I can't."

"You must."

She gave him a frightened look and went out. He heard her go into Mrs. Davidson's room. He waited a minute to gather himself together and then began to shave and wash. When he was dressed he sat down on the bed and waited for his wife. At last, she came.

"She wants to see him," she said.

"They've taken him to the mortuary. We'd better go down with her. How did she take it?"

"I think she's stunned. She didn't cry. But she's trembling like a leaf."

"We'd better go at once."

When they knocked at her door Mrs. Davidson came out. She was very pale, but dry-eyed. To the doctor she seemed unnaturally composed. No word was exchanged, and they set out in silence down the road. When they arrived at the mortuary Mrs. Davidson spoke.

"Let me go in and see him alone."

They stood aside. A native opened a door for her and closed it behind her. They sat down and waited. One or two white men came and talked to them in undertones. Dr Macphail told them again what he knew of the tragedy. At last, the door was quietly opened, and Mrs. Davidson came out. Silence fell upon them.

"I'm ready to go back now," she said.

Her voice was hard and steady. Dr Macphail could not understand the look in her eyes. Her pale face was very stern. They walked back slowly, never saying a word, and at last they came round the bend on the other side of which stood their house. Mrs. Davidson gave a gasp and for a moment they stopped still. An incredible sound assaulted their ears. The gramophone which had been silent for so long was playing, playing ragtime loud and harsh.

"What's that?" cried Mrs. Macphail with horror.

"Let's go on," said Mrs. Davidson.

They walked up the steps and entered the hall. Miss Thompson was standing at her door, chatting with a sailor. A sudden change had taken place in her. She was no longer the cowed drudge of the last days. She was dressed in all her finery, in her white dress, with the high shiny boots over which her fat legs bulged in their cotton stockings; her hair was elaborately arranged; and she wore that enormous hat covered with gaudy flowers. Her face was painted, her eyebrows were boldly black, and her lips were scarlet. She held herself erect. She was the flaunting quean that they had known at first. As they came in she broke into a loud, jeering laugh; and then, when Mrs. Davidson involuntarily stopped, she collected the spittle in her mouth and spat. Mrs. Davidson cowered back, and two red spots rose suddenly to her cheeks. Then, covering her face with her hands, she broke away and ran quickly up the stairs. Dr Macphail was outraged. He pushed past the woman into her room.

"What the devil are you doing?" he cried. "Stop that damned machine."

He went up to it and tore the record off. She turned on him.

"Say, doc, you can that stuff with me. What the hell are you doin' in my room?"

"What do you mean?" he cried. "What d'you mean?"

She gathered herself together. No one could describe the scorn of her expression or the contemptuous hatred she put into her answer.

"You men! You filthy, dirty pigs! You're all the same, all of you. Pigs! Pigs!"Dr Macphail gasped. He understood.

VIII

ENVOI

When your ship leaves Honolulu they hang *leis* round your neck, garlands of sweet-smelling flowers. The wharf is crowded, and the band plays a melting Hawaiian tune. The people on board throw-coloured streamers to those standing below, and the side of the ship is gay with the thin lines of paper, red and green and yellow and blue. When the ship moves slowly away the streamers break softly, and it is like the breaking of human ties. Men and women are joined together for a moment by a gaily coloured strip of paper, red and blue and green and yellow, and then life separates them, and the paper is sundered, so easily, with a little sharp snap. For an hour the fragments trail down the hull and then they blow away. The flowers of your garlands fade, and their scent is oppressive. You throw them overboard.

THE END